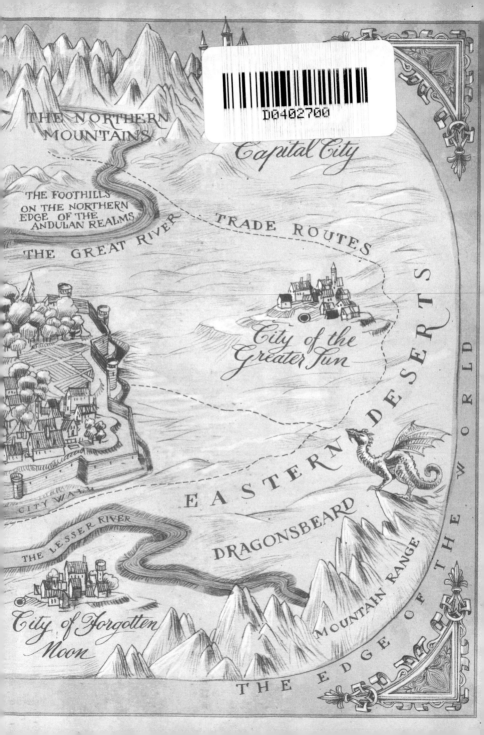

IRON HEARTED VIOLET

IRON
HEARTED
VIOLET

Kelly Barnhill

Illustrations by Iacopo Bruno

Little, Brown and Company

New York Boston

Copyright © 2012 by Kelly Barnhill
Illustrations copyright © 2012 by Iacopo Bruno

Little, Brown and Company

Hachette Book Group
237 Park Avenue, New York, NY 10017
Visit our website at www.lb-kids.com

Little, Brown and Company is a division of Hachette Book Group, Inc.
The Little, Brown name and logo are trademarks of Hachette Book Group, Inc.

The publisher is not responsible for websites (or their content)
that are not owned by the publisher.

First Edition: October 2012

Library of Congress Cataloging-in-Publication Data

Barnhill, Kelly Regan.
    Iron hearted Violet / by Kelly Barnhill. — 1st ed.
        p. cm.
    Summary: "Princess Violet is plain, reckless, and quite possibly too clever for her own good. Particularly when it comes to telling stories. One day she and her best friend, Demetrius, stumble upon a hidden room and find a peculiar book. A *forbidden* book. It tells a story of an evil being—called the Nybbas—imprisoned in their world. The story cannot be true—*not really*. But then the whispers start. Violet and Demetrius, along with an ancient, scarred dragon, may hold the key to the Nybbas's triumph...or its demise."— Provided by publisher.
    ISBN 978-0-316-05673-1 (hardback)
    [1. Fairy tales. 2. Princesses—Fiction. 3. Adventure and adventurers—Fiction. 4. Books and reading—Fiction. 5. Dragons—Fiction.] I. Title.
    PZ8.B254Iro 2012
    [Fic]—dc23

2011053213

10 9 8 7 6 5 4 3 2 1

RRD-C

Printed in the United States of America

In memory of Mary Roon,
who has gone on.

Loved in this world,
loved in every world.

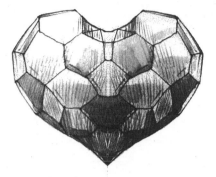

CHAPTER ONE

The end of my world began with a story. It also began with a birth.

Princess Violet, last of that name—indeed the last princess at all to be born in the Andulan Realms—was not a pretty child. When she was born, her hair grew in tufted clumps around her pink-and-yellow head, and her mouth puckered to the side whenever anyone peeked into her cradle. Her gaze was sharp, intelligent, and intense, leaving the visitor with the uncanny feeling that the royal infant was sizing him up, assessing his worth—and finding him wanting. She was the type of child whom a person wanted to *impress*.

Interesting, yes. *Intelligent*, most certainly. But not a pretty child.

When she was five days old, her round face broke out in a rash that lasted for weeks.

When she was twelve weeks old, the last of her feathery black hair drifted away, leaving her skull quite bald, with a lopsided sheen. Her hair grew back much later as a coarse, crinkly, auburn mass, resistant to braids and ribbons and almost impossible to comb.

When she was one year old, it became clear that her left eye was visibly larger than her right. Not only that, it was a different color, too. While the right eye was as blue as the Western Ocean in the earliest morning, the left was gray— like the smoke offered to the dying sky each evening by the magicians of the eastern wall.

Her nose pugged, her forehead was too tall, and even when she was just a baby, her skin was freckled and blotched, and no number of milk baths or lemon rubs could unmark her.

People remarked about her lack of beauty, but it couldn't be helped. She was a princess all the same. *Our* Princess. And we loved her.

On the morning in which the infant Violet was officially presented to her waiting and hopeful people, it was dark, windy, and bitter cold. Even in the Great Hall, where there were abundant fires and bodies to cheer us, our breath clouded about our mouths and hung like ghosts, before wisping away. The King and Queen entered quietly, without announcement or trumpets or pomp, and stood before us. The shivering crowd grew silent. In the months following Violet's birth, both mother and child recuperated in seclusion, as the birth itself had been treacherous and terrifying, and we very nearly lost both of them to the careless shrug of Chance.

The Queen wore a red wool gown under a heavy green cloak. She gazed over the Great Hall and smiled. She was, without a doubt, a beautiful queen—black hair, black eyes, skin as luminous as amber, and a narrow gap between her straight, white teeth, which we all knew was a sign of an open and honest heart.

"My beloved," she said. Her voice was weak from her long months in bed, but we hung on to it desperately, every breathing soul among us.

"The snow has drifted heavily upon the northern wall of the castle, and despite our best efforts, a bitter wind probes its fingers into the cracks, scratching at the hearts of the best and bravest among us."

We nodded. It had been a miserable winter, the most miserable in memory. And heartbreakingly long. We were well past the month in which the ice should have begun to recede and the world to thaw. People came in droves to the castle seeking warmth, food, and shelter. As was the custom of our kingdom, none was ever turned away, and as a result, we all contented ourselves with less.

"Rest assured, my beloved people, that though the cold has crusted and iced, though the winds still blow bitterly and without mercy, here, in the darkest winter, a Violet blooms in the snow."

And with that, she undid the top clasp of her heavy cloak and allowed it to fall to the ground. Underneath, a tiny creature was bound to her body with a measure of silk and a series of skillful knots. We saw the downy tufts of hair on the head of the new Princess and those large, mismatched, intelligent eyes.

Princess Violet.

As I said, not a particularly pretty child.

But a *wonderful* child, who, despite the multitudes present in the room, fixed her eyes on *me*. And on those tiny lips—a flicker of a smile.

CHAPTER TWO

Though both King Randall and Queen Rose longed for a large brood of happy children, alas, their hopes had been dashed. Each time the Queen's womb swelled with joy and expectation, it ended in pain and sorrow. Violet was her only child who lived.

Indeed, Violet's very existence was something of a miracle.

"A miracle!" shouted the citizens of the Andulan Realms on the yearly holiday commemorating the Princess's birth.

"A miracle," glumly proclaimed the advisers and rulers

of the Northern Mountains, the Southern Plains, the Eastern Deserts, and the Island Nations to the west, all of whom had harbored hopes that the King and Queen of the Andulan Realms would fail to produce an heir. They stared at map after map, imagining their borders with our country erased, imagining themselves able to reach into the great resources of our prosperous nation and pick plum after plum for their own.

But with the birth of the Princess, there would be no annexation without the bother of war. And, my dears, war is a terrible bother. So our neighbors seethed in secret. They spoke of miracles as they clenched their teeth and tasted acid on their tongues.

AH, hissed a voice, far away at the mirrored edge of the world. AN OPPORTUNITY. And that slithery, whispery voice slowly formulated a plan. It licked its yellow lips and widened its jaws into a grin.

CHAPTER THREE

By the time Violet was four years old, she had learned hundreds and hundreds of different ways to slip out of the reach of the watchful eyes that minded her—three sharp-faced nannies, a gaggle of pompous tutors, a quick-moving mother, and an easily distracted father. Each day she would go sprinting away through the twisting and complicated corridors of the castle until she reached my quarters, for the sole purpose of hearing another story. I was a storyteller—*the* storyteller, practitioner of a revered and respected occupation in my world, with a long and (mostly) glorious history.

Also, I don't mind saying, I was rather good at it.

While there was, in theory, a requirement that any castle resident or visitor must capture the fugitive Princess and deliver her, posthaste, to one of her nannies for the swift application of disciplinary action, this rule was routinely ignored.

Indeed, as it was well known where she would go, the Queen felt it was far simpler to retrieve the child from her intended destination.

The Queen, incidentally, liked my stories, too.

By the time Violet was six years old, she began telling stories of her own. My dears, my heart was filled to bursting! How proud I was! How vain! How delighted that this *wonderful* child should seek to emulate *me*!

Pride, alas, is a terrible thing.

Violet's stories, even at her very young age, went far beyond my own. She took stories—true stories, false stories, and those of questionable intention—and turned them on their heads, shook them up and down, making them new again. The child told stories with enthusiasm, verve, and wild abandon. And she was a *wonder*.

"There once was a dragon," the young Violet said one

night after dinner to a hushed, delighted crowd, her mismatched eyes glowing in the firelight, her untamable hair floating around her head like embers, "the largest and smartest and powerfulest dragon in all our mirrored world." She spoke with a slight lisp, due to the slow loss of her childhood teeth, but it only added to the charm. "His fire was hottest, his flight was fastest, and even the Greater Sun was jealous of his beauty. *But*"—she held up one finger, wagging it slightly—"it had a problem. This dragon fell in love with a princess. A *human* princess."

"Ah!" the assembled crowd cried out. "Poor dragon! Poor princess!" They pressed against one another, shoulder to shoulder, laughing all the while.

Violet raised her eyebrows and continued. "The princess lived in a faraway country, and they had never met. Dragons, you see, can spy halfway across the world if they choose to, and can fly from one end of the mirrored sky and back again in less than a day. But they usually don't." She pursed her lips. "Dragons are terribly lazy."

The listeners chuckled and sighed. *That child!* they thought. *That magic child!*

"But *this* dragon," Violet continued, "was not lazy at all.

It was in love. It didn't eat or sleep. It just sat on top of a mountain, its shiny tail curled around the peak, its black eyes searching the world for its love."

"All the time?" I asked incredulously. "Surely it must have had other hobbies!"

"Well," Violet allowed, "sometimes it enjoyed throwing snowballs at the head of the Mountain King." The crowd laughed. She cocked her head conspiratorially and raised one eyebrow. "It had perfect aim. And when the dragon passed gas, it made sure to point its rump right toward the Mountain King's gardens." The crowd roared. Violet leaned in. "They say the stink can last for a hundred years!" she whispered.

"Tell us about the dragon's lady love!" a young man said.

"Oh, she was an ugly thing," the Princess assured us. "She had moles in the shape of horny toads across her cheeks, and a crooked nose, and even crookeder teeth. Her smile was too big, and her eyes were too small, and her feet were of differing sizes. But the dragon loved her anyway. It loved her and loved her and loved her some more. The dragon loved her crooked teeth and loved her hairy wrists and loved her frizzy, frizzy hair."

No one laughed. An embarrassed silence pressed onto the crowd. They couldn't look at Violet.

(*Not a pretty child*, they thought. *And, alas, growing uglier by the day.*)

Violet waited for the praise that didn't come.

I tried to intervene. "Beloved Violet," I said, my voice tumbling from my mouth in a rush. "You have made a beginner's mistake! You have forgotten the beauty! A princess is never ugly. Everyone knows that a *real* princess is always beautiful." Violet didn't move. It was as though I had turned her to stone. Finally she fixed her large eyes on me. And oh! The hurt! The betrayal! I swallowed. "In a story, I mean," I added hastily, but it was too late. "Of course I mean in a story. Stories have their own *rules*, their own...*expectations*. It's the job of the teller to give the people what they want."

The crowd nodded. Violet said nothing. And oh, my dears! How I wanted to catch that child in my arms and tell her I didn't mean it! But the damage was done.

Finally: "You are right, beloved Cassian," she said quietly, tilting her eyes to the ground. "What was I thinking? The dragon, of course, was in love with a *beautiful* princess. The most beautiful in the world, with amber skin and tiny feet and eyes as green as spring grass and honeyed hair so thick it fell in great ropes down to her knees."

It was a line she'd stolen from one of *my* stories. I let it slide. But as she continued and finished her tale, I could feel that her heart was elsewhere, and when she excused herself to go to bed, she left without saying good night.

After that, the princesses in her stories were always beautiful. Always.

CHAPTER FOUR

When Violet was seven years old, she made her first friend. Indeed, her only friend.

Normally, the children of kings and queens were limited in their play to their siblings or their cousins or the children of courtiers. However, in Violet's case, she had no siblings, and as both her father and mother were without siblings, she had no cousins. Additionally, while the courtiers certainly had children of their own, they were all either quite a bit older or quite a bit younger, and therefore unsuitable playmates for a vigorous girl.

Still, Violet needed a friend. And as it turned out, a friend was waiting for her.

This is how they met:

Violet, being a terribly bright girl, had been placed under the intellectual care of tutors since the age of three and a half. By seven, she could read, do sums, recite historical facts, analyze, and debate. And what's more, she memorized everything she read, and most of the things that she heard, too. Unfortunately, the child detested her studies, so when she wasn't hatching schemes to play tricks on the sour-faced men and women who taught her, she slipped away from her tutors whenever she could.

One day, when the mirrored sky was particularly brilliant and when both the Greater and Lesser Suns gleamed to their best effect, Violet decided that she had no interest in staying indoors. So, using her very best imitation of her mother's handwriting, she wrote a note to her tutor that his advisory skills were needed in the throne room. *Urgently.* The old man flushed and tittered and told the child to work very hard on her translation until he returned. He left muttering, "At last, at last," and shut the door behind him. Once he was safely away, Violet slipped out the window, shimmied down the drain, and skirted into the fields west of the castle.

The day was so fine that the child decided to run. And jump. And climb. And after she had climbed over six different fences and sprinted across five and a half different fields, she found herself standing right in the middle of a grazing meadow, exactly opposite a very large bull. Its coat was brown and white and shining. It rippled and bulged over the bull's broad shoulders and back. The bull's damp nostrils flared and snorted.

Violet froze.

The bull stared at the child—her wild hair, her filthy cheeks, her red, red dress. It scraped one hoof against the ground and lowered its horns.

"Help," Violet called, her voice a tight squeak. "Help me!"

The bull bellowed and lunged forward, the weight of it shaking the ground as it thundered toward the Princess. Violet turned on her heels and raced for the closest fence.

"*Stop,*" a voice said. Her own? Violet didn't know. She looked up and, through her fear, she saw a figure launch itself over the fence and run straight toward her.

"No!" Violet said, panic making her vision go bright and jagged. "I can't stop." But just as she said this, her left foot hooked into a small hole. She pitched forward, fell head over knees, and sprawled onto the ground. She covered her head with her arms.

A boy leaped lightly over the cowering Princess and put his body between the bull and the girl. Violet shut her eyes, waiting to hear the boy's bones splintering under the hooves of the great beast, waiting to feel her own body trampled into the dirt, leaving nothing behind.

Instead, she heard this: "Stop screaming, will you? You're scaring him."

Violet tried to say *I'm not screaming*, but her mouth was wide and round, a scream tearing unbidden from her chest. For a brief flash, embarrassment eclipsed her fear. She shut her jaw with a snap and pulled herself to her knees.

A boy with a mop of black, curly hair stood between her and the bull. He was shorter than Violet, and scrawny, but with lean, ropy muscles twisting from his neck into his shoulders and down his arms.

Is he going to wrestle it? Violet wondered.

The bull, on the other hand, stood still, its eyes on the black-haired boy.

His hands were raised, palms out, and he made a noise over and over—something midway between a mother's cooing and a father's shushing. A sweet, soft, whispery sort

17

of sound. The beast was motionless, but its head remained lowered, its muscles bulged, and its eyes were bloodshot and angry and wild. They rolled and quivered as though about to burst. Still, Violet was incredulous.

"How could *I* scare *him*?" she asked. "He was the one—"

"Your dress," the boy said quietly, without turning around. His voice was infuriatingly calm. "Your dress is scaring him. It's not his fault. Stand up and walk slowly toward the fence. But walk backward. He needs to *feel* you watching him. You must not look away."

Violet's mouth dropped open. "But—" She paused, gaping. No one had ever spoken to her in this way before. And despite her terror, she was mystified. "I am the *Princess*. You're not supposed—"

"Do you *want* to be dead?" the boy asked. If he had any emotion at all, he certainly didn't show it. He said this as casually as if he were asking the Princess if she wanted a spot of cream or a spoonful of sugar.

"No," Violet admitted.

"Well then?"

Violet sniffed but got to her feet all the same and started walking backward toward the fence, maintaining her gaze on the bull in the middle of the field. It grunted and wheezed and whined. And the great muscles on the beast's shoulders and flanks trembled piteously. *He really is frightened*, Violet realized. And despite the terror twisting her insides into a knot, she felt a stab of compassion for the creature.

The boy kept pace with her, his hands still raised, his eyes on the bull, his mouth continuing its quieting sounds until both he and Violet were safely on the other side of the fence. Finally he slumped forward, rested his hands on his thighs, and sighed deeply.

Violet fidgeted, shifting her weight from one foot to the other. "I—" she stammered. "Or, I mean to say—" She paused. "Thank you."

The boy gave her a savage look. "*What were you thinking?*" he hissed, stepping aggressively forward. "Didn't you see the signs?"

"No," she said. "I was running."

"Don't you look on the other side of fences to see if it's safe?"

"No," Violet said, aghast. "I never have."

"Well, you're an idiot." The boy stepped away, jamming his fingers into his curly hair and hanging on tight. He looked as if he had more to say. He bit his lower lip hard.

"You are *not supposed*—" Violet said hotly.

"That bull would have *killed* you," the boy said. "And then they would have killed him, too, even though it was an accident and it was just because he was scared. So that would be two lives lost—for *nothing*. Just because you couldn't bother yourself to look." He kicked a loose stone on the ground. *"Stupid."*

The boy's eyes welled up. He turned his back toward her and quickly wiped his tears away. But it did him no good to hide it. Violet *saw*. She pressed her lips together and took a step closer. She was not used to talking to children her own age, and she wasn't sure how to begin.

"What's your name?" she said at last.

He wouldn't look at her, and he wouldn't answer.

"Please," Violet whispered, putting her hand on the boy's arm. "Tell me your name."

"Demetrius," he said at last. "Am I in trouble?"

Violet shook her head. "Of course not." And for an awful moment, she could see how easy—how *terribly* easy—it would be to get him, or anyone, into trouble. A hint. An accusation. A moment of manufactured tears. She would never need any proof. The very thought—*just the thought*—made her sick inside. She shook it away. "How did you do that?" she said, changing the subject. "With the bull, I mean?"

He shrugged. "You probably could, too. If you ever learned. You just have to *feel* with them." He wrinkled his eyebrows and thought a minute. "Or," he clarified, "they just need to feel you caring about them. Lots of people can do it. If they bother to. It's not hard."

"Will you show me?"

So Demetrius took her to the stables. He pointed to his house right next door, where he lived with his father, the stable master—a man Violet had met many times. Her father often called on the stable master to assist in his research. The two men would have lengthy and, Violet thought, ponderous discussions on the history and biology and physiology of dragons—though neither man had ever laid eyes on one. No one had for a hundred years. But Violet never knew that the quiet, gentle man had a son. She did know, though, that he had no wife. Or that his wife had died a long time ago. Violet knew that the subject of dead mothers was likely not polite conversation, but she wondered about it all the same.

The stable master, upon seeing the child Violet engrossed in a lesson on the care of horses, which was interrupted every once in a while by a game that consisted of the two children running and screeching around the yard, sent a message with one of his apprentices that the Princess had been found and was safe, and where she could be fetched. Within the hour she was dragged back to the castle, protesting loudly, by her mother, two nannies, and a rather embarrassed tutor.

Still, in the midst of her howls and pleading and threats, she shot a look at the boy Demetrius, and the two shared a quick and meaningful grin.

I'll be back in a bit, Violet's grin said.

I'll be waiting, Demetrius grinned back.

CHAPTER FIVE

After that, Violet and Demetrius saw each other nearly every day. They found excuses and schemes to leave their studies and their chores behind, to slip away from the adults who minded them, and to set off on their own mad adventures.

They made an unorthodox pair, but the King and Queen were of a modern view.

"They are only children, after all," the Queen said often.

"Why hamper them with the burdens of social class?

They shall have to trouble themselves with such foolishness soon enough!" the King agreed.

The court advisers argued against the friendship, voicing worries about *dangerous precedents* and *political implications* and the *prerequisites of propriety*. Violet's parents had the final say. "We simply don't see the harm," they said. And that was that.

Together, the children explored nearly every inch of the castle—or at least they thought they did. Every day the castle revealed new secrets, and every day it kept its most important secret cleverly hidden. Castles are tricky that way. The pair explored the castle grounds as well—its grazing fields and broad gardens and parks. They explored the twisting streets of the capital city and followed the wall that snaked around the city's edge, hugging it tight, and their fingers grazed against the ancient stones. And later they ventured farther out into the fields and forests beyond the city, exiting through the four gates that opened in the four directions. Those gates let the world inside. Or kept it out. Gates sometimes have a mind of their own.

Violet learned how to care for the horses and the goats and the falcons and the dogs. Demetrius taught her how to search for illness, how to communicate calm, how to listen to the voice coming from the animal's heart. Though he never, Violet noticed, taught her how to stop a raging bull, which, she felt, would have been a useful thing to know. (For his part, Demetrius assured her that it was a skill that *could not be taught*, and it was only in the moment when a person discovered whether he *could* or whether he was dead. Privately, the boy's dreams screamed with pounding hooves and pointed horns and a pair of livid, bloodshot eyes.)

Inside the castle, when we gathered for our nightly songs and stories and dancing, Demetrius proved to be nearly as clever a storyteller as Violet herself. And neither *alone* was quite as remarkable as the two of them *together*.

Together, they were a marvel.

"Shall we play at stories?" Violet said one day as they once again used my quarters as a hideout from the watchful eyes of the adults in the castle. I indulged them. How could I not? After all, someone would be here soon enough to fetch them.

"All right," I said, pouring steaming water from the kettle into the teapot and swirling the fragrant leaves in the water. There never was a story that didn't go down better with tea. "Give me a story about the beginning of the world."

"Which world?" Violet asked. "There are thousands of worlds in the multiverse."

"More than thousands," Demetrius said. "Millions."

"Millions of thousands of millions," Violet crowed, throwing her hands in the air. "They are endless."

"Fine," I said. "That is all very fine, but I, for one, am not impressed by the wonders of the other worlds in the multiverse. What care have I for wonders that I can neither see nor will ever visit? Tell me a story of *our* world, our twin suns, our mirrored sky. What use do I have for anything else?"

"Once, long ago, before the Old Gods formed the multiverse," Demetrius began, ignoring my request, "before the multitudes of worlds and worlds and worlds bubbled and foamed like a sea, there was only one world, one universe. And it was a *terrible* place."

(I *might* mention that the boy stole this story from me, but that would be terribly petty and small of me, so I shall let it pass.)

"The Old Gods breathed the same air and walked the same paths and bathed in the same rivers," Violet continued. "They tried their hands at creation. They placed bets and held challenges and produced unlikely creatures and forms. But they were foolish. Their ideas piled on top of one another, thick and fast, and the One World became jumbled. There was chaos and misery for its creatures. Reality jittered." She wiggled her fingers next to her face, and her mismatched eyes shone.

Demetrius jumped in. "Finally, one of the Old Gods went for a walk. He was a runty thing—stubby legs, stubby arms, and a merry smile—but he was agile and strong and low to the ground. He didn't mind so much when the land buckled and bubbled under his feet. He leaped from boulder to boulder and dodged the things that wobbled from *there* to *not there* as though they were shadows."

"The runty god is my favorite," Violet said fervently.

"He's everyone's favorite," Demetrius agreed.

"The runty god leaned down and took a handful of dirt from the trail and looked at it for a moment." Violet held her fist in front of her face and imitated as best she could the god's expression. "He had been walking a long way and was tired. And lonely. And cold. *A chair*, he thought. *A friend*, at the same time. *A fire.* All in one moment." Violet held up her hands, fingers splayed, and made a sound like the roaring of a fire, followed by a terrific BOOM.

"Oh dear," Demetrius said, laughing. "Oh dear, oh dear.

A clump of dirt in the hand of a god can become…*any-thing*. But it cannot be three things at once. The fabric of the One World trembled. It buckled and split. And where there was one, there were now three—a world with a chair, and a world with a friend, and a world with a crackling fire. The runty god shook his head. 'Nope,' he said. 'The others aren't going to like this one bit.' "

"That wasn't *our* world," I said. I could hear one of the nannies calling from down the hall.

"Close enough," Demetrius said. "You can't talk about a beginning unless you talk about *before the beginning.*"

"Impertinent boy," I chided.

"But we're missing part of the story, aren't we? It's incomplete," Violet said.

The nannies were growing closer. I resigned myself to having those dear children shooed away once again, and thought it all the pity. If it were up to me, the children would spend all day telling stories with me and not be shunted off to suffer through arithmetic and translations and chores. But it was not up to me. "What do you mean, 'incomplete'?" I said. "There's no such thing as complete when it comes to stories. Stories are infinite. They are as infinite as worlds."

"Oh, I know," Violet said. "But there was one book that

said in the One World there were thirteen Old Gods. But in the stories we *tell*, there are only twelve." She counted them off on her fingers. "There's the runty god, the goddess made of wheat, the god with the fish's tail, the blue goddess, the goddess of beauty, the god of giants, the Dark Lady, the god with wings, the stone goddess, the god of fire, the Great Ox, and the god who was a spider. Whatever happened to the thirteenth god? Did he vanish?"

I thought: *We don't ask about that.*

"Did he do something bad?" she pressed.

I thought: *No questions! There are things we do not question and things that we dare not know!*

Instead, I said, "I don't think I have ever heard of a thirteenth god. Perhaps the book you read was in error." I couldn't look at her. My breath rattled in my chest. My hands shook.

Which book? I thought desperately. *It must be found and destroyed. I'll destroy all the books if I have to.*

Demetrius's black eyes twinkled at the edges. His burnished cheeks swelled with a knowing grin. "You have," he said. "You've seen it and read it, or you learned about it along the way, but you don't want to tell us. I can see it in your hands."

I harrumphed. "You can see no such thing," I sputtered, hastily sliding my hands under my knees.

"Why does he not want to tell us?" Violet faced her friend and raised her eyebrows.

"It's a mystery," Demetrius said. And they both turned and stared at me.

My teeth chattered. "There is nothing," I stammered. "Nothing to tell. The Old Gods were twelve in number, but it was so very long ago that whether there were twelve gods or twelve thousand or none at all is irrelevant. We live in *this* world and *this* time and nothing else matters." I took a deep breath. "And that's that."

The children were quiet for a long, long moment.

"Beloved Cassian," Violet said as she folded her arms across her chest. "I do believe you are lying and hiding things from me. How dreadfully sneaky of you."

"Never, Princess!" I cried. "Never would I lie to you!" *I lie to protect*, I shouted in my heart, and I believed it. *Mostly.* Violet and Demetrius faced each other, their mouths mirrored in a thin, grim line.

But before Violet could question me further, three nannies burst in and shooed her back to her classroom.

"Until next time, dear child!" I called, and then

31

collapsed in my chair, covering my face with my hands and expelling a sigh of relief through my fingers.

When I finally removed my hands, I discovered that Demetrius had remained behind. His black eyes peered mercilessly through the fringe of black hair hanging over his brow, and his mouth puckered to one side in a half-smile. Was I only worth half a smile? My heart shivered in my chest.

"Do you have something to say, young man?" I snapped.

"Nope," Demetrius said. He was infuriatingly unrattled. His large black eyes were as implacable as two polished stones.

"Well then," I said, doing my best to affect a grown-uppish look of dignity. "Off you go. Your chores and such." My hands trembled. My voice caught. Did he notice?

Very slowly, the boy's half-smile began to fade. He shook his head and left without a word.

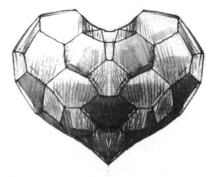

CHAPTER SIX

The children ignored me for a long time after that. It nearly broke my heart to pieces, not that they cared. Neither Violet nor Demetrius gave two figs for my heart—broken, unbroken, or missing altogether. There was a castle to explore. And both boy and girl were keen to do so.

Indeed, ever since my little outburst, they were keener than ever.

I suspect that you have not had the opportunity to spend a substantial amount of time in a castle, so you wouldn't know what it was like to be a child maneuvering through those endless cracks, crannies, and corridors. There were secret rooms, and forgotten rooms, and hallways that wavered between *being* and *nonbeing*. A castle, you see, needs more than stones to keep it standing. Magic is also required, as are mysteries, secrets, revelry, schemes, passion, mischief, and love. In fact, if one were to make a list of the multitude of things that a castle *is*, it would likely outstrip the list of things that a castle *is not*.

There was, for example, the abandoned workshop of an ancient chocolatier, which Violet and Demetrius were able to find only four separate times in their young lives, each time during the waning moon, and each time in the four farthest corners of the castle, starting in the west.

Also, there was a hallway that bent in one direction in the morning and quite another in the afternoon. The cause of this was unknown, but it was generally believed that the hallway itself was terribly vain and wanted nothing more than to display itself to its best advantage, depending on the light.

A castle, you see, is more than the sum of its stones.

It lives, my dears. It *breathes*.

So just as we could not expect your face to remain static and unchanging over time, nor could we expect your body to never grow, so too would it be ludicrous to assume that a castle remain fixed forever.

Imagine, then, young Violet and Demetrius set loose among those breathing stones. It is my belief that, even as children, they learned more about the castle than anyone in the history of the kingdom—and still, that knowledge comprised a mere fraction of the castle's secrets.

One particular discovery was a secret passage that led into a network of tiny corridors, its entrance in the farthest cupboard of the pantry—the one so far back that it was never used. Once inside, they had to lean against the panel until it quietly clicked open.

Violet found this passageway at the age of six when she was nearly caught stealing sweets. It was particularly curious because of its small size (even as a very young child, Violet still had to duck and crawl, lest she smack her head on the polished ceiling) and its intricate fashioning. The marble floor had been covered with a thick rug of the softest wool, and the walls and ceiling had been inlaid with thousands of tiny interlocking lengths of wood that gleamed in the low light with a fresh application of oil and wax. The passage was always impeccably clean, never given to smells · of dampness or must.

It was well known in our country that most homes had floor plans fitted with alternate walkways for the Hidden Folk—though, to my knowledge, no one had ever seen these rooms, nor had they been inside. No one save Violet and Demetrius.

Sometime in the months that followed the unpleasant conversation about the thirteenth god, Violet and Demetrius found themselves in an unfamiliar passage. It was far dustier here, as though the small residents who maintained the hidden corridors had simply run out of time or inclination. It happens.

But it was dingier, too, and in terrible disrepair. The wood was cracked and gray, and the swirling patterns on the marble floors were crumbling to bits.

"Is this passage getting smaller?" Demetrius asked, though he already knew it was. With each wriggle forward, the walls became closer, then touching, then tighter on his shoulders.

"It must be your imagination," Violet said, though her voice wavered and caught in her throat. Both children had the same thought running through their heads: *What if we get stuck?* The thought was itchy and shivery and made them want to crawl out of their very skins. *What if we get stuck? What then?* They shook the thought away.

Fortunately for the pair of them, they did not get stuck.

Eventually, the passage widened somewhat and then opened into a space not large enough to stand in but large enough to sit up comfortably. There were small chairs and small tables and small bookshelves covered and crammed with hundreds of very small books.

And it was dusty. Terribly dusty. Dust coated every surface. It heaped in corners, skittered across the floor in hazy puffs, and hung in the air like dull stars. Demetrius sneezed.

"I don't know how long I can stay in here," he said.

"It's light in here," Violet said. "Where is the light coming from?"

And indeed it *was* light. There were small round holes cut into the ceiling and the walls, each fitted tightly with a piece of glass, and the glass glowed and gleamed—though *separately*, and in its own way, no two shining with equal measure. "How does it work?"

"Mirrors, I'd suspect," Demetrius said. "The light bounces off mirror after mirror until it comes in here. But don't look too closely," he added as Violet leaned in. "It's too bright for your eyes." He looked around. "How long since anyone's been in here?" He coughed again. The dust pushed into his chest, making it hard to breathe.

"Who knows?" Violet coughed. "Tutor Rimi said that

the Hidden Folk disappeared from our world at the same time as the dragons. But Father says that dragons still exist and that Tutor Rimi is a pompous old windbag." She picked up a book. "It doesn't *look* as though anyone has been here for a very long time." A cloud of dust rose from the book as she opened it in her hands. Pages fell out and curled into strips as they hit the ground.

"What does it say?"

Violet gently turned page after page. "I don't know. These letters...I've never seen anything like them."

Demetrius coughed again. "I don't think—" A fit of coughing ripped across his throat. He folded his body over his legs and coughed between his knees.

"Just a minute," Violet said, running her fingers along the unfamiliar letters. "What language is this?" She didn't know. Violet was familiar with the three major languages spoken in our mirrored world, as well as their ancient predecessors. She was only just learning, of course, but she knew them well enough to know that *these* books were something else entirely.

She picked up another book. This one was beautiful and, despite its age, was still pristine. "Look!" she marveled. It had symbols that looked unlike any lettering she had ever seen. In fact they were more like pictures—a triangle, a stack of bars, a circle with spikes coming out of its edges, a star, wavy lines, a hand, an eye, a bulbous form like ripe grain, and other strange markings. She had no idea what any of it could mean.

And yet. The book wanted her to know. She could *feel* it wanting.

The book also was heavily illustrated and illuminated with gold. There was a picture of a man kneeling in front of a painting, or perhaps it was a mirror. And another showing the same man receiving gifts that emerged from the mirror—a sword, a shield, a crown, and finally a woman with hair that spilled over the floor, snaked up the man's legs, and wound around his throat.

"What is that book?" Demetrius asked. Though he didn't know why, he found himself wanting to snatch the book out of Violet's hands and throw it across the room. He'd never felt anything like it before. He shoved his fists into his pockets and tried to shrug the feeling away.

"I don't know what these words mean," Violet said, staring at the strange language. She thought she'd understand it if she just stared at it long enough. "But I *want* to know. I want it *so very much*." Indeed, she wanted it more than she'd ever wanted anything in her life.

Demetrius felt sick. He coughed and coughed and sneezed and sneezed. "We need to leave this place," he said. "I won't be able to breathe soon."

We're not supposed to be here, he thought, and the trueness of that statement rattled his bones. They needed to leave. They needed to leave *now*.

"Look," Violet said. She crawled toward the far wall. Reluctantly, Demetrius followed, sneezing all the while.

The back corner of the room was in shadow, but there was a glint of...something. The children squinted, letting their eyes adjust to the low light. As they approached, the ceiling sloped upward, and they came to a place where they could not only stand but could wave their arms and stand on each other's shoulders and still touch nothing. The ceiling towered above them, and the height of the space made its dimness seem cold and empty and bleak. Unconsciously, Demetrius shivered and rubbed his arms.

Leaning against the wall was a painting, delicately wrought and highly detailed, that stood almost as tall as the room itself, reaching a hand's breadth below the edge of the ceiling. It was *crowded* with dragons—hundreds of them—each one utterly unique in body and color and jaw. Each one gesturing differently with its haunches and its shoulders and its neck and its claws. Two things were the same on each, however. First, each dragon was chained—around the base of the neck and at each hind leg. And their chains cruelly cut into their skin, which bulged and reddened with pain. Second, each dragon—despite the fierce curling of its lips, despite the baring of its glinting teeth—had curiously and utterly blank eyes. Indeed, instead of eyes, each dragon simply had a white, hollow space, and the *emptiness* pressed against the children's very souls, almost taking their breath away. And though they wanted to, they couldn't avert their gaze. Violet reached for Demetrius's hand and held on tight.

At the bottom of the painting, heaped in the very middle, was a pile of hearts. Dragon hearts. The children had no idea why they were so convinced the things were dragon hearts, but they knew all the same. Below the dragon hearts was a series of symbols similar to those on the book that was still clutched in Violet's left hand. A name, maybe? A title? There was no telling. And above, on top of the pile of dragon hearts, stood a figure.

"What is that?" Demetrius whispered.

"I don't know," Violet whispered back.

It had two arms, two legs, and a head, but it was not human—not at all. Its head was too narrow, its arms and its legs too long, its shoulders too sloped. And instead of hands and feet, it had four sharp points. It stood on the dragon hearts. And the dragons were under its control.

They *knew* this, and the knowing was heavy and sharp at the same time. The children held their breath.

Curiously, the figure in the painting was not *painted* at all. It had instead been cleverly cut out from a mirror and affixed somehow onto the canvas—a marvel, really, given the delicacy and narrowness of the arms and legs and the sheer height of the figure itself. Instead of any identifying marks, they only saw the reflections of their own grasped hands, their pressed shoulders, their blinking eyes.

"Look," Violet said, pointing to the symbols at the bottom of the painting. "They're changing."

And they were.

Right before their eyes, the symbols wobbled and shuddered and deflated. They wriggled like snakes. They swapped places and re-formed. They became rounded, then angular, then looped, then tall. Violet and Demetrius stared at the changing script. They opened their mouths, but they could say nothing. And then—

"Violet?"

"I know," the Princess whispered.

"Is that...?" Demetrius asked.

"Yes," Violet said.

"But how—"

"I don't know," Violet said.

The first symbol transmogrified into a letter they knew. And then another, and then another.

"Nybb—" Violet began.

"*No*," Demetrius said, suddenly breaking into a cold sweat. "Don't say it. Please don't say it." He shook himself, as though waking up from a particularly bad nightmare, and found that he could move his feet. He stepped backward, pulling Violet with him. "There's something *wrong* with it. Everything is *wrong* here. We need to leave. *Now*." Even as they stood there, the letters were growing, covering up the dragon hearts, and brightening all the while. Demetrius squinted.

"But—" Violet began. *What could it mean?* She wondered and wondered and wondered. *And why does that word seem so familiar?* She thought she might die if she couldn't know.

"We'll ask Cassian," Demetrius said, though Violet could hear in his voice that he knew such a thing was futile. "He'll know."

But he won't tell, Violet thought as she followed Demetrius out, dropping the book onto the floor. Because there *was* something wrong. And the *wrongness* of it was sticky and foul, and it clung sickeningly to her skin. Suddenly, urgently, she longed to be *clean*. She left the book on the ground.

Demetrius waited and let Violet go first through the tiny corridor leading away from the library. He allowed one look back. The word was now so bright that it stood hot and livid, lighting up the whole dim space at the back of the room.

NYBBAS, it said. He shivered.

"We won't come back here," he said to no one in particular.

WE'LL SEE, a slithery, whispery voice sounded in his head. Demetrius jumped, grabbing at his ears. But the voice wasn't in his ears. He heard it *inside*.

"Are you coming or what?" Violet asked from the dusty corridor.

"Yes," Demetrius rasped, shooting one last look at the painting. He thought, for a moment, that the mirrored figure was smiling—a yellow, sharp-toothed smile. But then it flickered away.

A trick of the light, Demetrius told himself as he wriggled into the corridor.

YESSSS. A TRICK OF THE LIGHT. The Nybbas grinned.

CHAPTER SEVEN

The children were right, of course. There was a thirteenth god.

But we did not speak of it.

We did not speak its name.

Its story was forbidden.

CHAPTER EIGHT

Though they never talked about why they weren't talking about it, neither Violet nor Demetrius uttered a word about the hidden library—not for a long, long time.

I won't talk about it if he doesn't talk about it, Violet thought obstinately. *I already know what he'll say.*

I will never mention that place again, Demetrius thought fervently. *I will pretend it doesn't exist. And if she brings it up, I shall change the subject.*

Demetrius tried not to think about it, in hopes that by intending not to think about it, he actually *wouldn't*. He was wrong. The image of the hollow-eyed dragons haunted his nightmares. Night after night, he sweated and moaned in his sleep, his skin aching with the imaginary bite of the dragon's chains.

He would wake from these dreams with sore wrists and sore ankles and a great weight upon his heart.

What happened to them? he wondered. *And who would do such a thing?*

Violet, on the other hand, after getting away from that room with its sticky wrongness, was curious. So, so, so curious.

Her curiosity grew and festered. It lived in her brain, in her heart, and in her bones. It bubbled under her skin.

That name, she thought. *Why do I know that name?* She wondered and wondered and wondered. She scolded herself for dropping the book. And without telling Demetrius she was doing so, Violet started an unsuccessful campaign to find the corridor that would bring her back to that hidden library. But try as she might, she could not do so.

And she thought she'd never see the book again.

And for a long, long time, she didn't.

But books—particularly lost books—have a way of making themselves found.

CHAPTER NINE

On the eve of Violet's thirteenth birthday, her father, King Randall the Bold (the last of that name—indeed, the last Andulan king at all), prepared to lead an expedition into the border mountains on the hunt for a reported dragon. It was a decision hastily made and vociferously argued against.

"Think of the danger!" the King's advisers cried. "You could be gone for weeks, or months—an entire season, most likely. Think of your people. Think of your family."

But the King was undeterred. The terrain was dangerous, to be sure, and he didn't relish the notion of going so far to the north, where our country bordered the nation of the Mountain King—a greedy, cruel tyrant, and growing crueler by the day. But the King, in his soul, was a scientist, and his love of learning trumped his love of country. This particular expedition was for the sake of scientific research while also providing the King with an opportunity to test a new idea—a device to facilitate the live capture and transport of a dragon. It was a bold plan, and risky.

"The first dragon sighting in a century," the King said, his eyes shining. "To think that I should see this day!" And so the preparations were made. And all the citizens of the Andulan Realms worried together.

Demetrius, it was decided, would accompany the expedition. "It's high time for the boy to stand on his own feet," both the King and the stable master agreed. Indeed, in his ability to anticipate the needs of the horses and to heal their afflictions, Demetrius outstripped even his father's—a fact that his father would readily admit, and Demetrius never would.

And so both father and friend were to sally forth without Violet. She was incensed. And as the day grew nearer, she seethed and mourned and seethed again.

And though she had not yet seen it, she hated the dragon. You see, my dears, long ago dragons roamed throughout our world and were, for eons, more abundant than people. But many centuries before my time, their numbers began to dwindle and fade. Eventually, evidence of their existence was no more than rumor and supposition. This sighting—an Onyx—was the first verified proof that the species had miraculously escaped extermination. And the King wanted to be the one to find it, save it, and learn from it. And so a hunt was called for.

Princess Violet was unimpressed.

"You can't call it a hunt if you have no intention to kill it," she said. "All you are doing is playing a game of hide-and-seek with a bunch of grown-ups and an overgrown lizard." *And Demetrius*, she thought bitterly. *That traitor.*

"I've assembled the finest hunters in our nation. Men and women who have no equal as trackers, archers, trappers, and navigators," the King said. "It sounds like a hunt to me."

"Then why must Demetrius go?" Violet asked petulantly. "You are stealing my only friend. *On purpose!* Think of how bored I shall be!"

"Demetrius is coming because no one sees to the animals better. Not even his father." The King wrapped the last of his tools in an oilcloth and slid them carefully into his pack. "Besides," he said, "he *wanted* to come."

That, Violet thought, did not help. *She* wanted to come. But she was not asked. And therefore she would not ask. She crossed her arms across her chest and tried to suppress a glower.

"You should be happy for him," her father said, patting her head as though she were just a little child, and turned his attention to the organization of maps.

The King, as always, did his own preparations for his journey. He carefully compared the items in his rucksack with the items on his list. He arranged, checked, weighed, rechecked, and mended any weak spots himself. It would be hours before he was satisfied.

The King, like his father before him, was an engineer, devoting hours to the dreaming and building of devices and contraptions—much to the chagrin of his daughter. A *real* king, thought she, does not hunch over drafting tables! He does not tinker with hinges and levers and pulleys. A *real* king carries a sword into battle—he is brash and brave and *bold*. Just like the stories said. And though she knew it was wrong, Violet narrowed her eyes at her father's work and felt ashamed.

"Will you at least be fighting the dragon?" she asked, imagining the story she'd tell of her father's derring-do against a fearsome beast.

"Certainly not!" he cried. "We might hurt it!"

Violet threw her hands in the air in exasperation.

"Father," she said. "Do you never read? Great kings are supposed to fight great battles and slay fearsome dragons. Don't they call you King Randall the *Bold*?"

The King, temporarily satisfied that he hadn't forgotten anything, cinched his bags closed and hauled them over to the door.

"There are other ways to be bold," he said, "without demonstrating it with the sword. Most battles are won by changing minds and turning hearts. Sometimes that's all the bravery you need."

Violet scoffed, "And you intend to turn a dragon's heart? *That* is why you won't kill it?"

Briefly, a vision of the painting flashed behind her eyes—those long legs and long arms, those sharp feet digging into the pile of dragon hearts. And the eyes of the dragons—awful, empty, and blank, blank, blank. She shook the image away.

The King smiled slightly and sat next to his daughter on the sofa, leaning as he did so toward the fire. "In a manner of speaking," he said, "yes." He stretched his feet as close to the flames as he dared, trying to warm them through.

Spring had come early that year—a blessing, of course—but the nights were still windy and cold and damp. Still, the King was undeterred. "Many of the stories you've heard about dragons come from the days when their will was not their own. When they were enslaved. Worse than enslaved. Controlled."

Violet snorted. "So, they're forgiven? Just like that? Their nature is still their nature. The stories—" Her voice caught, and she stopped. *Those eyes.* She tried not to think about it. *Those blank, blank eyes.*

"Indeed," the King said, not noticing the catch in his daughter's voice. "Simply stories. There are risks to irresponsible storytelling." He paused, then folded his arms across his chest and narrowed his eyes at his only child. "And you, my dear, ought to be going to bed."

Now Violet, like many children, had her own ideas of when she should sleep, wake, eat, read, and pursue her own plans. But after several minutes of negotiations, offers, and pleading, Violet agreed with her father. Besides, she had several stacks of books squirreled under her bed that she had stolen from the library, her father's study, and my room. Violet had not yet found any more mentions of a thirteenth god, nor had she found any of its stories, but she had not stopped trying. It was there somewhere. She just knew it. Violet threw her arms around her father, kissed each cheek, and wished him pleasant dreaming.

But when she reached the door, she paused.

"Father," said she, "do you know the story of a creature called the Nybbas?"

The room was lit with the rich light of beeswax candles and the bright coals in the fireplace. Even still, it appeared to Violet that her father's face began to darken, then pale. But she blinked and he looked quite himself, and she wondered if she had only imagined it.

"Now where would you have heard such a name, child?" her father asked, a curious hoarseness grating the edges of his voice.

"Oh, I don't know," Violet said casually. "A book or a painting or something. Or perhaps I just dreamed it. But I haven't been able to come up with a reference no matter how hard I look."

"I don't believe I can help you, my dear," her father said. "I simply haven't heard of it. And if Cassian doesn't know it either, I daresay no one does."

And Violet went to bed wondering.

That night, she was troubled by strange dreams. She

dreamed that the castle foundation became, quite suddenly, beset by cracks—fine as spider silk. And like spiderwebs, each filament intersected with countless others, making an intricate and infinite pattern that stretched from the ground to the midpoint of the castle walls. The cracks began to widen, then crumble, then yawn open, and they gave way to an army of golden-skinned lizards, each with hard, glittering jeweled eyes. They were beautiful, quick, and without mercy.

Violet woke just as the castle fell.

Her father, on the other hand, did not sleep at all. He remained seated by the fire, his brooding heart troubled by worry. Exhausted and distracted, the King, along with Demetrius and the rest of the party, left the next morning into the fresh, damp world as the early sun lit their way with a thin, cool light. Before the castle disappeared from view, he stopped, turned, and looked at his home, the place of all he held dear.

Instinct made him raise his hand and wave, though he couldn't see anyone on the parapet waving back—he was too far away. Still, he could *feel* himself being waved at and missed. And in that moment he had half a mind to turn around and head home.

The light shone tenderly on the stones and moss and leafless vines, and he could have sworn he caught a glimpse of something hard, bright, and glittering along the castle's foundation. Like a thousand jeweled eyes. He blinked twice and it was gone. With a jerk of his heels and a quick whistle, he set his horse onward toward the mountains, a tight knot of anxiety curling around his heart.

CHAPTER TEN

Violet's birthday had been observed and celebrated in the days prior to her father's departure, and though at the time she had felt happy and content and *loved*, she watched the retreating figure of the King and his entourage (*Including that rat Demetrius*, she thought scathingly. *Traitor!*) with a growing emptiness. She stood with her mother at the top of the northern wall as the hunting party's horses thundered down the broad road and disappeared into the wood. The Queen rested her hand upon her daughter's shoulder, a faintly hummed lullaby drifting from her tightly pressed lips.

"I don't want to sound ungrateful," Violet said, keeping her eyes on the forest that had just swallowed her father, hoping vainly that he might change his mind and come home.

"I know, my love," the Queen said.

"It isn't that I need anything more," Violet continued. "Because I don't. And I had a wonderful birthday, honestly I did."

"I know, Violet," the Queen said, still humming under her breath. Violet recognized the song. It was the same lullaby that her mother had sung to her as an infant. It didn't occur to her at the time to wonder at it. "Would you like to play at stories, my love? It does so often cheer you up. We could begin with a beautiful princess stealing away from home in the dead of night, setting off on a desperate journey."

Violet bit her lip. "No, thank you, Mother," she said. *A beautiful princess*, she thought, and her heart sank just a little bit deeper.

"It's just..." Violet hesitated. "It's just that he'll be gone so awfully long. And for what? A stupid dragon. I don't understand why he thinks it's so important."

"And yet he does. Your father is not one to stop learning.

Nor is he one to stand aside when there are those who need his help. It's part of who he is." There was a catch in the Queen's voice.

Violet didn't notice.

"It's just this—" She paused again, gesturing to the empty road, as if her father's and her friend's absences each had substance and mass. Each absence felt palpable and crushing. A terrible weight. A gift gone wrong. "It's just a rotten birthday present, that's all." She pulled away and hurried down the worn stone steps without looking back at her mother.

If she had paused, if she had looked back, she might have noticed the tears in her mother's eyes. If she had turned, she might have noticed the pallor in her mother's face, or the recent tightness of her gown around her belly, or the deepening lines of worry around her mouth.

But Violet *didn't* turn. And she didn't notice.

At the bottom of the stairs stood a mirror in a heavily polished wood frame. It was two and a half times as tall as Violet herself, and four times as wide. Carved at the top of the mirror was the likeness of a dragon, its jaws wide open, each tooth glinting with inlaid mother-of-pearl. Gnarled claws curled around the upper rim, and two beady eyes made of cut glass gleamed over the top. All along the edges of the mirror, the artisan had carved no fewer than three hundred (Violet had counted) tiny lizards, so supple and delicate as they twisted and writhed that their wooden bodies seemed ever to be in motion. The mirror was old—more than five hundred years, people said—and had endlessly fascinated Violet from the time she was a very little girl.

She stood in front of the mirror, facing her own reflection—her mismatched eyes, her inconsistent skin, her slightly lopsided face. Normally, Violet wasn't much of a mirror-gazer. "I already *know* what I look like," she'd say impatiently. And she knew that she was ugly. No amount of mirror-gazing would change that, ever. But on this day, her reflection caught her attention, arrested her on the spot. She stared at the ooze of tears making its way down the edges of her cheeks, at her lips weighting into a frown.

Selfish, she thought.

Dull, she thought again. She closed her eyes, her heart caught between wishing that she was useful enough to have been invited on her father's excursion and wishing that she was clever enough to have convinced him to stay.

She opened her eyes and stared at her reflection.

Not pretty enough, a voice whispered in the back of her mind. *Not enough for a* real *princess*, it said even more quietly. It was a thought that had been surfacing quite a bit lately. Violet shrugged it away.

"Yes I am," she said to no one in particular. She glared at her reflection. Her reflection did not glare back. "I'm *real*." No one answered. She closed her eyes, turned away, and hurried down the hall.

Violet didn't notice that there was something...*odd* about her reflection in the mirror. If she had been paying attention, she might have seen that her reflection did *not*— as reflections typically do—mirror her movements and vanish into the limit of the mirrored space.

No. Her reflection remained.

It *remained*.

And as Violet—the *real* Violet—reached the end of the hall, wiping her tears away as she did, the reflection in the mirror—the *wrong* Violet—spread its lips into a cruel yellow grin.

CHAPTER ELEVEN

The hunting party had been gone for a double phase of the Lesser Moon when something that was once known only to a select few became known to all: The Queen—our dear, beautiful, and wise Queen—was expecting another child. Given the sorrowful conclusion of her other pregnancies (besides the miraculous birth of Violet, that is) and the increasing danger to her life and health, we worried for her. Every breathing soul among us.

Still, the entire castle was under strict orders not to

enlighten the King—not even when a supply team was sent to replenish the dwindling stores of the hunting party. "The King must not know," she said.

"He has been searching for a dragon for as long as I have known him, and he may never have another chance," she reasoned. "Why give him cause to worry? Either the child will live or it will not, and there is nothing that the King can do about it."

And perhaps that was true. But *oh*, how we *worried*! And though she pretended not to, so did the Queen.

Violet, for her part, became like a shadow to her mother. She went where the Queen went, ate when the Queen ate, slept when the Queen slept. She fetched drinks and foodstuffs and reading material. She sat in on meetings and hearings and councils—even those that were the *most* boring and the *most* tedious.

The Queen indulged this, calling Violet "my little apprentice."

"Remember, my darling," she said seriously, "the more tedious the meeting, the better the training for later. I wish I could tell you that the tedium becomes enjoyable as one grows old, but alas, I cannot." She laughed at this, but then the laugh became a grimace, and the grimace became a cry, and our gray-faced Queen found herself beset by physicians once again.

After a particularly long meeting, the Queen retreated to her chambers to lie down. Violet remained at her mother's side for a bit to tell her a story—a tale about an apprentice storyteller who had fallen in love with a painting, and how the painting tried to take over the world. But her mother didn't hear the ending, for she drifted off to sleep somewhere in the middle. Violet leaned against the pillows, holding her mother's hand.

How can a painting take over the world? she found herself wondering. The story itself—like many of her stories—spun out of her mouth unbidden and unplanned. She was sure that parts of it were from the stories she had heard or read and that other parts were built of her own invention. But how *much* she had gathered from elsewhere, she couldn't say.

And in any case, she was sure of this much: She had no idea how the story ended.

A painting that took over the world? Or wanted to. Was it possible?

Once again her mind drifted to that hidden library, and

its strange painting, and the book that she had dropped so many years ago. It haunted her dreams still—all flipping pages and dusty pictures and open eyes. Every morning, she woke with the uncanny belief that she was *meant* to be able to decipher the strange lettering in the book, that it would rewrite itself, just as the letters at the bottom of the painting had rewritten themselves, if she just had the chance to see it again.

The sleeping Queen shifted and murmured. She threw her arm across the side of her face, and the lines around her mouth tightened. Violet slid off the slick coverlet, her feet slapping softly on the stone floor. "I'll be back, Mother," Violet said, picking up her mother's hand and kissing the knuckles. And very quietly, she hurried out of the room.

What Violet did not know was that she was being watched. In the opposite corner, standing in the shadows, were two figures, one young (more boy than man) and one very, very old. And they were *small.* So small that if Violet had been standing there, they would have only reached the knob of her knee. Once Violet closed the door behind her, the older one crossed his arms and gave a low, glowering grunt.

"Something you ate?" the younger one said.

"Don't be an idiot, Nod," the older one said absently. It was a phrase he said a lot. "The real question is *why*. Why does that girl know about the painting?"

The younger one—the one called Nod—leaned back on his heels. "P'raps she doesn't. It's a common enough story."

"It's not common at all, you dolt. We haven't heard a soul breathe a word of it for the last five hundred years. And did you hear her? She described that wretched painting to a T. I thought we hid that room well and good, that's what I thought. A lot of work for nothing, wasn't it?"

"*I* didn't help hide the room," Nod said. "I wasn't born yet." He gave the old man what he hoped would be a significant look. He paused. "So I am not at fault," he added, driving the point home.

"And we can all thank the gods for that. If you'd been a part of it, we would've been cooked long ago. Oh, come now! Don't hang your head like that. We all have our own gifts." Though his tone suggested that he had deep doubts as to the existence of any gift possessed by the boy. Nod shoved his hands into his pockets and let out a low, sad whistle.

The older man rubbed his stubbled chin and curled his lips around his toothless gums, grunting all the while.

Finally: "Well, it doesn't do to sit around all day." He clapped a hand on Nod's shoulder. "Go fetch Auntie. Tell 'er the Queen's right poorly again, and she'd better do something before she makes a turn for the worser."

"Auntie," Nod said, screwing up his forehead to force the words to stick in his memory. "Worser. I'll do my best to remember." He hesitated. "You're not coming with me?" A note of pleading in his voice.

"I'm following that girl. Everything's... *wobbly*. Wobblier than I seen it before. And that thing's been bump, bump, bumping around and slithering and mucking about, no matter *what* Auntie says. And getting worser all the time. I *seen* it. With my own eyes. Just yesterday in the mirror, there it was, looking as self-satisfied as a full-bellied snake is what. If it thinks it can pull one over old Moth here, it's got another thing coming." Sighing deeply, he reached into the pocket of his furry brown coat and pulled out a pipe. He gripped it thoughtfully in his teeth. "Go get Auntie," he said. "And tell her I was right."

CHAPTER TWELVE

After the runty god's unintended creation of three whole and distinct universes, and after the inevitable grumbling that followed, the Old Gods discovered that the new worlds were stable and *whole*. They didn't wobble. They didn't jitter or bend. And so twelve of the Old Gods set about making universes of their own. They built universes based on mathematics and universes based on magic and universes based entirely on whimsy. They built worlds clustered together and worlds scattered apart and worlds *within* worlds, fitting inside one another like nesting dolls. Each world shimmered like bubbles in a surging sea. And they were beautiful and unique and *loved*. The gods loved their worlds and they were loved in return.

However, while the twelve Old Gods were creating the many worlds of the multiverse, the thirteenth god—the Nybbas—made nothing. It couldn't be bothered. It pursued its own pleasures instead. It spread malaise, division, mistrust, and despair. It fed on unhappiness and pain.

But soon it longed for more. Power. Control. It saw how the other gods were venerated in the universes they made. Cherished. Adored. *Loved*. The Nybbas was loved by no one.

And it seethed and seethed.

And in its seething, it concocted a plan: The Nybbas began to follow the dragons.

Long ago, you see, dragons were the only creatures of the multiverse who were able to travel from world to world. They could press themselves against the skin of one universe and pass into another as easily as through water. They were bold fighters, long-lived and resilient, but they lived in fear of one another. Indeed, their fear was so great that even their own reflections terrified them. And so they spent their lives alone.

Fully grown dragons, you see, do not have hearts in

their bodies. How could they? Hearts are tender, breakable things and would be burned to cinders in the terrible fires blazing inside the dragons' chests. When dragons reach adolescence, they remove their hearts, encase them in scales and dragon tears—a substance that when dry is as luminous as pearls and as hard as diamonds—and cleverly hide them away. They must keep the location of their hearts a secret, lest they be found and stolen. Whoever controls the heart controls the dragon.

The Nybbas knew this, of course. It also knew of my world—its mirrored sky was the perfect prison for the fearful creatures. And so the Nybbas, using trickery and cunning, stole the heart of every dragon in the multiverse. It brought the hearts to my world and waited for the dragons to come looking. Once they arrived, the dragons were unable to face their own reflections, and could not leave. And so it was fear, their own debilitating fear, that gave the Nybbas the key to their enslavement.

AN ARMY OF DRAGONS, the Nybbas whispered.

THE MOST POWERFUL SLAVES IN THE MULTIVERSE, the Nybbas crooned and crooned.

AND SOON I SHALL BE POWERFUL ENOUGH TO INVADE WORLD AFTER WORLD AFTER WORLD. EACH SHINING UNIVERSE

STRUNG AROUND MY NECK LIKE BEADS ON A STRING. AND EVEN THEIR GODS SHALL LOOK UPON ME AND TREMBLE!

The rule of the Nybbas was short by a god's standards, but for us it was many generations of slavery and misery and subjugation. It was a dark time for my world, a miserable time, until one day the groans and pleading of my world were noticed by the stubby, runty god.

And he roused his brothers and sisters from their godly dreaming and prepared for war.

Now, I don't suppose that you have ever seen an attack led by an army of gods. I myself have not, but there are surviving accounts of what happened that day. The seams along the western edge of the mirrored world stretched, then bulged, then split like a melon, and the gods rained down.

The Nybbas fought but lost. A god cannot kill another god and so, after conferring, the Old Gods decided to imprison the Nybbas inside the very mirror that once corralled the dragons. The dragons themselves were to remain in my world to stand guard and ensure that the Nybbas never escaped.

"You will," the runty god said to the Nybbas, "watch the world that you will never control. You will be forced to mimic and reflect, to display only what the world shows you and nothing more. You will be forced to do as you are told, that you may know the pain of subjugation. The creatures that you once enslaved—the dragons—hold in their power the key to your destruction. Pray they do not use it. Furthermore, we shall transform your heart. We shall give it use and purpose. It will be stones and corridors and rooms. It will bear witness to birth and death, love and treachery. It will be protected, guarded, *loved*. And your magic will never touch it."

Then the gods returned to their worlds. Remembering too well the perils of distraction, they spread themselves widely throughout their universes. They touched and loved and *knew* each rock, each plant, each living cell. They became wind, breath, and dreaming. They coursed through rivers and rumbled in stone and felt the pounding beat of every heart in love. They became everything and everywhere and nothing and nowhere.

And in time their worlds forgot them.

The Nybbas contented itself to bide its time. The dragons, it knew, would die out eventually. Everything does. And anyway, the runty god was wrong. Its heart was not beyond its magic. Some magic works very, very slowly.

And what's more, some magic is patient. Very, very patient.

CHAPTER THIRTEEN

Though Demetrius missed Violet, he was, truthfully, having the best time of his life.

As the youngest member of the expedition, he was expected to see to his work with the same focus and vigor as any of the grown men and women in the party. Each evening, he would inspect the horses' hooves for gravel and cracks, check their teeth and gums for the telltale signs of stress and disease. Then he'd rub their muscles with a soft cloth, wringing out the sweat, and brush them till they gleamed.

All the while, he whispered and crooned.

And all the while, his heart said, *Thank you, thank you, my beloved. Thank you for your work.*

And from the hearts of the horses: *Beloved boy, beloved boy. Doubly beloved.*

The Andulan people were particularly known for our deep connection to our animals. We *loved* our animals, and were loved in return. It wasn't as though we could speak to our animals—clearly, we couldn't. But we *understood* them. Our hearts called out to our horses and our dogs, our milking cows and our shearing sheep and our hunting falcons— and the animals reached out to us in return. And no one was as adept at this as Demetrius. He had a knack for listening.

The dragon hunt was considered by most—even by members of the hunting party—to be a dubious operation. The King—our studious, bookish, endlessly fascinated King—in his thorough and detailed and *profound* research into the history and biology of dragons, discovered the method by which the ancients had trapped and subdued their dragonish quarry. *Mirrors.*

The hunting party—on the whole—grumbled about this scheme. (*Madness!* they groused. *Insanity!*) But they kept their concerns to themselves. Demetrius, on the other hand, thought it would work—no, *knew* it would work—but believed it to be a terrible idea all the same. He brought his concerns to the King.

"I know it's not my place," the boy said, his eyes on the ground. "But I'm here to see to the animals, and the dragon, once it is caught, will be partially my responsibility."

"No, dear boy," the King said kindly. "I would never put that kind of responsibility on the shoulders of one so young. The dragon, though hobbled, will still be terribly dangerous. And I daresay it will be more dangerous to *you* than to *most*." Demetrius waited for the King to clarify this, but he did not.

"It isn't that I think the dragon will be hurt," the boy continued. "It clearly won't. But it is old. And it will *remember*. The dragons were enslaved, and you are capturing it in the same way the ancients did." Demetrius could barely look up. "I fear that the beast won't take it well."

"Nonsense!" the King said jovially, clapping Demetrius on the shoulder. The boy saw a curious gleam in the King's eyes—like the gleam of someone who has been terribly hungry for ever so long, and has just learned that food is on its way. There would be no reasoning with him, Demetrius knew. "The beast will be frightened, to be sure, and angry. But if we do not intervene, its kind will be extinct from our world. Indeed, we may already be too late. But we must *try*. Even when hope is lost, we must still *try*. Now, son, I wonder if you'll see to my horse. He seemed to be treading softly on his front left, and I worry that he might have the beginnings of an injury." The King paused and gave Demetrius's shoulder a fatherly squeeze. "I do wish our Violet could be with us! I had so hoped she could come, but her mother wouldn't allow it. At least she'll have you to tell her the tale, dear boy. And what a marvelous tale it shall be!" And with that, Demetrius was shooed out of the King's tent. He walked back to where the horses were tethered, worrying all the while.

For weeks they searched but found nothing, and the hunting party began to despair. Finally, on the twenty-fourth day of the expedition, the falcons began swooping in excited spirals across the sky, screeching a new call to the ground.

Beast, the screeches seemed to say. *Beast beast beast!*

And the company followed.

Demetrius understood these calls. Everyone did.

But Demetrius understood other things as well. He

could hear that the falcons noticed that the dragon's body was not entirely sound. And while he couldn't tell what exactly was wrong with it, he could hear the alarm in the falcons' voices. He could hear their compassion for the creature. And he worried.

On the morning that they finally laid eyes on the dragon itself, Demetrius had gotten up before anyone else. After feeding and visiting the horses, he ate a bit of salted meat and hard cheese and climbed the nearest tree to clear his mind.

Like the other trees on that mountain, it was old, broad-branched, and impossibly tall. Demetrius climbed as high as he dared. He dangled his feet on either side of a thick, sturdy limb, leaned against the trunk, and looked out at the land as it tumbled away down the side of the mountain and rolled and waved toward home. He couldn't see the castle, but he knew where it was. It shimmered and vibrated in his mind. And somewhere in the center of it was Violet, as bright as a beacon. Demetrius knew he could find his way blindfolded if he needed to.

He climbed a little higher.

In the opposite direction, where the mountains became high and sharp and cruel, lay the castle of the Mountain

King. Demetrius couldn't see that, either, but he could feel it all the same—and it was as cold and vain as the heart of the Mountain King himself. Demetrius didn't like how close they were coming to the border—none of them did. But it couldn't be helped. The dragon must be followed. Never mind if they hadn't—

Wait.

Demetrius froze.

He was up so very high, and the slope beyond the mountain upon which they were camped dropped precipitously. At the bottom of the slope, the woods gave way to swamp and marsh and flowers. And there, gobbling mouthful after mouthful of flowers, was a dragon.

The dragon!

Demetrius didn't move. The beast was terribly far away, but the boy's eyes were keen and his gaze sharp.

And *oh*, it was beautiful! Demetrius felt his breath catch and his heart pound and his eyes well up. Its black scales gleamed in the morning light as it thoughtfully chewed its flowers. Even from his vantage point, the boy could see that the beast had been lamed. Its left wing drooped oddly to one side, and it seemed to be favoring its left haunch. It bit another mouthful and, still chewing, tilted its great

head upward and fixed its stare right at Demetrius. The boy was so startled, he nearly fell out of the tree.

And then a strange thing happened.

Though dragon and boy were separated by a several-hour-long scramble through the woods, Demetrius felt as though there was no space between them at all. That they were boy-nose to dragon-nose. He could smell the sulfur on the beast's breath and had to squint at the bright glitter of the dragon's diamond eye. Its other eye was gone—whether by illness or accident or cruelty, the boy did not know.

Beautiful! the boy thought. *So, so beautiful.*

And then—so close that he might have thought it himself—came the voice of the dragon, ringing inside Demetrius's skull.

OF COURSE.

Demetrius didn't move. Neither did the dragon.

YOU NEED TO GO HOME, BOY, the dragon's voice sounded in his head.

"No," Demetrius whispered out loud. "We're here to see you. We're here to find you and learn from you and help you. Surely you understand this."

I'VE HAD MY SHARE OF HUMAN "HELP," THANK YOU

VERY MUCH, came the dragon's voice. AND DESPITE MY GRIEVANCES WITH YOUR WEAK-WILLED RACE, I WILL OFFER THIS BIT OF ADVICE: YOU NEED TO GO HOME TO YOUR ACCURSED CASTLE. RIGHT NOW. EVEN AS WE STAND HERE, A TERRIBLE EVIL GROWS IN POWER AND INFLUENCE, AND IT MAY NOT YET BE TOO LATE. BUT IT HAS NOTHING TO DO WITH ME, NOT ANYMORE. I AM OLD AND TIRED, AND I WOULD PREFER YOU LEAVE ME OUT OF IT. GO HOME. NOW.

And with that, the dragon turned away, giving the boy a view of its shining rump, and after taking a few more mouthfuls of flowers, the creature disappeared into the forest.

Demetrius climbed down and walked through the forest to the camp, wondering all the while.

"Why would the dragon call our castle cursed?" he asked out loud. The trees didn't answer.

"Our castle has always been good. There's never been any kind of evil." The horses munched on their breakfast and said nothing. Though in the back of his brain—*That room! That painting!* He shivered and fussed.

Finally, Demetrius brought his story to the King.

But alas, any message the dragon communicated—or

the fact that the dragon communicated at all—was lost to Randall's exuberance.

"The dragon!" he exclaimed, upsetting his breakfast bowl and grabbing the boy in his arms, spinning him around and around. "I knew it was wise to bring you along, you marvelous, ruddy, *brilliant* boy!" The King kissed the boy loudly on both cheeks and set a very dazed Demetrius on the ground. "Everyone!" he shouted. "To your horses!"

"But—" Demetrius said.

"Dragons are very tricky and terribly clever," the King said to everyone. "It will likely try to convince us to abandon our mission. Be sure to close your minds to its influence, and let us be off!"

Good advice, Demetrius reasoned. But still he couldn't shake that ancient, craggy voice echoing in his head as he gathered his supplies and saddled the horses, and followed the party at a gallop.

TOO LATE, TOO LATE, TOO LATE.

CHAPTER FOURTEEN

Moth searched for Violet in the hidden passageways in the castle's walls, but in vain. Perhaps his memory of the layout had failed, or the corridors had rearranged themselves (again!), or something was simply redirecting his path. ("Moth knows what you are. I *seen* you," he muttered to the quiet darkness as an invisible *nothing* slithered away.) He returned home in a foul mood.

Violet couldn't find the right corridor, either. But she could *feel* that hidden library, with its strange, indecipherable book. She could feel it breathing. And that same itchy, bubbly curiosity grew and grew under her skin.

Though soon Violet had bigger worries.

That night the Queen's belly seized, and her laboring began all too soon. The infant died before it reached the air. Another son. Another loss.

The Queen continued to bleed. And the bleeding devolved into fever.

"It's manageable," the harried physicians said as they rushed in and out of the room, their faces tight and set. Violet tried to believe their words. She didn't want to leave her mother's side, and stayed as long as she was allowed—waiting, red-eyed, in the corridors during the times when the physicians tried to shoo her away.

She did not go away; Violet, after all, was a girl of her own ideas.

"My mother needs stories," she said, her voice stout and resolute. "This is not a request." And, finally, the physicians had no choice but to obey, though they grumbled about it in private.

Whether the Queen was alert or asleep, Violet sat by her side and told her story after story until her mouth was as dry as sand. She told stories when she should have been eating and stories when she should have been sleeping. She spun stories as though her life depended on it. Or her mother's life. Or every life.

She told her mother about a storyteller who dreamed the world.

She told her mother about a heart that burned, a heart that was lost, a heart fashioned from gold and glittering jewels so sharp they cut the eye.

And she wondered just what would make a story forbidden. And she wondered at the power a single story could wield.

And far away, at the world's edge, a creature shifted and wriggled and tugged at its bonds.

ALMOST, hissed the Nybbas.

CHAPTER FIFTEEN

While the Queen lingered in bed, her fever raging, her heart pounding, her life growing thin and weak as dry grass, King Randall and Demetrius and the rest of the party pursued the Onyx dragon. It was a beautiful creature, though quite old. Its skin was as luminous and deep as the night sky, with a spangle of glinting flecks like stars scattered across its back. Its one eye was a bright jewel set beneath its brow. Its wings had been clipped—a poor, ragged job by someone who cared little for the creature's well-being—and one had been broken at some point in its long life, and healed badly. It could leap and it could glide, but it could not fly.

That it had survived this long stumbling half blind through the woods was something of a miracle.

Even more amazing, the creature was clever and quick and devilishly difficult to apprehend, despite its handicaps. King Randall and his hunters pursued the beast day and night, hemming it in, blocking its escape. The trackers led the charge on the ground while five swift falcons pursued from the air. Snares were laid, decoys hidden, traps set, and yet still the dragon slid through the narrowest gaps like a snake, needing no rest, nor food, nor water—and would not for some time. Dragons, after all, can go many months without food or drink, and while they prefer a sedentary life rich with naps, they do possess a surprising stamina.

Soon the hunters began to tire. They were a thin, ragged bunch.

And all the while, Demetrius could hear the dragon's voice in his head: GO BACK NOW BEFORE IT'S TOO LATE, the voice whispered urgently. YOU STILL MAY SAVE HER.

But who *her* was exactly, the dragon did not specify. No one else seemed troubled by the dragon's voice, and whether they were simply able to ignore it or the dragon was talking only to *him*, Demetrius did not know. In any case, he had a job to do, and he was going to do it to the best of his ability. He bit his tongue to keep from collapsing and crooned to the horses to keep his spirits high.

They gave chase to the dragon for nine days, beginning in the forested hills of the kingdom's northern edge and moving straight north to where the land became steep, jagged, and treacherous.

In the midst of their hunt, they disturbed an ancient-looking crow that had been squatting on a clutch of eggs. The eggs had long ago gone bad, and when they spilled onto the ground and were trodden upon, they let up a dusty cloud of foul odors that clung to the hunters' noses for hours. The crow hovered near their faces for a moment, cawing angrily, before launching in a huff toward the sky.

So intent on their quarry, the King and his hunters didn't think for a moment where the crow was flying *toward*. If they had known, perhaps the archer would have nocked her bow and loosed an arrow into the bird's heart. Instead, the crow soared over the ragged lip of the ridge into the snowy slopes ruled by the Mountain King. There, she whispered the news to the court magician, who whispered the news to the Captain of the Guard, who whispered the news to the Mountain King himself.

The Mountain King nodded grimly and set a plan in motion. Twelve horsemen swung leg to saddle and thundered over the drawbridge to apprehend what they believed to be a war party from the Andulan Realms. Meanwhile, in the forges under the castle, the blacksmiths and sword makers worked both day and night, building arms for every man, woman, and child in the kingdom.

"If it's war they want," the Mountain King said again and again, "then good. The Lowland King will weep for his lost kingdom, and his wife and daughter will spend their lives in the bowels of my castle, scrubbing chamber pots. The time has come to make low the Lowland King."

CHAPTER SIXTEEN

Violet needed her father.

She *needed* him. But he was off on some crazy adventure, leaving her alone. And she felt *oh so* alone. The physicians had insisted that Violet allow them to do their jobs without her incessant meddling, and so she wandered. Having nothing better to do, Violet decided to sneak into her father's study. Read his books. Go through his papers. She wanted to look for... something. She knew not what. Clues, maybe?

Finding and stealing the key to her father's study was

easier than Violet would have guessed—so easy that she was quite appalled that she had not thought of it before. She slipped away, darting from corridor to corridor, until at last she arrived at the polished door. Checking first behind her to make sure she was quite alone in the hallway, she slid the key into the lock and turned until it clicked. Holding her breath, she pushed open the door, wincing at the creaky moan of the hinges, and looked into the darkened room.

It was, as usual, a mess. Violet stepped carefully over the debris on the floor, walked to the desk, and sat down.

Her father had no fewer than six ledgers scrawled to the margins with notes and covered over with diagrams, drawings, charts, and figures. There were precise anatomical renderings of the insides of dragons, detailed descriptions of their musculature and physiology, lists of hormones and glands that were responsible for fire-making. There were several drawings of the heart of the dragon—both the external heart, encased in its shell for its protection, the dragon itself bending over and tending to its heart, and drawings of the heart inside the open chest of the beast. There were also several pages on the subject of mirrors. "If dragons are terrified of their own reflections," her father had written, "if the fact of their heartlessness makes them prisoners to that fear, then how in heaven's name did they find themselves in our world? Of all possible worlds in the multiverse, what led them to the world with the mirrored sky—from which there is no escape? I am beginning to suspect that, ever so long ago, dragons were brought here by trickery and deceit, and discovered too late that they could not leave. But why? And by whom?"

Was it possible, she wondered, that the creatures that haunted the most fearsome stories and the most frightening nightmares would be this weak? This frightened? That the only thing they did *not* fear was a dragonling—and that any dragon, regardless of family or tribe, would fight to the death to protect it? Violet shook her head. *This can't be right.*

She continued to turn the pages, pulling out more loose scraps of paper that her father had scrawled notes or questions or drawings on and had folded several times before shoving them at random into the ledger. "Does the dragon know when its heart has been moved?" one scrap said. "Can the heart be replaced?" said another. This question had been underlined several times. And indeed, Violet found it again and again, all on its own, on other pages, scrawled in margins, scribbled on the backs of pages, and on scrap after scrap after scrap.

The question seemed to be a bit of an obsession.

"Have you gone mad, oh my father?" Violet murmured to the empty room. "And if you have, what are we to do?"

On another page there was a rough sketch showing a young woman reaching toward the chest of a dragon. In one hand she held a knife; in the other was a heart. Below it King Randall had written "Traced from the Wanderer's Chronicles, supposedly written before the Great War. Possible?"

Violet gathered the ledgers, as well as a large stack of loose notes, and slid them into her satchel.

"Why now, Father?" she whispered. "Why did you have to do this *now*? Please, please come home." And just as she was about to start in on the bookshelves, Violet heard something that made her heart go cold.

A bell.

At the top of the western wall hung a bell. It was huge, black, made from cast iron. It had rust along its edges. It was a call to prayer—a call to hope when all hope was gone. It had been rung once before in her lifetime, when she was only an infant, and both her life and the life of her mother hung on the tiniest thread of hope. On that day the magicians rang the bell, and the entire country hoped and prayed as one. Violet had no memory of it but knew its ringing all the same. There was nothing else in the castle that could make that mournful boom, so deep it rattled the bones and stole the breath.

The Queen, the bell tolled. *The Queen is in danger.*

Pray, pray, pray, pleaded the bell. *And hope without ceasing.*

Violet tore out of the room, slamming the door behind her.

CHAPTER SEVENTEEN

The Mistress of the Falcons, a tall woman with a fierce, brusque way of speaking that made Demetrius simultaneously terrified and amazed, sent forth her birds, which reported back the existence of a natural corral in the high cliff not one-half league ahead. The King ordered the wagoners to bring the transport into the rocky grotto and to hang canvases over the mirrors. The hunters gave chase, bounding after their fleeing dragon, listening for its breath, catching its scent. They could smell the beast's panic and its exhaustion. They could smell its frustration over its broken wing, its rheumy joints, its sense of its own diminishment. And they grieved for the dragon. Even as they hunted they grieved.

After seemingly endless days of chase, the King and his party finally had the upper hand. The dragon had no choice but to back defensively toward the grotto.

Demetrius and four hunters waited at the entrance, partially hidden in the foliage. They waited until the dragon was close, and they stepped into the clearing, holding their mirrors before them like shields.

The dragon, though old and infirm, its prime days a thousand years past, was still a terrible thing to behold. The sharp sheets of its armored skin overlapped one another, the edges glinting like knives as they skimmed the beast's sinewy shanks. It hissed and snarled and snapped. It reared, uncurled its fibrous tongue, and brandished the yellow curve of each war-worn fang.

And yet.

Before the mirrors it trembled.

Before the mirrors, it postured, roared, and backed away, its ears pressed flat against its skull.

The hunters—every last one of them accomplished, professional, and celebrated—let their mouths drop open

in surprise. Inwardly, the good King Randall rejoiced. And advanced.

Once the dragon had backed entirely into the transport, Randall gave the word, and the canvas curtains inside dropped away. The dragon, seeing its reflection on all sides, believed itself surrounded, and, with a sound that was something between a roar and a whimper, laid its great head on the transport floor and covered its brow with its forearms.

The lead tracker, standing next to the King, removed his hat and shook his head. "If I hadn't seen it myself, sire," he said, "I would never have believed it could be done. In fact, I'm not sure I believe it even now."

Demetrius frowned. *Just because it* can *be done*, he thought to himself, *doesn't mean it* should.

The Mistress of the Falcons set about securing the enclosure while two trappers checked the vehicle for cracks and weaknesses. However, both Demetrius and the King knew those tasks weren't necessary. The dragon would not move until it must, and if the King's research was correct, it would not require food or water for a month, at the very soonest. It was well and truly trapped. Demetrius laid his hands on the wooden doors and closed his eyes. He could hear nothing from inside, no indication of the dragon's voice—and whether this was from dragonish contempt or abject fear, he did not know.

The King patted Demetrius's shoulder tenderly. "It's unfortunate and unpleasant, I know," he said with a sigh. "But think of what we'll *learn*." He rested his hand on the boy's back as they and the lead tracker left the rocky grotto and went to their horses in the clearing. The King's horse was stamping and whinnying, and if Demetrius were not so exhausted, he may have investigated the cause. At the very least, he would have taken the time to listen to the horse. Instead, he reached into his saddlebag and pulled out a morsel of salted meat, which he chewed thoughtfully.

"Indeed," the King continued, "I knew that it *ought* to be done as well. But oh! My heart aches for the creature. First imprisoned by loneliness and now imprisoned by fear. It seems terribly unfair."

And whether the trapper agreed with the King, I do not know, my dears. For at that very moment, the horsemen from the castle of the Mountain King emerged from the tangle of spring green. Their swords were drawn, their arrows nocked, and their eyes narrowed pitilessly.

"Drop your weapons," the Captain of the Guard said, holding the tip of his sword to King Randall's exposed throat.

CHAPTER EIGHTEEN

Back at the castle, Violet lay next to her mother on the bed, feeling the heat from the Queen's body radiating like coals.

"Bring him back," her mother pleaded again and again. "Please bring him home." And whether she was talking about the stillborn son or her husband, Violet didn't know.

The castle physicians and midwives and magicians and apothecaries all collected in the corners of the room, conferring quietly as though to protect Violet from any harmful information. In truth, they needn't have bothered. Violet didn't care much for them and instead focused all her attention on her mother, cradling the Queen's hot, papery fingers in her own.

"I had so hoped," the Queen said, touching her thumb to each of Violet's fingertips and gazing vaguely at the ceiling. A midwife applied a foul-smelling plaster to the Queen's belly to heal the infection and a pale blue poultice on her chest to soothe her broken heart. "I thought that the hoping would be enough. I should have told him before he left. I should have known that every secret has a sting."

She then fell into a deep swoon, and a suddenly panicking—and uncharacteristically insistent—group of physicians shooed Violet out of the room.

"Just for a moment, Princess," the head nurse said. "Just give us a moment," and the old woman wiped at her creased eyes with the back of her hand and closed the door. Violet walked alone through the many corridors of the castle and out into the stable yards.

Demetrius should be there. But he wasn't. *That rat*, she thought.

The castle, meanwhile, was in an uproar. Councillors called emergency meetings; magicians, mages, and holy men and women led prayers; and scribes worked around the clock to pen notices and pamphlets and proclamations. Courtiers and ladies-in-waiting and librarians and scholars met in small groups around the castle, speaking in hushed voices as they dabbed their eyes. An elite team of four soldiers was outfitted, supplied, and sent in search of the King to gather him back home.

I, for my part, took to my room. There was something... *odd* about the Queen's illness and the King's absence. A strange simultaneity setting a disturbance in my soul. Something I couldn't quite put my finger on—a slippery, wily grin, ever out of reach. And I was afraid. I told myself that I was creating a comforting place of stories for whoever wanted to slip away from the grieving castle for a moment or two. But that was a lie.

So Violet was alone.

And she was miserable.

She sat down on the hard gravel and leaned against the rough boards of the stable's exterior. The Greater Sun had dipped below the castle wall, but the Lesser Sun was high and full, its brightness thin, clear, and warming. She squeezed her eyes shut, dimly aware of the red glow under her lids, and let the pale heat sink past her skin and into her bones.

And then she heard it.

"That one," a voice said. "There."

Violet sat up and opened her eyes. She was alone. Who had spoken?

"Hello?" she said, peering up at the leaves, then down to the undergrowth and the shadows. No one was there.

A second voice. "Are you sure? You've thought that before, you know."

"No," the first voice said with a bite of exasperation and annoyance at the center of the sound. "No, that is not what I said at all. Before I said *maybe*. There is a great difference between *maybe* and *definitely*. Now I know for sure. Definitely."

The second voice snorted. "Tosh!" it said.

"Who's there?" Violet asked, scrambling to her feet. "What do you want?"

"Ooooh, look at that, loudmouth," the first voice said. "She can hear you. Now you've done it."

"She can*not*," the second voice said. "None of 'em can. Big'uns are as deaf as iron."

"Hush up, featherbrain."

"I *can* hear you, you know." Violet took a step back to look at the roof, when she heard a gasp and a clatter and then nothing. Only silence.

"Hello?" she called.

The yard was quiet. Even the field and the trees and the undergrowth hushed, though it was a brittle and uncomfortable silence, as though the whole world was bracing itself. But for what? Violet did not know.

Her skin prickled and itched. It grew hot, then cold, then hot again, and she knew, as sure as she knew that the sky was clear and the day was cool, she *knew* that she was being watched.

"Fine," she said, more loudly than before. She turned on her heel in a huff. "Please yourself." She began walking across the gravel yard. But just as she rounded the corner of the stable, she heard the first voice once again.

"See? I told you she'd be able to hear us. And I told you she was the one—the right one. Or one of them, anyway."

CHAPTER NINETEEN

The King and his hunters did not move. And though the blade upon the good King's throat pressed cruelly into his flesh—so deep that a tiny bead of blood, bright as a ruby, shone at the top of the blade before oozing lazily downward—the King's face remained implacable and detached. Demetrius couldn't take his eyes off the bead of blood. Indeed, the redness of the blood, and the horror of it, were all he could see. They eclipsed the world. Very slowly he balled his hands into fists.

"Well then," said the Captain of the Guard. A cruel smile creased his face. "My dear friends. Look what I have caught. A lowland rat scurrying into our fair kingdom. What was it thinking?"

The soldiers of the Mountain King laughed.

It was more than he could stand. Demetrius (oh, that good boy! and, oh, that terrible fool!), without thinking, without planning ahead, pawed the ground like a bull, lowered his head and shoulders, and with an animal grunt, rammed his skull into the Captain's rib cage. It was a very brave and very stupid thing to do. The Captain was a giant of a man, and cunning, too. The weight and force of Demetrius's body caused hardly a jostle in the big man's stance and certainly didn't pull the tip of his sword from the throat of the King. In quick succession, he grabbed the boy by the back of his tunic, tossed him up into the air, and threw him down hard onto the ground. And before Demetrius could even breathe, the Captain had unsheathed his stiletto from his belt and, with a casual flick of his wrist, sent the blade directly into the boy's shoulder.

The pain nearly blinded him.

"Damn," the Captain said. "I missed."

The King swore, and the assembled party shouted, but Demetrius was too astonished to make a sound.

"I was going for the throat," the Captain said casually, narrowing his eyes at the King, "but perhaps, given the reaction of your overly emotive crew, it's best if I let the boy live. For now." He spat on the ground. "He may be useful."

Demetrius, panting in pain, pulled up to his knees, yanked the blade out himself, and stanched the bleeding with the heel of his hand.

"Bind him," the Captain of the Guard said. He kept his sword on good King Randall's neck. The King did not flinch. After his brief eruption, his face no longer betrayed even a hint of fear or worry but instead remained as calm and unreadable as stone.

"We are always delighted to see the emissaries of our cousin to the north," the King said slowly and formally, as though he was standing in the Great Hall. "May we inquire the nature of this visit, sir?"

The Captain paled. He had expected the captive to beg, insult, or even engage in a foolhardy attempt at an attack. He was not expecting the address of a King.

Still, he was not the Captain of the most elite unit of

the Mountain King's guard for nothing. He set his jaw and twisted his lips into a sneer. "We are responding, *Your Majesty*, to an act of war."

The King raised his eyebrows. "Our hunting party?"

"I don't care what you choose to call yourselves," the Captain said, waving at the disarmed hunters and their weapons piled on the ground. "What I see is a fierce assembly, armed to the teeth, one mile within our borders and heading, apparently, to the castle."

"Indeed," the King said thoughtfully. "Indeed."

It was, I believe, an act of sheer will for the King to refrain from glancing into the rocky grotto where the dragon, its transport, and the Mistress of the Falcons and the two trappers lay in wait. From where the Captain stood, the entrance to the grotto was invisible, and as he had not yet ordered a soldier to gather any strays, the King knew it was unlikely that the Captain had seen them enter or exit with the dragon.

And thus did our beloved King permit his hands to be bound, his ankles tied with a lash that looped under the belly of his horse, and his horse tethered to the others. He looked out at the faces of his companions, all bound, and said, "I am truly sorry, my friends."

He turned to Demetrius, the boy's face an ashy mask of pain. "I don't know how I shall face your father, beloved Demetrius. My heart aches with sorrow for this attack on you, for the danger I have put you in." The King's voice halted and broke. "It is unforgivable, dear child, and I am sorry."

The hunters, all grave-faced, said nothing.

For they, too, knew that three of their number hid and listened at the rocky lip of the grotto's entrance. They knew that once they had plodded away, they might—should they look behind them—see the shadow of a flank, the wisp of a tail, and the broad-winged beat of the five falcons on their launch to the sky as the two trappers and the Mistress of the Falcons thundered their way toward home.

Slowly, quietly, they whispered to their horses. Slowly they breathed courage to one another. And as they looked at the Captain and his men with an expression of unabashed contempt, they thought this:

Just wait.

CHAPTER TWENTY

There was little the physicians could do. They could only wait. Both the Princess Violet and I were called back to the sickroom and took turns sitting next to the feverish Queen. A nurse laid a pallet and blankets on the floor, where we could catch an hour or two's rest from time to time. We whispered story after story after story to the failing Queen. Tales of mages and deadly spindles and true love transformed yet undeterred all rasped from our dry mouths, our lips chapped and cracked from worry and weeping.

Some of our stories might be familiar to you, my dears,

did you know? Stories have a tendency to seep across the shining membrane walls separating the universes. They whisper and flutter like the feathers of birds, from island to mainland and back again. They fall into dreams like rain.

Do you know, for example, the one about the broken-hearted maiden, cheated out of marriage by a false youth, who goes to live on a remote, rocky shore and swears off love forever—only to win the heart of a fearsome leviathan that lurked in the dark, treacherous reef?

Or the one about the young man who, after refusing the attentions of a very persistent and very powerful goddess, chose to transform himself into a tree rather than submit to a marriage without love?

Or perhaps you've heard of the king who grew tired of the world and shut himself inside a tall tower with a single window from which he could gaze at the stars—and of his patient wife, who waited for his beard to grow long enough to allow her to climb up and fetch him home?

If not those, I assure you there are others that have drifted back and forth from time out of mind.

As we told our stories, the Queen's fever deepened. She gasped and sighed and moaned, and whether she was vaguely awake or vaguely asleep, she was always imprisoned by her strange and desperate dreaming. She sweated and shivered and went pale to flushed to pale again. And Violet—poor Violet!—did her best to soothe her mother. She tenderly dipped the cooling cloth into a silver bowl of fresh-drawn water and dabbed her beautiful mother's fevered face. She applied salve to the Queen's blistered lips, ice to her palms, and scented oil under her nose.

Toward the end of the sixth day, the Queen's ravings began to clarify into words.

"The dragon is the least of your worries," she said in midafternoon.

"The hunters are hunted," she said as the cook brought in tea, and the grim-faced physicians listened to her breathing and pulse.

"*Run!*" she screamed in the waning light, her body thrashing nearly out of the bed. *"Run, my love!"*

And then: "The King has been taken. They've taken the King!"

Violet and I—along with the nurses and midwives and magicians—told her again and again that what she saw was merely a dream, but the Queen couldn't hear us.

But of the four riders sent to fetch the King, only one returned. And the King was not with him. Instead, he was accompanied by two trappers and the Mistress of the Falcons.

Within the quarter hour, they stood before the Princess, the High Chancellor, the four generals, and the Council of Scholars. I was there, too, though by rights I should not have been. But Violet insisted, and no one had the heart to refuse her.

During the meeting, the escaped members of the King's hunting party ignored the senior members of the council, with their grave voices and their pompous ponderings. Instead, they kept their eyes on one person, and that was Violet. Imagine, my dears, the child Violet! She would not release my hand, and I was therefore privy to information far above my rank and station. And *oh*, it was terrible! The grim faces of the men and women of the hunting party. The shivering child standing before them.

"The King has been taken," the Mistress of the Falcons said, and though of course she already knew it was true, still she gasped sharp and high, as though in pain. Her given name was Marda, and she was tall and very strong. She wore a leather tunic and leggings—both well worn and soft—and a gray hood that shadowed her features. Though it would have been right and proper for her to remove the hood in the presence of the court, it was clear to all of us that her eyes were red and heavy from weeping, and we thought better than to mention it.

"Three of us remain in the mountains to track the prisoners," the rider said. "The trail will be marked—a leftward slash at regular intervals while the prisoners remain alive. A rightward slash for each death. An X if their captors should have the audacity to—"

"Enough!" Violet commanded, her voice trembling, though her body was still and calm, her eyes locked on the Mistress of the Falcons. Violet gripped my hand so tightly that she left finger-shaped bruises under my knuckles. She drew herself up to her full height and turned to face the advisers.

"Who here are the generals?" Violet asked.

The four generals, large and gruff women and men, stepped forward and knelt before the Princess. "We are, Lady," they murmured.

Violet knew them all, though not very well. And she had no idea, not really, what exactly they *did*. She simply knew they were in charge of...well, a *lot*. Soldiers, horses, stores of equipment. They looked up at her expectantly. Violet cleared her throat.

"Assemble as many soldiers as you need. Bring the fastest, the strongest, and the best. And bring him home." Tears leaked from the corners of her eyes. "Please," she added before returning to her mother.

Later, as she laid her head on the pillow next to the Queen's fevered face and whispered a story about a clever mouse that helped a girl win the heart of a prince, she listened to the rhythmic rumble of horse hooves assembling on the cobblestoned square and thundering away.

And that night she dreamed that she rode a black dragon. In her dream she wore a white dress, black gloves, and a flaming, pulsing heart attached to a red ribbon, tied around her throat.

CHAPTER TWENTY-ONE

The journey from the point of capture to the castle of the Mountain King should not have taken more than two days—with an hour break at midnight to rest and restore.

At the rate at which they were currently traveling, however, it was sure to take ten times as long.

"What is wrong with your horses?" the Captain shouted again. He raised his leather strap and gave the King's horse a cruel smack on the rump.

"It's not their fault, sir," Demetrius said. He was weak

from loss of blood, and the world swam around him. "Our horses have been ridden hard and fast for days. They know that they are no longer in pursuit of their quarry. You may shout and threaten all you want, but these animals are intelligent, and you have not persuaded them."

This, my dears, was a lie, and a clever one at that. But the Captain—given that he was a man of the mountains and not of the Andulan Realms—would never have guessed the truth of the matter. You see, the people of the Northern Mountains, as well as the people in the Southern Plains and the Eastern Deserts and the Island Nations to the west, all saw their animals as simple beasts of burden. But we in the central kingdom felt differently.

And so it was that Demetrius and the King and all the captured party, in their deepest hearts, whispered to their horses. *Slow down*, their hearts breathed. *Delay. Plod and shuffle, my beloved.* The horses knew and understood. And no amount of barked orders or cruel lashes on the back would persuade the animals to hasten.

The King watched the far rim of the horizon and was soon rewarded with the sight of five falcons, flying in formation in the distant sky.

And they were growing nearer.

CHAPTER TWENTY-TWO

Violet rested her chin on her fists as she lay sprawled on the floor next to her mother's bed, her father's papers strewn before her like stars. She had tried to organize them according to topic—the stacks of notes on dragon biology here, the notes on the mathematics and science of flying over there, the pages and pages of history and lore over there—but there was too much *in between*. Too many pages that *might* be story and *might* be science and *might* be history and *might* be complete balderdash, but she had no way of knowing.

She read, "The fact that dragons once roamed freely throughout the multiverse before finding themselves trapped—en masse—in our mirrored world is something of a puzzle. I have kept, as have my fathers and mothers before me, the details of the Forbidden Tale a secret, guarding it deep in my heart, though I never believed it to be true. I have never believed in the Old Gods, and certainly never believed in their rogue sibling. But the secret is tradition, and I have kept it, just as my child will after me."

Violet felt her blood turn to ice.

"Still," she read on, "there are facts that cannot be ignored. In which case, the successful regrafting of the dragon's heart might be of a larger importance than the simple continuation of the species. Indeed, this may be the most important task ever undertaken in the history of the mirrored world."

Violet felt her breath quicken.

She thought of the painting in the hidden library.

The mirrored figure standing on the dragon hearts.

The chained dragons with the fierce teeth and fierce jaws and blank, blank eyes.

Violet shuddered and turned the page.

And then she read this:

"The writings of Odd the Obscure and Reginald the Wanderer and B'thindra the Other all point to the same conclusion—the Forbidden Tale is true, the thing whose name we do not speak is as real as worlds, and it did, ever so long ago, bring dragons here as slaves, and it did take over our world, and it did have plans to control the rest of the multiverse before it was stopped by the Old Gods. What Cassian has always told me is wrong: The tale is *true*."

The tale is true.

Violet gathered her father's notes and slipped them into his ledger before binding it shut and shoving it into her satchel. *If this story,* she thought, *this Forbidden Tale is true, then what other stories are true? And if the stories are true, then why is the world so removed from the way it is supposed to be?*

Violet stood for a long time in front of the mirror in her mother's room. Her mismatched eyes were red-rimmed and bloodshot. Her unruly hair had achieved new levels of unruliness. Her normally blotchy skin was now raw and chapped and livid.

She was well and truly and *terribly* ugly. She couldn't close her eyes. She couldn't look away.

She had been, day after day, telling her mother stories, and each of these stories depicted valiant kings, radiant queens, and impossibly beautiful princesses. *This is the world as it should be*, the poor girl thought. *But somehow everything has gone wrong.*

I have made it wrong.

I am all wrong.

The Queen stirred and murmured in her sleep. No words escaped her dry lips, just an assortment of sounds. Violet went to her mother's bed. She kissed the Queen's feverish hands and her feverish cheeks and her feverish lips.

"Don't worry, Mama," she said. "There's a way to make this right. I *know* there is. And I am going to find it." And with that, Violet set off with new determination to find that dusty corridor.

She would find that library.

And she would find that book.

And she would find that painting that tried to take over the world. Anything that could do *that* would have powers. And answers.

She would find all these things, and she would set the world right. She *had* to.

"I'll be back soon, Mama," she said as she shut the door behind her.

"*No!*" cried the feverish Queen in her feverish dreaming. But Violet was already gone and didn't hear her.

YYYYEEEEESSSSSS, whispered the Nybbas.

CHAPTER TWENTY-THREE

Demetrius, despite the injury to his shoulder that, even now, continued to slowly leak blood onto his shirt, crooned to the horses. Everyone in the hunting party did. But Demetrius could *feel* the horses' desire to run, to protect the people they loved. He could feel their growing frustration.

Horses, as you may know, my dears, are loyal creatures, devoted to their masters and families.

Demetrius had to be firm. *Soon, beloved. Plod. Shuffle. Limp. Be ready.*

It was almost time. He knew from the wide circling of the five falcons that their friends had arrived.

Quick, his heart urged the King's horse. *Go lame. Now.*

The horse grumbled silently but did it all the same. With a stumble and a sharp whinny, the King's horse wobbled dangerously—nearly falling over and crushing its rider. It righted itself with a snort, lifted its left foreleg, and refused to place it down again.

"What now?" the Captain cried.

"I don't know," the King said slowly, an inscrutable look on his face. "I only hope that it is merely a bruise. I would hate to lose this horse."

The Captain smiled. "Oh, *Your Majesty.*" His upper lip curled, showing his long, yellow teeth. "I suspect you'll lose much more than that. There are rules about the crimes of war. Morality is merciless, after all."

The King gazed back, his face expressionless. The Captain cleared his throat, dropped his gaze to the bonds cutting deeply into the King's wrists, and shrugged. He unsheathed his dagger.

High in the sky, the falcons soared in a wide arc, their mouths open and screeching. *It's him! It's him!* their voices seemed to call as they tumbled over updrafts and spiraled through the wind. *Strike when the hands are free.*

They kept their eyes on the man with the long coat. They saw him lean toward the King. They saw the bright slice of a blade in his hand; they squinted at the glint of its edge in the sun.

"I think, Randall, that I shall have you ride with me," the Captain said, cutting the strap that bound the King's ankles. "This pathetic excuse for a horse will be far more useful as food for those vultures over there once its throat is cut."

He brought the blade to the King's wrists and cut the first strap.

"I should let you know," the King said casually as the second strap snapped free under the blade. "Those aren't vultures." The third strap snapped. The King lifted his hand. "They're falcons."

And before the Captain could react, the King fell lightly to the ground, and the falcons attacked.

When the first falcon shot forth, the King's soldiers unsheathed their swords and leaped out of the thickets and into the battle.

Though it seemed to Demetrius to take an eternity, the battle lasted little more than an hour's quarter. Two Andulan soldiers lay dead on the ground, their mouths still open and aghast, and the bodies of four guards from the mountain kingdom were crumpled in heaps under the trees. Those who remained—including the Captain, bleeding heavily from one eye—were rounded together, swords leveled at their hearts.

The King sat astride his horse, his sword pointed casually at the Captain, who, despite great pain, managed to force a look of sullen malevolence onto his bleeding face.

"The Mountain King will answer to this brazen act of violence," King Randall said, his voice low and cold and even. "In the meantime, I want you and your men to mount your horses and quit this place. Immediately."

"And go without weapons?" the Captain sputtered. "The wild animals will tear us to pieces."

"Which means that you shall have your speed and your hands, in addition to your wits, as means of survival. I assume the mercy I show you now is greater than what you or your monarch were willing to afford us. Indeed, I daresay it is more than my men- and women-at-arms likely wish that I would grant." In response, the hunters and soldiers raised their swords, baring their gritted teeth. "Still," the King continued, "the right is mine to offer mercy or retribution. I choose mercy. You have your lives, and we will bury your dead with honor. Go. Now. And do not look back."

The Captain attempted to mount his horse but, because of his injuries, could not do it on his own. In frustration, he kicked at the ground and punched the animal hard in its flank. The Captain's men helped him onto his horse and followed behind. They moved in single file down the trail in a slow plod until they were quite out of sight, when, with a smack on the hides of a dozen horses, they galloped away.

"My beloved," Randall said to his soldiers, his strength escaping in a sigh, "I owe you my thanks. But we cannot tarry. See to the boy first—his wound has festered too long. And to our fallen comrades. And then let us ride, my friends. The faster we get to the border, the safer we all are, I expect."

The King looked into the face of his lieutenant, a young, tall woman with a scar across one cheek.

"Sire," she said. She hesitated, cleared her throat, and stared hard at the ground. "When the three uncaptured members of your party neared home, they were met by messengers from the castle. Because of the"—she cleared her throat again—"*situation*, the message is now carried . . .

I carry the message, sire." Her eyes, quite suddenly, filled with tears. "The Queen—"

King Randall heard no more. He leaped onto his horse's back, pointed its nose toward home, and flew into the green.

CHAPTER TWENTY-FOUR

It was as though the hidden library *wanted* Violet to find it. She had searched for hardly more than an hour when she suddenly stumbled into a corridor choked with dust, which shortly opened into a vestibule, which opened into a room.

It was silent.

It held its breath.

She went to the painting—the enslaved dragons, the pile of hearts, the oddly lengthened figure in the center. And the symbols at the bottom that, even now, were trembling, shifting, their curves and slashes snaking into new curves and new slashes, until they finally wrote themselves into letters that she knew.

She wished Demetrius were there.

She wished her father were there, too.

And yet... in a strange way, she was glad to be alone. She was glad that the room, and the library and the painting and the dust and the strange symbols, exactly as they had been before, were hers, and *hers alone*, to find.

They were *beautiful*.

The painting was silent. *NYBBAS*, its letters said. Violet didn't say it out loud, though she could *feel* the painting wishing she would. She stared at the figure wrought in delicate mirrors. She saw herself staring back—and then, quite suddenly, she was not alone in the mirror. In the shining center of its narrow face was a pair of yellow, blinking eyes. Violet gasped.

"What are you?" she asked out loud.

DO NOT ASK WHAT YOU DO NOT CARE TO KNOW. It wasn't a voice in her ears. It was in her head. It skittered around her skull with its spidery legs. She shuddered. AND DO NOT ASK WHAT YOU HAVE ALREADY GUESSED.

She took a step backward, her foot landing on something hard and square. Violet looked down. It was the book

NYBBAS

that she had dropped all those years before. The book that haunted her dreams. Keeping her eyes on the painting, she reached down, grabbed the book, and slid it into her satchel. *At last*, she thought.

"Don't tell me what I know or what I wish to know," Violet said. Her voice shook. Her eyes burned. Her mother lay dying, and it was Violet's own fault—she was sure of it. Her father was missing, and this was her fault as well. "What are you? What kind of painting speaks?" Her skin tingled, and her stomach flipped. Her heart urged her to turn, to stop her ears, to run away. But she resisted. After all this time *wondering*, she had to know.

GO, CHILD, the painting said, as though hearing her thoughts. GO AND FORGET. YOU DO NOT WANT TO STAY HERE.

"I am a perfectly good judge of what I want, thank you," Violet said, her eyes narrowing on the mirrored figure in the painting. It had lips now. And blushing cheeks. "Tell me what you are, or I shall have my soldiers burn this library to cinders."

I AM THE ONE YOU HAVE BEEN LOOKING FOR, CHILD.

"I haven't been looking for anyone." Violet clutched her satchel to her chest. "And you haven't told me what you are."

OH, BUT YOU KNOW.

"I don't. And you are playing games. Tell me what you are this minute. I command it."

The mirrored figure in the painting closed its yellow eyes. It grinned its golden grin. AND I OBEY. INDEED I MUST.

Outside, the bells rang and rang and rang. Prayers, mourning, or welcome? Violet did not know. She couldn't move. Dust clouded the air around her, making her cough.

IT'S A STORY THAT YOU KNOW. IT'S A STORY THAT YOU'VE TOLD. I'VE HEARD YOU TELL IT. LONG AGO, YOU SAID, THERE WAS ONLY ONE WORLD. ONE UNIVERSE. I LIS- TENED WHILE YOU WOVE THE TALE, AND I SMILED. BECAUSE THE TALE IS TRUE. I WAS THERE, AND I KNOW.

"No," Violet breathed.

AND MY BROTHER—THAT RUNTY IDIOT—MADE THREE WORLDS WHERE ONCE THERE WAS ONE. I WAS THERE.

"It's not possible," Violet said.

AND MY SIBLINGS, IN THEIR JEALOUSY, IN THEIR... LIMITATIONS. THEY TRAPPED ME HERE. FOREVER. AND THE MULTIVERSE FORGOT ME. AND NOW I MUST ONLY OBEY. NOW I LIVE TO SERVE.

"But no one believes... it's not supposed to be..." Violet tried to swallow, but her mouth was dry. "It's not *true*."

136

OH, BUT IT IS, CHILD. AND YOU KNOW IT IS. INDEED, I CAN SEE THE RECOGNITION ON YOUR FACE.

"I—"

VIOLET. POOR, WEAK-HEARTED, UNATTRACTIVE VIOLET. I'M HERE TO HELP YOU.

"No one can help me," Violet murmured.

I CAN, I MUST, AND I WILL.

"What are you?"

MY DARLING CHILD. I AM THE THIRTEENTH GOD.

Violet turned and shot across the dusty library at a run.

OH, DON'T GO! (The voice crept its fingers up her spine.) COME BACK.

The satchel fell to the ground. She stopped to grab it, chanced one look at the painting. At the figure in the center, cut from mirror. Its yellow eyes were large and wet with tears. She snatched her bag and book and kept running.

SAY MY NAME. PLEEEEASSSSE. (The voice was in her hair. It was in her eyes. It scattered across her skin.)

She dropped to her knees and skidded into the corridor.

SAY MY NAME, AND I CAN HELP YOU. SAY MY NAME, AND I CAN MAKE EVERYTHING RIGHT. (The voice spun about her feet. It wound around her arms and legs like spider silk.)

But she couldn't. Not yet. She clutched her satchel to her chest as she scrambled through the dark passageway. She didn't look back.

Behind her, the voice from the painting opened its throat and howled.

CHAPTER TWENTY-FIVE

When King Randall arrived—bloody, panting, and utterly spent—he threw himself at the foot of his wife's sickbed, weeping on the covers. The Queen gave a startled, strangled cry—but that was the only sign that she sensed her husband's presence in the room. Her fever deepened and worsened. The King had an hour—perhaps two. He held her hands—so pale now they were nearly gray—and mourned the loss of their son. He kissed her hair, her cheeks, each eyelid, each blessed fingertip.

Before the setting of the Lesser Sun, the Queen was dead.

My dears, I remember the moment that she expelled her last breath—when her body transformed from warm flesh to cold clay. I stood in the corridor just outside the chamber, waiting for Violet to return, but I waited in vain. From the room there was a sudden commotion of voices. A rush, a panic of clattering dishes and tools, and a splintering of glass. And then it was terribly silent.

I couldn't move. *She is alive*, my heart whispered. *She is alive. She is alive.*

A moment later, from that harsh, tight silence erupted an anguished cry—the sound of loss, and grief, and love broken to pieces.

Violet, meanwhile, found herself in a pasture on the western side of the castle, the strange book clutched in her hands—its language infuriatingly familiar yet still indecipherable. She refused to greet her father or to return to her mother's bedchamber. She didn't even ask about Demetrius, whose wounds had been tended in the field; who was at present being carried, weak and feverish, by Marda, the Mistress of the Falcons, and who would soon be fussed over by a worried father and a team of physicians sent by the King. But not by Violet.

Violet stayed away. She felt no grief, no worry, no

sorrow. She only felt a terrible numbness like ice encapsulating her heart. She refused to acknowledge the black flags that flew from the roofs of the castle or to listen to the funeral bells that rang, even now, without ceasing. Instead, she climbed to the roof of the summer stables, lay down on the mossy planks, and watched the sky.

Violet let her fingers drift through the book's pages, as though the touch of paper would make clear the meaning of those strange, unknowable words. She paused at a picture of a girl in front of a mirror. The mirror was wide and very tall, its wood frame intricately carved with tiny lizards, twisting and writhing up the sides. She sat up.

"I know that mirror," she said out loud.

The girl standing in front of the mirror was mousy and plain, but the girl *in* the mirror was another matter entirely. She was a thing of beauty, delicate, red-lipped, and black-haired. She looked like the Queen. Violet squeezed her eyes shut to stop the tears, and rested her chin on her knees. The Greater Sun had just dipped under the rim of the world, while the Lesser Sun lingered at the edge like a shadow. This caused a bleeding of light all along the horizon—a glowing golden hoop encircling the world.

A story, Violet mused. *A forbidden story*. How can a story be forbidden and impossible to forbid at the same time? And why would it make everyone so cross just to have it mentioned?

Now, Violet's imagination was a powerful thing. She knew that stories had their own sorts of magic—beauty can be given or taken away, as can power and love and even hope. Sometimes even the dead come back. And if the dead could be brought back *within* the story, what if the story's magic could be unlocked? What then?

What if her mother could live, not just in the stories about her but *all the time?*

What kind of power can a story gain when people forbid its telling? Violet wondered and wondered, until the wondering swelled to bursting in her heart, and she could no longer bear the suspense. She decided to try an experiment. Violet opened her eyes and cleared her throat. She stared hard at the shining rim of the sky.

"Good night, Nybbas," she said, testing the word on her tongue. Instantly, the gold at the edge of the world grew brighter. Then brighter again. It rippled and hummed and buzzed before fading into the glittering stars and vanishing.

Still, the name *did* something.

The name had *weight*.

Interesting, Violet thought as she stood, leaped lightly onto the ground, and walked toward the castle.

Had she looked backward, even for a moment, Violet would have seen this: a very old man, a very young man, and an ancient woman. All were dressed in strange clothes made from woven grass and petals and horsehair. All had bows and tiny arrows slung across their backs. And not one was any taller than the knob of her knee. The very old man spoke first.

"Oh dear," Moth said. "Oh dear, oh dear."

"What?" the very young man said.

The ancient woman—the one called Auntie—pressed her hand onto her brow and shook her head. "Nothing, Nod, dear. Nothing at all. It's just that we have our work cut out for us, don't we?" She turned to the young man and laid her hand on his cheek, giving him a loving smack. "Would you be a dove and follow that child for a bit longer? And do try to keep your big mouth shut."

The very young—and very *small*—man shoved his hands deep into his pockets before disappearing into the tall yellow grass and following Violet inside. The old man and the woman watched the empty grass for a long time as the shadows deepened and the world grew dark. Auntie reached over and rested her hand on Moth's shoulder.

"Come, Moth," she said briskly. "We have work to do." And they turned their faces into the sighing wind and vanished in the gloom.

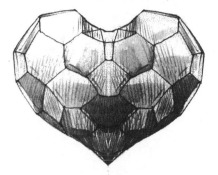

CHAPTER TWENTY-SIX

The nation mourned for twenty-two settings of the Greater Sun, as was proper and expected for a Queen—both beloved and loved, both good and wise—cut down too soon. The castle walls had become littered with flowers—new flowers, wilting flowers, flowers collapsing to rot—as well as hand-drawn likenesses of the Queen.

Soon, though, the memorials spoiled in the sun and had to be gathered, swept, and hauled away. And we had to resume our lives, all cognizant of a loss, a gap, something that *should* be there but *wasn't*.

It took a good deal of time for the hunting party to arrive with the transport vehicle and the dragon. They moved slowly, carefully, afraid of hurting the creature inside. The dragon shook and trembled in its prison; it wept, huge dragonish tears splashing onto the floor and leaking out of the corners.

Violet stood on the northern wall, watching the transport approach. The book was in her satchel—it was always in her satchel—but she hadn't looked at it for eight settings of the Greater Sun. *Not yet*, she told herself, *not yet*. Whenever she walked near the entrances to the Hidden Folk's corridors, she could feel her skin shudder and crawl. The painting was calling to her. Or *something* was calling to her.

NOW, she could feel it whisper. NOW, NOW, NOW. A desperate recitation. Though now, *what*, exactly, she couldn't be sure.

An invitation?

An accusation?

A warning?

Violet did not know. She had the book, and that's what mattered. She had no reason to return to the library. Instead, she let her fingers graze on the book's edges, over and over again, reminding herself that it was still there, comforting herself with its presence.

The wind blew hard from the north, and the castle wall where Violet stood was damp and cold. She shivered. Her eyes stayed pinned on the wooden transport approaching the stone enclosure where the dragon was to live, a short walk from the castle. She hated the dragon.

Hated it.

Her hatred for the creature pierced her heart like a needle, over and over again. She winced, patted the hidden book with her fingers, and buttoned her satchel closed.

She wanted to see the dragon. She wanted it to *feel* her contempt. She wanted it to know just how much it was hated. She wanted to look into its heartless face and peer into its heartless eyes and spit. But not yet. There were too many soldiers, too many opportunities to be caught. Violet would bide her time.

Besides. She wanted Demetrius to come with her.

The King began dividing his days in half, spending the mornings attending to matters of state—or pretending he did. In truth, the King sat as still as a corpse at his desk while his council and advisers and magicians and scholars attempted to turn his thinking away from grief and toward the more pertinent matters involving the state of the castle (strangely wobbly, people said, with a proliferation of cracks and gaps the likes of which no one had ever seen), or the state of the nation (oddly restless, people said, with more than the usual amount of grumbling).

Meanwhile, the Mountain King had flown into a rage. The wealth of the Andulan Realms—its rich farmland and fat animals and abundant trade—had been in his grasp! And now, thanks to the treachery of the Lowland rats and the ineptitude of his guards, his opportunity was lost. Lost! Rumor had it that a whole forest had been laid low to feed his weapons forges. There were whispers that all the villagers on the mountain slopes—from the littlest children to the oldest men and women—had been conscripted into military service and were, even now, practicing drills and swordplay and perfecting the art of killing.

Only rumors, the councillors said in public, but behind closed doors they worried and fussed. Every morning they presented their reports to the King. Every morning they debated and fretted and argued. They begged the King to engage, but he barely acknowledged them.

"Your Highness," they said. "A decision. You must make a decision on how to respond."

But poor Randall cared only for the dragon. *His* dragon. He kept his notebooks on his lap, and his ancient manuscripts open across the desk and on the floor. If he had noticed that any ledgers were missing, he did not mention it. With each passing day, he worried less and less about the threat of war and more and more about the dragon. *If I cannot save it, then the death of the Queen will be in vain,* he told himself as he pretended to listen to his advisers. *There must be a way. There must be a way. I will—I must—save it. I promise.*

The meetings ended at the midday meal with no decisions made, our nation one day closer to war. The King's afternoons were dedicated entirely to the care and study of the dragon.

It was not as though the King intentionally ignored the Princess, nor she him. But both, in the days following the funeral, were loath to weep and reluctant to witness weeping by the other. And so they gave each other a wide berth, regarding both father and daughter at times as strangers— affectionate strangers and loving strangers, but strangers all the same.

Violet didn't mind. It saved her the bother of lying. In any case, she was ready to pay the dragon a visit, and she was ready to see Demetrius.

CHAPTER TWENTY-SEVEN

Demetrius, his wounds now almost fully healed, woke early one morning to find Violet standing outside his window. Her exhausted face was as pale as milk, the spangle of freckles as bright and sharp as pinpricks. Her blue and gray eyes were red-rimmed and puffy, with darkened smudges underneath. She looked as though she had not slept—and would not sleep. Not for days. In truth, Demetrius looked the same way. Ever since his injury, he had been weak and wan—a shadow of himself. He attempted a thin smile.

"Are you awake finally?" she said. She did not mention

her absence. She did not explain herself. Though she did find that she was—quite unexpectedly—tearful. Biting back her frustration, she wiped at her tears with the heel of her hand.

"How long have you been out there?" Demetrius asked. He didn't ask what he wanted to ask. *Where have you been? Or, Why have you not come to see me? Or, Are you all right?*

"Forever," she said. "I thought you'd never get up. Come on. Put on your coat."

"Where are we going?" Demetrius said, hunting around for his shoes.

"Where do you think?" She turned on her heel and started walking away. "And don't think I've forgiven you. I won't. Not ever."

"I know," Demetrius said. "And I'm sorry, Violet. But it wasn't the cause—" His voice broke. "I mean...it didn't—"

"I know," Violet said, and she kept walking. Demetrius followed close behind, and the weight of Violet's grief and the memory of her mother pressed heavily on their grim, silent mouths.

The Lesser Sun was now fully risen, but the Greater Sun would not emerge for another hour or more. They walked down the stony trail in silence, Violet wrapping her arms around her middle and clutching it tight, and Demetrius shoving his hands into his trouser pockets as far as they would go. His father had told him that now that both had lost their mothers, he and Violet would need each other more than ever. That Demetrius's words would be exactly what Violet needed to hear.

But he had no words. And in the face of his friend's grief, his tongue was as cold and heavy as the stones at their feet.

Violet quickened her pace, and Demetrius tripped and stumbled, trying to keep up.

The dragon's enclosure stood about an hour's walk for a sauntering adult, and half that for a couple of impatient, quick-footed children. Once it came into view, both Violet and Demetrius slipped into the thick underbrush that crowded the sides of the pathway, to assess the situation without fear of detection. Sure enough, posted on opposite sides of the oval walls were two sentries, sitting on partially covered platforms. One was asleep on his chair, a book open on his lap. The other stood at attention, his eyes focused on the ground, though darting around at the smallest sounds. He seemed particularly frightened of birds.

"Jumpy bugger, isn't he?" Violet whispered.

The enclosure was a renovation of an old structure—the King believed that it had once held enslaved dragons in the dark and wicked days of my world's faraway past—and made of stone. The King had shored up the crumbling sections, braced the outside of the entire structure with timbers, and seen to the gaps.

But not all the gaps. Violet slid her fingers around Demetrius's hand, hanging on tight. She gave a little pull and led him through the thickest part of the undergrowth. She didn't let go.

"There's an open spot. It's small. I saw it last night."

"You were here last night?" Demetrius said incredulously. "By yourself?"

Violet shrugged. "I couldn't sleep." She pointed. "It's right over there."

Demetrius couldn't see it at first. Violet pulled him forward, leading him to where two large trees stood an arm's length from the old stone wall. There, at the bottom, was a gap large enough for the two of them to fit side by side and look in.

"Is this safe?" Demetrius asked, crouching down and crawling into the gap.

"Probably not," Violet said, crawling in after him.

The walls were thick—so thick as to swallow up the

entire length of their bodies and still stretch beyond their feet and ahead of their faces.

"Don't go all the way to the opening," Demetrius said, laying his hand on Violet's shoulder. "The guard might see you."

"The guard can boil his head." Violet shrugged off her friend's hand. "I didn't come all the way out here to see nothing. I already saw nothing last night in the dark."

She crawled ahead, bringing her face right up to the opening, resting her chin on her fists. Demetrius inched forward while keeping himself well in shadow. He needn't have bothered. The guard, well spooked by now, was on the far end of the platform and out of view. The two children peered out of the gap, directly into the cave on the other side of the enclosure. Two thin ribbons of smoke curled out of the darkness.

"Is that it?" Demetrius asked. He hadn't laid eyes on the dragon since it was captured, but in his dreams of late, the image of the dragon had enlarged to grotesque proportions. Large enough to swallow the whole of the mirrored world in its jaws.

"Yes." Violet fanned her fingers over her mouth. "It's in there."

"Has it moved since last night?"

She shook her head. "It's an old, decrepit, useless thing. And my father is an idiot."

Demetrius laid his hands on the ground. He squinted toward the darkened cave. The ribbons of smoke stopped abruptly.

"Did it stop breathing?" Demetrius asked.

"We can only hope so," Violet said.

Demetrius kept his hand on the ground, trying to call up an image of the beast in his mind. To Violet he said, "You don't have to be unkind. It's hurt and old and frightened and probably sick. You don't have to—"

But Violet interrupted him. Her body shook, and two thin tracks of tears blurred her eyes and oozed down her cheeks.

"I hate it," she said, her voice rasped and ragged with anger. *"Hate it."*

The ground shook slightly—just the tiniest tremor—but Demetrius felt it. Smoke erupted in a round puff from the mouth of the cave. The dragon was moving. *Come on,* Demetrius pleaded silently. *Come out.* But the dragon stayed in the cave.

"If it weren't for that stupid dragon," Violet said, "my mother would still be alive."

"You don't know if that's—"

"Oh yes I do. I *know* it. I wish it were dead." Her mouth twisted and churned, and she looked away. "I wish *it* were dead and *she* were alive." She turned to Demetrius. "And I want you to wish it, too."

Demetrius blanched. "What?" he said, and Violet's face darkened. "But... Violet..."

"Are you my friend or not?" she said.

"Of course I..." He paused, pressed the flop of curly hair out of his face. "Death doesn't work like that, Violet. Surely you know that."

"Never mind," she said, turning her back to Demetrius and scrambling out of the gap. "You wouldn't understand." She struggled to her feet and ran away.

"But Violet," Demetrius called, though he didn't go after her. "Of course I understand," he muttered. "Does she forget who she's talking to?"

PROBABLY.

Demetrius gasped. Was the thought his own? Was it the dragon's? He wasn't sure.

The dragon, Demetrius could feel, had stopped moving. Demetrius kept his eyes on the black mouth of the cave. And in the darkness, a single eye—bright and hot like an ember—blinked once, twice, and glowed open.

CHAPTER TWENTY-EIGHT

Nod ran down the empty corridor looking for Violet, his mouse-leather slippers making no sound on the stone floor. He leaped behind potted plants and velvet drapes— sometimes going so far as to pose as a figurine on a shelf— hiding from servants and advisers, hurrying from room to room. He needn't have bothered. The whole castle had fallen into a tizzy of distraction. No one would have noticed him even if he had sauntered down the center of the long table at suppertime. Such was the growing discontent in the castle.

Still. Auntie had said, *Follow the girl.* And Auntie had said, *Mind you are not seen.*

And so Nod watched Violet. A lot. And he hid.

All the time.

Nod crept into the library and found Violet at the far end of the room with books piled into crooked stacks and papers scattered across the table. She hunched over a particularly large and dusty volume. Nod stood in the leaves of a potted plant and observed.

Violet spent the rest of the morning copying out passages from the books onto small pieces of paper, just as she had done for the countless days prior. Or at least Nod thought they were countless, because they had extended beyond the limit of his own fingers. He had noticed that as the days passed, the Princess seemed thinner, paler. She hunched and ducked and scurried. He noticed that her fingers were ink-smudged, that the skin under her eyes was stained with exhaustion. The girl read and wrote and wrote and read. She was a thing obsessed.

The more Nod followed the girl, the more he guessed that the things she was *reading* and the things she was *writing* were terribly important. Nod understood that *reading* and *writing* were profoundly connected, in the same way that rain and rivers were connected—one flows ever into the other. Nod couldn't read, but Auntie could. And since Auntie wanted him to find out what the girl was up to, Nod thought to snatch a bit or two of what the girl was writing.

It was, Nod thought, a particularly good idea, and he was frankly astonished that he had come up with it at all.

Now, Nod had a knack for mimicry. In fact, he was quite excellent at it. After spending weeks following Violet around, Nod had found himself *also* following a boy called Demetrius, and thus had acquainted himself with the exact rhythm and cadence of the boy's voice. He could match it perfectly.

Nod climbed carefully to the open window and slid outside, hanging on to the mossy stones for dear life. Then, throwing his voice as far as he could, he called, "Violet! *Vi-oh-let!*"

Violet looked up, turned toward the open window. "I'm busy."

"You've got to come out here, Violet," Nod said in his very best Demetrius voice.

"Can it wait?"

"Can anything?"

Violet sighed, shook her head, and closed the book with a dusty thud. "Fine," she said. "But it had better be good."

The moment she left the room, Nod swung his body onto the sill and dashed to the book-covered table, where he grabbed three pieces of paper. He rolled them up and tucked them under his arm and ducked into one of the many tunnels that his people had built into the castle centuries earlier.

Later, Violet returned in a foul mood. Games were all fine and good, she thought, when she was the one playing them. The very idea that Demetrius would interrupt her work and run off and hide—well, that was more than Violet could stand. She sat down at the table, closed her books, and gathered her notes into a pile.

If Nod had stayed in the library, if he had watched her as she replaced the books (as, Auntie later pointed out, he had been *instructed* to do), then he would have seen her trudge from shelf to shelf, hefting heavy books into their gaps. He would have seen the shelves sigh dusty breaths each time a book was replaced.

He would have also seen this: a small book—thin, worn, and old—that remained in Violet's hands after the rest of the books were replaced. He would have noticed her furtive glances over her shoulder, and the way she clutched the book to her chest as though it were a treasure in danger of theft.

But Nod did not see this. Nod had already run off to Auntie to report on what he had seen. "*Reading*," he told Auntie, inclining his head knowingly. "The girl is reading." And he handed Auntie the three pieces of paper.

They said: "There is a magic in storytelling when the story is bigger than the teller. This is important."

And: "The dragons, I believe, were in league with... something terrible. Father should kill that thing when he has a chance."

And: "Once upon a time, a good King and a good Queen gave birth to a girl who was not a real Princess. And then everything went wrong."

If Nod had grabbed the note that said "The Nybbas knows. The Nybbas will help me. The Nybbas knows what to do," then perhaps we would have avoided catastrophe.

But Nod could not read, and he did not grab the right paper, and catastrophe was, as sure as snow, on its way.

"Thank you, Nod," Auntie said, patting the boy on the back. "This is terribly helpful."

And from its prison the Nybbas grinned its yellow grin. NOW, it crowed. NOW, NOW, NOW.

CHAPTER TWENTY-NINE

The Princess Violet sat on the edge of the dragon's enclosure, her legs dangling down the stone wall. She had a tall stack of books teetering next to her, and one of her father's journals open on her lap. The book from the hidden library remained in her satchel.

Thus far she had resisted leafing through the pages (*So old!* she thought. *So fragile!*) and had kept it primarily hidden in her leather bag, preferring to let her fingers slide along its edges from time to time. If she had been truthful with herself, she would have had to admit that she was afraid of the thing. But now she grasped it, pulled it out of its hiding place, and held it in her hands.

It was warm, almost alive—its cover more like skin than leather. Its paper insides whispering like a breath. The book seemed to respond to her touch, settling into the curve of her hands.

The dragon sniffed at the ground and cautiously moved through the broad green space. Since the enclosure was terribly old, it was also overgrown with shrubs and sapling trees, which the King hoped would be reminiscent of home for the displaced dragon. There was a mud pit, a sand pit, and ample foliage for munching. (Dragons, if you didn't know, dears, are carnivorous; however, they do chew on leaves and grasses to settle their stomachs, much as house cats do. And if you've ever seen what a house cat does with the remains of its chewed-up grass, you have an idea of what a dragon does as well. Except that dragon vomit is much, much nastier than cat vomit. Additionally, it is often on fire.) The dragon sidled up to the low-hanging branches of the raginaw tree and sniffed at it suspiciously.

"It's not poisonous or anything," Violet called down testily. The dragon jerked its head and snorted. It didn't look up at the girl on the wall, though she could tell it *wanted* to.

Still, it stretched its telescopic neck to a higher branch and pulled off a jaw's worth of leaves, and, turning its rump toward Violet, settled down in the shade to chew in peace.

The wall around the enclosure was nearly twenty feet high and six feet thick and was made of stone on the inside and sun-baked clay fortified with a tight web of rushes on the outside. It was built to withstand heat and to resist cracking (should the dragon decide to use its considerable speed and weight to ram through a section of the wall). So far the creature had done neither, which had surprised the King and his advisers and had sent rumors spreading throughout the castle that the dragon was either dying or simply biding its time until the day it would destroy them all. Violet felt sure that neither was true. The dragon, she felt, was something of a dud. It was nothing like the stories said it should be. Nothing at all.

You're the worst dragon I've ever seen, she found herself thinking toward the slumped creature under the tree.

AS FAR AS I CAN TELL, YOU'VE NEVER SEEN A DRAGON BEFORE. She felt the words itch at the midpoint of her ear canal. She waved them away like a fly.

"It doesn't matter what I've seen," she said out loud. "Cassian says that knowing a story is the same as being there, and in fact it's even more real than real. I don't have to *see* a dragon in order to know what it *is*. And I don't have to look at you very long to know that there are better dragons than you."

NOT ANYMORE. The whispery voice was hot and sharp in her ear—or perhaps not her ear. She heard it with her skin, in her mouth, at the tips of her hair. She felt it in the sudden prick of tears at the corner of her eyes. THERE ARE NONE BETTER AND NONE WORSE. THERE IS ONLY I.

"I don't believe you."

The great beast didn't answer but merely moved its rump from side to side in a way that Violet thought was intentionally rude. It passed gas. Violet *knew* it was on purpose. She nearly gagged on the smell.

"Dragons have always been a plentiful menace," Violet choked. "Everyone knows that." She gathered her books into her arms and stood on the wall. "They burn crops and eat cows and steal princesses. They've just gotten good at hiding. Dragons are *sneaky*."

THINK WHAT YOU'D LIKE.

"I will think exactly what I'd like." Violet flushed and clenched her teeth. A very small part of her wondered at her sudden anger at the captured animal, just as it wondered at her agitation over—well, a growing number of things. It was as though she had a well of anger inside her that would never run dry. And that same small part of her quietly suggested that perhaps—just perhaps—she should put the book away, or burn it, or forget it altogether. However, since it was a very small part, Violet ignored it easily. "I always think *exactly* what I'd like. Besides, I have proof." She held up the book at the top of her stack. "The Nybbas brought thousands of you into this world. Thousands and thousands."

DON'T SAY THAT NAME.

"I will say any name I feel like saying. You're not in charge of me. You're just a miserable excuse for a captured dragon. The Nybbas would have made you into a warrior."

DON'T SAY THAT NAME.

"The Nybbas appointed strong kings and beautiful queens and gave them dragons to serve them."

DO NOT—the voice tore into her heart like a sob—DO NOT SAY THE NAME. PLEASE.

Violet felt her connection to the dragon deepen, as close and raw as a slap. She gasped.

"Why am I bothering to talk to you?" Violet asked, reaching one hand out to the closest branch of the acacia tree and swinging herself onto a broad, curved limb. "I could probably weave a tale with a dragon ten times as good as you." And with that, the child disappeared from the edge of the wall, and the dragon was alone.

Chewing the leaves in its mouth thoughtfully, the beast pressed its paws against the ground.

Silence.

The beast sighed and took another mouthful of leaves in relief. Then, in midchew, the left paw felt it first.

A beat.

A beat.

That cursed heart beating.

OH DEAR, the dragon thought. OH DEAR, OH DEAR.

CHAPTER THIRTY

Demetrius continued to worry about the Princess. I say this with some shame, as I was the one who loved her best—or so I told myself, anyway. Demetrius, as I mentioned earlier, was by nature a shy boy, both hardworking and kind. He was the sort of person who listened far more than he ever spoke, and who helped people before they even realized that they needed helping.

But it was not only the Princess who worried him. The whole castle seemed...off. Tempers were rattled, cools were lost, skins thinned. Demetrius noticed that people were spending more time than usual staring at mirrors.

And more troubling, they were *talking* to the mirrors as well. "*Yes, yes, yes,*" people whispered at the mirrors.

Demetrius brought these concerns to me, but I brushed them off. I didn't want to listen.

(*Coward.*)

And so, Demetrius worried alone.

It was at the same moment that Violet was having her terse conversation with the dragon that Demetrius was, for the first time in his life, in the middle of a fistfight.

What had happened was this: Demetrius had just led the four horses of the four visiting scholars—one scientist, one alchemist, one theorician, and one animal surgeon, all gathered to discuss the dragon—out to the smaller pasture, where they could sip from the stream and rest in the shade. As he was closing the gate to the paddock, he noticed two of the baker's apprentices leaning against the bakery wall, eating their midday meal. The apprentices, one boy and one girl and both only three years older than Demetrius, smiled at him over their sandwiches and waved him over. Demetrius had a long list of chores to do before he could begin his studies, and was reluctant to tarry any longer than necessary—particularly given that bakers' apprentices were notorious for their poor work habits. Still, he didn't want to be rude.

Now, the southern wall of the bakery was a popular place to linger, since it was heated from both within and without by oven and sun. Also, because some years earlier, it had been painted over by the apprentice of one of our artisans with a large mural depicting the King, the Queen, and a five-year-old Violet, holding on to her mother's hand. It was a picture I had always admired, for the artist managed to skillfully capture the hearts of the three subjects. King Randall had his hand in his unkempt red hair, and he looked simultaneously amused by his child, distracted by a passing thought, and ever so pleased to see the viewer of the painting. The Queen's face was lovely, loving and sad. Her black hair draped down her shoulders and fell nearly to her knees. Her one hand clutched that of her child while her other was open, its palm toward the viewer, like an invitation. Violet, as painted, looked entirely like herself, which is to say, wonderful. Her mismatched eyes sparkled and danced, and her auburn hair flew about her body, tangled and wild. Her dress was torn, her nose smudged, and she had a slight chip in one small tooth. It was one of my favorite places to sit and think, and was for Demetrius as well. Which is why he was surprised at the apprentices, who pointed with their thumbs at the image of the Princess and sniggered unpleasantly.

"What's so funny?" Demetrius asked.

"Nothing," said the boy apprentice—both older and much, much bigger than Demetrius—nearly choking on a hunk of bread.

Demetrius slipped his hands into his pockets and rocked back on his heels. He pointed at the painting with his chin. "I like that painting."

"'Course you do," the girl said. "You have to be friends with her."

"I don't *have* to be friends with anybody. No one does." Demetrius, who had never hit anything in his life, found that his palms were itching. He balled his hands into fists, but he didn't take them out of his pockets.

"Do you want a pastie?" the boy said, offering up a honey-sweetened roll. Demetrius took it, bit off a hunk, and slowly chewed.

"You still haven't told me what was funny," he said.

"It isn't anything," the girl said. "It's just that—well—it's kind of silly, isn't it?"

"What is?" Demetrius said with his mouth full.

"Nothing," the girl said. "I mean, it's just that they're not what you'd expect, are they? King Randall? He looks as though he could be frightened by a mouse. He's not what you'd call *kingly*, is he? The Queen was all right, but she's gone, so what use is her picture anymore? And Violet—I mean, I'm sure she's *funny* and *smart*, and I'm sure she's a perfectly fine *friend*."

"Can you imagine if the King offers her hand to some poor prince as a *reward*? One look at her lopsided face and he'd ask if there was a second option."

Demetrius didn't hear the whole sentence. At the word *lopsided* he crouched, and by the word *second* he had flown at the boy, his fists hurling into any body part they could find. Since he hadn't any practice with fights, Demetrius didn't really know what he was doing. The older boy, however, had plenty of experience and knew exactly what he was doing. In quick order Demetrius lunged too far, and in one smooth move the boy swiveled his torso from left to right, hooking his arm around Demetrius's hips as he did so, and flipping him onto the ground.

"They're fighting, they're fighting!" the girl screeched excitedly, and by the time the baker emerged, ghosted with flour and shouting a long string of curses, the boy had Demetrius pinned to the ground and was happily pummeling his face.

"He started it," the boy said when the baker grabbed him by the back of his collar and hoisted him up.

Demetrius attempted to say something in response—"Did not," for example—but found himself unable to speak because of the pool of blood overflowing his lips and spilling down his chin.

Later, as his father applied poultices to his bruises and cool rags to his blackened eyes, Demetrius maintained his silence.

"It's one thing," his father said, shaking his head, "to engage in every sort of stupid and childish prank with the Princess. We expect it from her. She has grown wild from the outset, and a certain level of wildness is acceptable from those who will one day bear the burden of leading their people." His father dipped another rag into the earthenware bowl of cool well water. "The rest of us, son, must maintain appearances. If your beloved mother were alive today, no doubt she'd tell me that I have done a dreadful job of raising you and that I must be more firm."

His father sighed, and still Demetrius said nothing.

"I don't know, son," his father continued. Demetrius noticed that the old man's eyes were wet and wide, as though torn between grief and dreaming. "Everything seems to be turned upside down, doesn't it? The Mountain King rattles his saber, and our King can do nothing but bury himself in his studies." He stood, went to the basin, and washed his hands. "And, well, it's a pity about the Princess, isn't it?"

Demetrius went to his feet. "Explain what you mean by that, Father," he said in a voice as sharp as he could manage with his swollen lips.

His father ran his hand over his balding head. "Son, I'm talking about war—a thing you, thankfully, have no experience with, and I'd like to keep it that way. Now, if *I* were king—"

Demetrius, his patience at an end, smacked his hand on the wooden table. "Not about the King, Father. About the Princess. What is the pity?"

"Who said anything about pity?"

"You did. Just now. You said it was a pity about the Princess. What did you mean?"

"I did?" His father shook his head. "No, son, I believe you are mistaken. I never said any such thing." He reached into his pocket, took out his pipe and his tinderbox, and walked toward the door. "We all love Violet. All of us." And then he added, in a voice so small and slippery that it was little more than a whisper, "Of course, if she were a *real* princess, she would be beautiful."

Demetrius followed his father out the door. "Father, I'm sorry," he said, "but could you repeat that last bit?"

"What's gotten into you, boy? I said that we all love Violet. End of story."

He nodded. "I see. Thank you, Father."

"Of course, my son. But wait! Come back here this instant. Demetrius? Where are you going?"

But it was too late. Demetrius ran past the stables and disappeared from sight.

CHAPTER THIRTY-ONE

Demetrius looked for Violet for the better half of the next day. When he finally found her, the Greater Sun had already set, and the Lesser Sun hung low and broad in the sky. Violet was in the library in a darkened corner at the very back, surrounded by stacks and stacks of open books. Each book, he noticed, was open to an illustration of a princess—both Andulan and foreign. In each illustration, the hair of the princesses hung down in great cascades to their knees or ankles. They shone at their edges with illuminations of silver or gold. Each princess had large, wide-set eyes that matched each other perfectly. Each princess had skin like ivory or amber or onyx, unmarred by freckles or moles.

Violet didn't see Demetrius at first, nor did she hear his approach. Instead, Demetrius noticed, she pored over a small volume that was hidden slightly by her curtains of unbound hair. It rested open on her forearms, with her hands curled around its top edge like claws. Her shoulders rounded over the top of it, and her whole body curved inward, as though she were going to curl right into its pages and disappear. Her breathing was quick and shallow, and her head and shoulders slumped toward the book, as though they had become, quite suddenly, too heavy to bear. Demetrius crouched low and rested his forearms on his knees. Violet still didn't see him. He cleared his throat. Still nothing.

"Violet," he said out loud. "I've been looking everywhere for you."

Violet made a sharp snort in the back of her throat, as if she was suddenly waking up. She lifted her face, and Demetrius saw that her eyes were glittering strangely in the half-light, like jewels. Or broken glass.

"What happened to your—" But Violet blinked, and her eyes were back to normal, one larger and gray, one smaller and blue, as always. "Never mind," Demetrius said.

"I'm rather busy, as you can see," Violet said, quickly shoving the small volume into her satchel, followed by the rest of her papers and ledgers. She didn't mention his swollen lips or his cut chin or his two black eyes. In fact, it seemed that she barely saw him at all. She pulled one of the open books—one with a picture of a princess with wavy black hair—onto her lap and stared at it. "I don't have time for any of your mad adventures, Demetrius. No time at all."

"I can see that," Demetrius said, his voice low and soft. "That's quite a collection you have there. And I know you're working hard." He gestured to the bulging bag on her lap. "But what are you working *on*?"

"Just getting ideas," Violet said without looking up.

"What kind of ideas?" Demetrius asked. He picked up a dusty book from the far end of the table. It was a volume he remembered, crowded with stories and pictures. "Can you imagine?" he said, pointing to the painting of the princess. It was a particularly ridiculous image, showing the poor girl with hair hanging in ropes the size of a grown man's upper arm and falling into a heap on the floor. Artists, it must be said, are as bad as storytellers. Perhaps worse. Fancy having a head of hair that weighed more than a child!

"Can I imagine what?" Violet said.

"Here." He showed her the page. "It's ridiculous. She wouldn't be able to stand with all that hair, much less walk."

Violet glanced up, and once again her eyes glittered hard and sharp. It took two blinks this time to make them right. "I don't see the issue. She's just beautiful, that's all. Like a real princess."

Demetrius felt as though he had just accidentally swallowed a rock. That phrase! That blasted phrase. "A *real* princess? Seems like I'm hearing that a lot lately."

Violet lurched forward and grabbed her friend by his collar. "What is that supposed to mean?" she asked savagely. "*Who* is saying that?"

"No one," Demetrius said quickly. "No one at all. Just making conversation."

Violet let go and sank back into the chair. She humphed at him. "Well," she said, "you're not very good at it, are you?"

"I guess not."

"Anyway, it doesn't matter. I'm going to make everything right. They'll see." Violet swallowed hard. Her eyes sank toward the book, though it seemed to Demetrius that she struggled against it and tried hard to keep her eyes away from the words on the page. "*Everything*," she whispered, "*will be perfect*."

"Violet—" Demetrius began, but she held up her hand, setting her mouth into a hard, thin line.

"If you wouldn't mind, beloved Demetrius, I am frightfully busy and would prefer to be left alone." Demetrius winced at the formal address and tried hard not to show her how much it hurt him. She lifted her face and gazed at him, a hard, sharp, cold stare. "This audience is over."

"Fine," he said, standing up. Already, Violet's body seemed to collapse around the lure of the open book on her lap. "By the way, *Princess*," he said. "What's that you're reading? The book you stealthily shoved into your bag so I wouldn't see? I'm not blind, you know."

"It's none of your concern," she murmured, burying herself back in the pages. "It's a book for princesses," she said in a softer voice. "*Real* princesses," even more softly. And then she said nothing more.

Demetrius turned and left the room, his head swimming with questions. He stumbled into the hall.

Little did the boy know that the one person who could answer his questions was, at that moment, standing with her great-grandnephew under the window seat.

Auntie shook her head. "I gave you one job, Nod. Just one."

"But, Auntie, I swear I—"

Auntie cut him off with a swift smack to the center of his forehead with the blunt end of her knitting needles.

"What was that for?"

"Idiocy," Auntie said simply, but since she could never be angry with the boy for very long, she gave his shoulder an encouraging pat. "I know you tried, dear, truly I do. But facts are facts, Nod, and we must accept them. You failed. And now we must act." Auntie sighed and began to absentmindedly smooth over the patchwork pattern of her apron. "Four thousand years of silence, and now it wants out. And here we are, only three. How can three defeat a god?" She shook her head. "There's no good in fussing. Only action matters. Tonight we talk to the boy. The girl is beyond us, I'm afraid. The boy will help, though. He *wants* to help. And we must get ready."

They turned and walked into the dark tunnels that had been carved and maintained by generation upon generation of ancestors. For all those years, the stone floor, walls, and ceiling were silent and still. But not anymore. Now the stone rumbled with the beat, beat, beat of the buried heart. And it was growing louder.

CHAPTER THIRTY-TWO

In my own quarters, I was unconcerned with heartbeats or stone beats or dragons or gods or anything outside my own cursed cleverness. You see, I had, just the night before, been visited by a dream. A *marvelous dream*. It was the sort of dream that storytellers can only *dream* about.

A story. A brand-new, magnificent story. Normally, you see, the hardworking storyteller must glean the world around him for bits and pieces to assemble into stories. Men and women are taken apart, reassembled, and transformed into characters. But sometimes, my dears, sometimes a story comes in a dream. Sometimes it is fully formed, shining, and new—a gift from the broad multiverse. Such a dream had visited my sleeping brain but six other times in my life, and those were the six best stories I had ever told. This dream was the seventh. A lucky number, I told myself. And I spent days in my quarters ruminating on the language, perfecting the delivery. It would be, I felt, the finest day of my career.

I did not know that the dream was no dream.

I did not know who—or what—had *sent* me that story. And truthfully, I do not know what I would have done if I *had* known.

What I do know is this: Right as I was in the middle of my solo rehearsal, right as the heroine of my story was unlocking the secrets to eternal beauty and power and love, there was a rattling, panicked knock on the door. My concentration broken and my mood soured, I stomped to the door. Threw it open.

"What on earth do *you* want?" I barked at Demetrius.

The poor boy paled and recoiled from me—and for good reason. I had been in my chambers for three days at that point, without emerging to eat, bathe, or converse. The story had, I'm afraid, consumed me. But Demetrius was a brave and good boy and wanted to do right by his friend. "Don't shout, Cassian," he said quietly. "I am worried for Violet. Actually, everyone has been acting strangely ever since..." The boy looked down at his shoes and shut his eyes tight. He wanted, I learned later, to say "ever since the Queen died," but he couldn't bring himself to say the words and couldn't bear to hear them spoken. Instead, he said, "Ever since the King came back with that dragon. It's strange. They say cruel things without remembering that they've said them. And they're saying terrible things about Violet."

Now, I have no memory of what I said in response. I can only assume that what Demetrius told me was true, though it makes my heart sick to even consider it.

"Well," I said—according to Demetrius—"what can you expect? We lost our beautiful Queen. And now everything is wrong. A castle needs a proper princess."

"What did you say?" Demetrius said.

"Nothing, child," I said impatiently. "I've said nothing at all."

"I see," the boy said. He breathed slowly and ran his hand through his black curls, though inwardly his mind was racing. He drew himself up to his full height and looked at me straight in the eye. "Beloved Cassian," he said, taking the formal address, "I appreciate this audience. Would you be so kind, sir, as to check in with the Princess? She suffers, sir, in her mind and in her heart, and I have reason to believe that a story is to blame for it. Or maybe something that is rather like a story and rather like..." He searched for the word. "Something *else*."

"Thank you," I said coldly, "for the suggestion."

Demetrius gave a curt bow and took the corridor at a run.

And *oh*, my dears, how it pains me—nay, it *disgusts me*—that I must tell you this! As I stood at the doorway, watching that dear, brave boy disappear into the gloom, my mind thought this: *Storytellers do not take orders from stableboys*. And with that, I retreated into my quarters and shut the door.

I did not tell the King.

CHAPTER THIRTY-THREE

The slippery insinuations from the mirrors moved quickly beyond the baker's apprentices. Soon the castle was filled with narrowed eyes and cupped hands carrying whispers from mouths to ears. Every smirk, every shake of the head, every sidelong glance cut Violet so deeply she thought she might bleed to death.

Worst of all were the whispers.

Not a proper princess, the whispers said.

We lost our beautiful Queen, and now look what we're stuck with.

Not what we deserve, other whispers agreed.

Violet bowed her head, clutched at her arms, and scurried out of sight.

Meanwhile, the castle groaned with grievance and division. Those with rank and status—good people all of them, who had always chosen cooperation and humility over subservience or prejudice—began to see their daily tasks as beneath them. They barked orders at assistants and apprentices; they formed secret societies and enjoyed the power of exclusion. And resentment spread, as thick and foul as smoke, until we choked on it.

And as for King Randall—was it grief or distraction? He might have noticed—*should* have noticed—but he spent all day and all night watching the dragon, tracking its movements, writing notes on its biology, all the while wondering why he could communicate so well with his horses, with his dogs, with his falcons, but the dragon, for him, was as cold as any stone. *Talk to me*, the King pleaded daily, but the dragon was silent.

Come back to me, he pleaded to his dead wife, but she was just as silent.

Far away, the Mountain King continued his preparations for war. He would not admit it, but it was true. Troops were armed and massed at the borders. ("Military exercises!" the Mountain King said.) The forges billowed forth giant columns of black smoke, lifting nearly to the limit of the mirrored sky. ("The development of skills and trade!" the Mountain King soothed. "For the good of my people.") And the King's council, acting (they hoped) under the orders their King surely would have made had he not been…altered by grief, sent out pleas for alliance and aid from the other three kingdoms.

"We must do what is necessary, sire, to protect your people. *You* must do this," the councillors told him.

"Fine," the King said absently. (*Come back*, pleaded his heart. *Come back to me*.) "Whatever you think is right, of course."

Violet continued to read the story of the Nybbas. She read it and read it and read it again. She read until her face paled and her lips chapped and her fingers trembled and the dark circles under her eyes became puffed and black as bruises. She took her meals in her room. She wouldn't see me. She wouldn't see Demetrius. She simply read.

Is it possible, she wondered, for a story to remake the world? For a story to remake a person? Can a story bring back the dead?

YESSSSSSSSS, hissed a tiny, itchy voice at the very back of her mind.

Now, the book of the Nybbas was a special volume—a magic volume. Each page carried an enchantment to bind the reader closer to it. It was a shifty, tricky thing, a cowardly sort of magic that did not announce itself or state its purpose.

Every time Violet came to read the story, it changed. In fact, the moment her eyes passed a sentence, the words rearranged themselves, so with each read the story was bigger, wider, and more gripping. It transported her beyond the limits of our mirrored world and showed her the wonders beyond.

But worst of all, the conclusion of each story was the same: FIND THE NYBBAS. IF YOU WANT POWER, FIND THE NYBBAS. IF YOU WANT BEAUTY, FIND THE NYBBAS. IF YOU WANT THE WORLD AS IT SHOULD BE, THE WORLD YOU DESERVE, FIND THE NYBBAS. THE NYBBAS MUST DO AS IT IS TOLD. IT IS A WILLING, HELPFUL SERVANT. YOU HAVE ONLY TO ASK.

"But how can I find the Nybbas?" Violet said out loud.

In answer, the book flew from her hands, spun three times, and fluttered back to the table, its pages rustling like leaves and opening to the beginning of the story. A new story.

ONCE, the story began, THERE WAS A TELLER WHO LOOKED AT THE WORLD AS IT WAS AND THOUGHT IT WAS NOT RIGHT. HOW SHABBY ARE OUR FORESTS! HOW FEEBLE ARE OUR RIVERS! INDEED, HE ALONE WAS ABLE TO SEE THAT THE WORLD HAD BECOME GRAY AND WEAK AND UGLY—A PATHETIC SHADOW OF WHAT IT MIGHT BE.

BUT THERE WAS A WAY TO BUILD THE WORLD ANEW, TO MAKE RIGHT WHAT ONCE WENT WRONG.

"A STORY," THE TELLER SAID. "I NEED A STORY TO REMAKE THE WORLD." SO HE PACKED UP HIS RUCKSACK AND WENT OUT IN SEARCH OF THE NYBBAS.

CHAPTER THIRTY-FOUR

It was, my dears, the story that was supposed to make my career. I believed at the time that it would place me among the giants of my field—those tellers whose stories still rang through the ages, whose words made them immortal.

I put on my best robes, and I oiled my beard until it shone. I gazed at the mirror for a long while—hours, perhaps—before I was satisfied and ready to sweep into the hall.

Did I notice, dears, the subtle glitter of jeweled eyes that flashed with each fluttered blink? Did I notice the shimmered tongue flicking out again and again to lick those golden lips? Perhaps. I certainly remember it, but memory is tricky business, after all. Memory invents itself. If I did notice it at the time, I certainly did not notice myself noticing, if you understand me. Only the story mattered. Only the story.

The great hall swarmed with people, though I'll admit that it was not as crowded as I would have liked. Or, to be more specific, it was not as crowded as I believed that I *deserved*. Surely, thought I, the servants that I sent scurrying off with my adamant orders did not spread the word of my magnificent story as they were instructed. Surely, I thought, they had been lazy, defiant, and slovenly in their duties. And indeed, I may have been right on that point. Ever since the capture and return of our dear King, a cloud of disdain had settled over every resident of the castle— from the lowliest page to the highest-ranking generals. We, all of us, took to spending more time in front of mirrors, imagining ourselves more powerful, more beautiful, more exalted. Each of us felt that we *deserved* it.

The wine had been poured, the bread broken, the first songs sung, and I, with a grand gesture, raised my hands and stood. The room mostly quieted, and I cleared my throat.

"Good evening, my beloved," I said, using the formal voice as I swept low into a bow.

"Good evening, beloved Cassian," the crowd responded. (BUT OH! that unpleasant voice whispered. THEY DO NOT MEAN IT. YOU CAN TELL.)

"As you know," said I, "our dear King pursues at our expense a marvelous folly involving the care and study of one heartless and overgrown lizard just west of the castle." Many at their tables brought their hands to their mouths and tittered. I had expected the King to shift uncomfortably in his chair, but he remained motionless, his gaze trending toward the far windows. HE'S NOT LISTENING TO YOU, the slippery voice in my head taunted again and again. I gritted my teeth and continued.

"Now, all of you, from your varied infancies, have listened to stories about dragons. You've learned how to track dragons and how to trick them. You've learned how to find the holes in their armor, and the ashen caverns in their chests where their hearts should be. But all of you—and indeed, I blame myself for this gap in your collective educations—know nothing of how dragons first arrived in our world. You know nothing of the person who once sought to control these beautiful and terrible beasts, nor of the power that such control can bring."

The King was standing now, his eyes blazing on me. I bowed toward him and, with a casual swish of my robes, turned back to the listening crowd. "Therefore, my dears, I will begin with the tale of a god—one of the Old Gods— who, after a long day of walking, found himself wanting a chair, a fire, and a friend."

"STOP!" bellowed the King.

"CONTINUE!" shouted the crowd. They clinked their glasses; they pounded the table with their fists; they shouted for the story. I nearly wept.

"Guards," the King ordered, "please escort our dear friend to his quarters. Do not let him leave until I arrive."

The crowd rose to their feet. They shook their fists and stamped their feet. And truly, I have no doubt that they would have revolted, or rioted, or ... well, I shudder to think of it. So agitated and unhappy was every last man, woman, and child in the castle, it was quite possible that the unthinkable could have come to pass—revolt, unrest, revolution—and I would be telling a very different story indeed.

Fortunately for all of us, the riot was instantly averted by two simultaneous entrances into the Great Hall.

First, from the main doors, four riders burst in, their uniforms filthy and torn, their hats askew, their faces red and blotchy and damp. Two had been bloodied, and one held her arm with her good hand, and we noticed that it had twisted sickeningly in its socket, its fingers quite swollen and blue.

"The Mountain King," gasped the young woman with the broken arm. "His armies are coming—a thousand regiments are marching down the southernmost slopes. They've crossed the border. We have two days at best to prepare."

Those words created a silence as absolute as stone. Indeed, we would have remained silent for some time had it not been for another entrance, this time from the side door.

Princess Violet's primary governess—the woman who saw to the girl's education, who coordinated the work of her teachers and instructors, who ensured that our dear Princess would grow in wisdom and grace—was not a flighty person. She was broad-shouldered, strong-armed, and stern. So you can imagine, my dears, the shock we felt when we saw that woman burst through the door, smacking it open

with such force as to leave a hole in the plaster where the handle hit. Her black-and-gray hair, normally smoothed back into a severe knot at the nape of her neck, flew about her head like feathers, as though she had been tearing at it, and tears poured from her eyes and ran in rivulets down the deep creases in her dark skin.

"The Princess!" she cried. "The Princess is missing!"

If the world had ended then and there, I doubt many people in that room would have minded very much. Indeed, for most of us, the end had already come.

CHAPTER THIRTY-FIVE

And where was the Princess?

King Randall's normally pale face grew paler by degrees. In short order he divided the roomful of people into groups: one to search the grounds for the Princess, one to assess the castle walls and to fortify the weak areas, one to send messages to the outlying farms and villages, and so on.

"She will be found," I told the King after I had been forgiven and kept near, as though I might draw the Princess in the way that metal draws lightning. "She will be found."

But where was Violet?

The King called a meeting with the generals, advisers, ambassadors, and regents and discussed the developments and strategies. They dispatched three riders on the three fastest horses to the kingdoms to the south and the east and to the Island Nations to the west to beg for aid and assistance, while a small delegation rode northward in an attempt to persuade the Mountain King to resist the temptations of war.

But there were rumors of madness coming from the north. It was said that the Mountain King neither slept nor ate, that he spoke of a lover no one had seen. And recently he was never without an ornate hand mirror, exquisitely wrought, and clutched in his fists. He called it "my love." Could such a man be reasoned with?

"Tricky business going to war against a madman, sire," an elder general said, her two long braids hanging down her body like silver whips. "It could go either way."

The delegation murmured. There had been no war in our world for five hundred years. And the thought was terrifying.

"It is imperative," the King said slowly, addressing the assembled men and women before they left, "that we resolve this conflict peacefully. I do not want a single drop of blood—not from the citizens of the Andulan Realms, nor from the subjects of the Mountain King—to defile this great and beloved country. The Mountain King's control over his people is oppressive and absolute. My heart breaks for his people, but that yoke is theirs to overthrow; it is not ours. However, I will do everything in my power to prevent the oppression of *my* people. Make sure he understands that." The delegates nodded, pressing their hands to their hearts as they bowed low. Their hopes of survival, let alone success, were minimal. A suicide mission. They set their faces and stopped their tears. "Stay safe, my beloved," whispered the King.

Armies mobilized; people built barricades and armed catapults; hospital tents were erected and supplied throughout the kingdom.

And still the question remained:

Where was the Princess? Where could she have gone?

Where indeed, my dears?

CHAPTER THIRTY-SIX

In the hours before she disappeared, Violet read the story of the Nybbas, over and over and over again. She couldn't stop. She couldn't slow down. The story had weight and meaning and *voice*. It breathed in her ear and whispered against her skin. Its voice spun a tale around her heart and pulled it tight, and all the while it *told* her things—*awful* things—and Violet believed them.

YOU ARE NOT A REAL PRINCESS, the story told her.

It was a thing that she always believed. That she always *knew*. But still she found herself arguing, using the same tired truisms that she had heard her mother say. "But I am," Violet tried to argue. "I know I am. I always—"

LOOK AT YOURSELF, the story said. PRINCESSES HAVE SKIN THE COLOR OF AMBER OR EBONY OR IVORY. THEY DO NOT HAVE FRECKLES. THEY DO NOT HAVE MISMATCHED EYES. THEY ARE NOT LOPSIDED.

Violet hung her head. She was supposed to be beautiful. She was supposed to be *perfect*. And now the kingdom was ruined, and it was all her fault. The thing that she worried over was *true*. The Nybbas said so.

"Still," Violet said, raising herself up. "The people love me."

ONLY BECAUSE THEY MUST.

"And my father loves me," she countered, feeling her voice deflate. "And my mother loved me."

ONLY BECAUSE THEY MUST.

"My mother..." Violet began desperately.

IF YOU HAD BEEN BEAUTIFUL, SHE LIKELY WOULD NOT HAVE DIED. IF YOU HAD BEEN BEAUTIFUL, HER WOMB WOULD HAVE STAYED STRONG. YOU WOULD HAVE HAD BROTHERS AND SISTERS.

"If I was beautiful..."

THEN EVERYTHING WOULD BE BEAUTIFUL, CHILD. EVERYTHING WOULD BE AS IT SHOULD BE.

"My mother—"

IF YOU WERE BEAUTIFUL.

"My mother—"

EVERYTHING WOULD BE RIGHT AGAIN.

Violet carried a stack of books to her room and locked herself inside. In addition to the story of the Nybbas, she had histories and biographies and explorations of art. Her collection had increased over time, and now she struggled under the weight of her books. She had reproductions and paintings of every princess of the Andulan Realms as far back as anyone could remember. Girls with faces that glowed on the page. Shimmery lips. Sleek hair. Eyes fresh as rain. She stood in front of her mirror, looked at her dull masses of hair. Her face unbrightened by her usual smile. Her mismatched eyes shadowed by circles as dark as ashes. She grimaced. Shuddered.

IT CAN BE FIXED.

"But how?"

YOU KNOW WHO CAN HELP YOU.

"But I can't. The story says—"

FORGET THE STORY AS IT WAS. THE ONLY THING THAT MATTERS NOW IS YOUR STORY. VIOLET'S STORY.

Violet closed her eyes, expelling her breath in a long,

rattled sigh. "All right," she said. "There once was a girl who made a wish..."

AND WITH THE WISH THERE WAS A PROMISE.

"What sort of a promise?"

THERE IS NO GAIN WITHOUT LOSS, CHILD. THERE IS NO GLORY WITHOUT RESPONSIBILITY.

"What will I lose?"

A TRIFLE, CHILD. YOU'LL NEVER MISS IT. YOUR NATION DESERVES A REAL PRINCESS. YOU DESERVE BEAUTY. WHAT WOULD YOU GIVE UP FOR THAT?

"Everything."

EVERYTHING.

"I wish..." She leaned toward the mirror.

YES...

"I wish..." She felt herself falling, and falling, and falling.

"I wish..." And she saw the mirror growing bigger, opening up like a door, and then a lake, and then an ocean, and then the sky.

YESSSSSSSSSS...

And just like that, the Violet we knew, the Violet we *loved*, was gone.

CHAPTER THIRTY-SEVEN

In the meantime, I must confess, I was in a bit of a snit. My story had been ruined, my moment ruined. There was no salvaging the situation, no reclamation of the lost story. Even if I had attempted, it would have been a shadow of what it *ought* to be—the pathetic ramblings of an old man past his prime.

The war was to blame.

Violet was to blame.

The world, it seemed, turned against me and sought to mock me in my defeat.

And worse—*worse!*—after the King was finally pulled from the room with the generals and advisers, he turned to me.

"You know her better than anyone, Cassian," he said. "Find her. Please."

I left the Great Hall in a foul temper, my best robes flowing behind me. No doubt, thought I, she was hiding. Another selfish game from a selfish Princess! How I chafed at the thought of it! I imagined Violet quashing her giggles under her hands, listening with that infernal Demetrius as the footsteps of their elders pounded hither and yon, as our voices grew hoarse with worry.

And in that moment, I detested that girl. In fact, I detested them all: all girls, all boys, all children. Everyone.

I continued on to Violet's room. I had thought, you see, that Violet's governess and teachers had simply not looked thoroughly enough through the length and breadth of the room, nor had they checked its many nooks, crannies, and secret places. But I did not find her in the room at all. On the bed there was a small handheld mirror. It was a beautiful thing and reminded me of our dear, departed Queen. I picked it up and gazed at my reflection.

But then something very odd happened. My grizzled

beard, my tired eyes, my sagging skin all vanished. And in their place, very briefly, an image of Violet appeared. She pressed her hands against the glass, tilted her haunted eyes upward until they found mine.

Help me, Cassian, mouthed her lips.

And Violet vanished from sight.

CHAPTER THIRTY-EIGHT

Despite your concern over the fate of our dear Violet, I must redirect your attention for a moment to the actions of Demetrius. You see, on that terrible day when Violet disappeared and war was declared and the world as we knew it shattered before our eyes, Demetrius was *also* nowhere to be found. He had left the castle an hour before and walked toward the dragon's enclosure. On the western wall, the King had built a small platform with a spyglass to more closely watch the dragon in its new home, and a tiny hut to keep out the rain. There was a ladder at the back, and a system of ropes and pulleys to supply the small observation station with quills and paper—not to mention food and drink.

"Sire," Demetrius called. "King Randall!" He climbed up the ladder in a flash and swung his legs onto the platform with a thump. For the previous hour, Demetrius had practiced what he would say to his King once the moment arrived. He would explain the incident involving the two apprentices of the baker, and the words that his father had spoken and immediately forgotten. He would explain what he and Violet had found in that hidden corridor ever so long ago. He would describe the sudden and troubling change in Violet—something *different* from grief. Something *else*. He would, Demetrius told himself firmly, keep his voice steady and his eyes dry.

"Hello!" Demetrius called, but the platform was empty, and Demetrius was alone. He sat down at the edge feeling very miserable indeed.

One yellow eye glowed from the manufactured cave at the far end. Two nostrils poked their way into the light, with two ribbons of smoke curling lazily toward the sky. The dragon stepped out of its cave and blinked. It limped into the center of the enclosure and looked up at Demetrius.

"What are you looking at?" Demetrius said to the dragon.

The dragon sat on its haunches and tipped its head.

"This is all your fault, you know," Demetrius went on, feeling a growing anger burning his neck and ears, hissing like acid in his mouth. "Everything was *fine* before we went looking for you. Now everything is *terrible*."

The dragon said nothing. It took a long, slow breath in, showing its brown-and-yellow teeth, and lay down heavily on the ground.

"You're old and broken and pathetic. You don't care about any of us. You're *heartless*."

"Well, that one is obvious," said a voice behind him.

Demetrius froze, then turned around. No one was there. "Who said that?"

"Dragons keep their hearts elsewhere, don't they?" the voice continued. "Everyone knows that. Using 'heartless' as an insult to a dragon is simply cruel. Like insulting a blind person by calling him sightless. It's not like you're telling them something they don't already know."

"I don't recognize your voice," Demetrius said, craning his neck. "And I can't see where you are. And anyway, I have work to do, and I don't want to sit around and play games." He pulled himself to his knees, adding, "It was nice meeting you, though," because it seemed polite.

"It doesn't much matter what you want, you ridiculous boy," said another voice entirely. This one was a woman— an old woman, by the sound of her. "Your services are needed, child. And there's not much time."

"Why can't I see you?"

"Because you can't see through wood, *obviously*," the first voice said. "He sure does think a lot of himself, Auntie."

"*Hush, Nod*," the woman's voice said. "We're under here, dear. Under the platform. And Demetrius, if you wouldn't mind, please keep your exclamations of surprise to a minimum. We do have—"

But Auntie couldn't finish. Demetrius, belly on the floor, limbs splayed outward, had already peeked over the edge of the platform, had already seen both Auntie and Nod—human-*looking*, but not human at all—and had already screamed. Still screaming, Demetrius scrambled to his feet, swung down the ladder, and ran through the woods toward his home.

Under the platform Auntie sighed, shook her head, and

brought her palm to the back of Nod's head with a quick, sharp smack.

"It wasn't my—"

"Of course it was, Nod, dear. Still, it doesn't change the fact that we do, indeed, need the boy. Go get your uncle. We'll all of us visit the child tonight."

CHAPTER THIRTY-NINE

By the time Demetrius returned home, the world he thought he knew seemed to be shattering to pieces. Violet, first altered and now gone. A nation, once peaceful, gearing up for war. You must understand, my dears, the early millennia of my world were rather similar to your own—tribalism, infighting, wars over land or water or power or beautiful maidens. But that was in the past, you see, and while there were still *stories* of war and *stories* of battles, we had not had even the inkling of polished swords and distant drums for five hundred years. And while each nation in the mirrored world kept standing armies and knew well the techniques and theories of warcraft, there is a great difference between the *theory* of warcraft and war *itself.*

What Demetrius found was chaos.

In the weeks after the dragon's arrival—after the brazen capture and then release of the King—the castle and the surrounding city had been a thicket of activity. War was in the air—no matter what the council said—and people from the countryside had been gathering within the castle walls. Militias formed, pantries were stocked, and ad hoc training exercises became common in the city squares and in the yards.

The announcement of the Mountain King's act of aggression had sent a worrying population into action.

Messengers had been dispatched into the towns and villages throughout the kingdom, announcing the imminent war and calling for all men and women of able body and spirit to come with horse and bow and sword in defense of their country. Demetrius slowly made his way home, jostled by the crush of people.

Once he reached the stable yards, he saw his father calling orders to a group of youths whom Demetrius didn't know. The horses, susceptible as they were to the fluctuations in emotion of their beloved masters, were in a terrible fright. They reared and whinnied and kicked, and no amount of shushing or pulling on the part of his father or the new helpers could soothe them.

"You, in the green!" his father called. "Lead your mare this way into the run. And what's your name? Gherta? Girl in the red. The chestnut trusts you, see that? Lead him into the side pasture. Those others will follow once they see him moving. We just need to break up this mob a bit, and they'll all calm down. *Demetrius!*" He spied his son, and his face went from gray to pink. "Thank the gods! Come over here and take hold of this fellow here and bring him into the stables. He needs to be rubbed down, but he can't be when he's this worked up. Quickly now!"

Demetrius, his head spinning, did as he was told. The horse, a stallion so black he was nearly blue with a sharp white star on his forehead, pulled at the reins. His nostrils flared, and his eyes bulged. With each jerk of the horse's head, Demetrius slid a few feet forward, his legs flailing out from under him momentarily, before he could whip them forward and right himself.

"Hush, beloved," he whispered, blowing gently toward the horse's face as his father had taught him. "Hush now."

The horse, his ears laid back and his eyes overly wide, submitted himself to be led, though he still gave the occasional pull, as though wanting to let Demetrius know who, *exactly*, had the upper hand.

"Yes, yes, beloved," Demetrius soothed, "you could certainly throw me aside like a rag doll and trample me into a bloody pulp. But I trust you, you see? That means you must trust me. Fair's fair, after all." The horse snorted with a shake of his head. Still, his ears came up, Demetrius noted with some satisfaction. He led the stallion into the stall and carefully, making his movements as slow and deliberate as he could, fetched the brush. "I know you're feeling poorly," he said, slowly laying his hand on the animal's belly, "and this will make you feel better, I promise." And with that, he started brushing.

His father was deep in conversation with two men from the army and a woman whom Demetrius recognized instantly. He smiled at her, but she didn't see. She was clad entirely in leather and had a variety of tools and weapons attached to her belt and an archer's quiver slung around her back. Her leather hood had been replaced by a helmet that had already been dented and scratched. Her name was Marda, Mistress of the Falcons and now Captain of the

Front Guard. She scanned the stable, and her eyes narrowed on Demetrius.

"Why is he not training with the front guards? We need everyone we can get."

Demetrius's father choked a bit and stepped backward, as though trying to right himself. "Excuse me? Do you have any idea how young that child is?"

"Demetrius," she said, ignoring his father. "I know you can throw a punch, and I certainly know you are an excellent rider. But can you lift a sword?"

He looked at his father, who mouthed, *Say no.* Demetrius shrugged. "I've had some practice. I'm not bad."

"And can you shoot a bow?"

"Yes," he said. "Very well."

She gazed imperiously at Demetrius's father, who shrank before her. "He's not strong enough to arm the horses, that much is clear. He'll break his neck as sure as he breathes. He's no good to you here. Send him up to the guard. They need fighters who are quick and small and good shots. This war may be nothing but a spoiled brat shaking his spear, but we need to be ready regardless."

"But if the Mountain King attacks, the boy will be killed." His father's voice was as light as ashes.

"Better dead than enslaved," Captain Marda said, and the two lieutenants nodded grimly. "Boy, run to the main gates. And follow instructions."

Demetrius couldn't move. He stared at his father.

"*Now!*" the woman yelled, and Demetrius turned and ran as though burned.

As he darted through the narrow gap between the stable and the forge, he heard his father say, "But he's my only son. He's the only family I have." And the old man's sobs echoed strangely on the old stone walls.

But tears were useless now. War had begun.

CHAPTER FORTY

The first attack happened that night, along the wooded border—small scouting parties coming upon one another by accident, and surprise giving way to skirmish.

The dead were few, the injured many, and the cloud of war pressed heavily on the city.

Demetrius worked hard, avoided sleep when he could, and tried to prevent himself from thinking. Thinking, he discovered, was dangerous and led to fruitless worry that did nothing but fill him with a sense of impotent rage and despair.

Still, even in the din of warfare, his thoughts wandered. *Where is Violet?* he wondered again and again and again. *What were those creatures?*

And most troubling: *Why now?*

Indeed, my dears, *why?* It was a question that I myself was troubled with, and if it had not been for the necessities of our respective circumstances, perhaps Demetrius and I would have been able—but no. No. The damage was done.

By the fourth night, the fighting was still far away, but as Demetrius stood watch at the northern section of the western wall, he could see the first ripples of red light spreading across the horizon, bleeding from the land into the mirrored edge of the sky. The land was burning. And whether it was a farmhouse or a wheat field or a grain silo that was the original target, the result now was the same: a broad swath of burning earth raging as the battle raged. As though the ground under the soldiers' feet, too, had become an adversary.

"Captain? Captain!"

Captain Marda appeared from a makeshift tent below. Her eyes flashed in the dark.

"Speak," she said.

"Fire," Demetrius said, pointing northward. He returned

his gaze to the horizon and saw with a sinking feeling that the fire had spread.

The Captain shook her head. "That's all we need. Stay at your post, boy. I'll send out the alert. We'll need a crew to dig a fire line. And this on top of everything else." She sprinted down the narrow walkway and out of sight.

Demetrius turned back toward the widening fire. It wasn't as though he had never seen a fire before. He had. Not two years earlier there was a terrible fire in the western wastes, and he had traveled with his father to lend their skills in the care and healing of the many displaced livestock and other animals. The fires raged while they corralled and soothed hundreds of beasts, salving their burns and tearfully easing the dead into pits, where they were buried. As a child, he was terrified of fire—it was a fire in the stables, after all, that had killed his mother—so terrified that he could hardly bear to look at his own home's bright hearth, and even the smells of bubbling stew and baking bread filled him with horror and grief. Now, though, as a youth, his fear had been replaced with awe. Fire was, Demetrius knew, a transformative force. A fire did not *destroy*; it simply *changed*. His mother, after shooing her son, all the goats, most of the cows, and half of the horses

out of the barn, only to find her own exit blocked, was ushered out of this world and into another.

Still, this fire was different. Though uncannily bright, and so hot it bent the light above it, the fire made no smoke. Instead, a strange, unnatural smell wafted over the field. Everyone shuddered. The fire shimmered and swelled—more song than flame. Demetrius curled his fingers around his eyes and squinted, trying to extend his vision as far as he could. It was so far away, and yet he could have sworn that he saw thousands of tiny glints scurrying through the flames. He shivered, and though the night was chilly and damp, he realized that he was sweating uncomfortably under his leather-lined tunic.

"Don't like this," grumbled a voice he recognized. "Don't like this at all."

Demetrius gasped, whirled around, and nearly fell off the wall. "Who's there?" he demanded.

"What are those things, Auntie? What's wrong with their eyes?"

"I'm warning you," Demetrius said, noting with humiliation that his voice was squeaking like wet fingers on clean glass. "I'm armed." He attempted to add some gravel to his voice, but that just made it worse. Someone, somewhere in the darkness, snickered.

"We're not about to show ourselves to you, dear. Remember what happened last time?"

"There wasn't a last time," Demetrius said. "I was tired and worried and starting to see things. It happens. In fact, it's happening now, which means there's no *this* time, either."

"He does have a point, Auntie."

"Hush, Nod."

In the dark, somewhere near his knees, there was the sound of a quick, sharp smack and a cry of pain.

"Demetrius, dear, there isn't much time. If they reach the castle—"

"I know, I know. We'll all be slaves to the Mountain King."

In the darkness a very old woman clicked her tongue and sighed. "My dear child," she said, "the Mountain King is the least of your worries. The being behind this mess is more powerful than you could possibly—"

"You! Boy!"

Demetrius turned, stood at attention. "Yes, Captain!"

"Come down and grab a shovel. I need fresh eyes above. You strong enough to dig?"

"Yes, Captain."

"Good. There are twelve teams going out to dig a trench

around the city. You're not going for depth but breadth. Don't leave anything that could burn."

"Don't go down there," the old woman's voice commanded. "We are running out of time. By the time that fire reaches the line, all will be lost. Are you listening to me?"

Demetrius shook his head, but instead of clarity, he only felt the lack of sleep and the worry and the fear rattling around his head. Something small and strong latched onto his leg, and the poor boy froze.

The Captain's voice shot out of the dark. "Are you coming to me, boy?"

"Yes, sir," Demetrius said. "I mean, ma'am. I mean, Captain. My foot's just caught on—there, that's better." With one quick jerk of his leg, the invisible—*something*—dislodged and disappeared, with a cry, into the smoky gloom. Demetrius swung his body onto the makeshift ladder and clambered to the ground. He grabbed a shovel and a rudimentary hunk of wood that he supposed was to act as a hoe, and ran to the outside of the city wall.

The fire was closer. So was the fighting, from the sound of it. Demetrius tied his kerchief around his face to block out the smoke, and began to dig.

On the top of the wall, Auntie, Moth, and Nod sat at

the outer edge, their shoulders pressing close to one another as they shook their heads and sighed.

"Well," Auntie said, clucking her tongue again and again, "I suppose it's better than nothing."

"Don't see how you could think that," Moth said, spitting prodigiously into the dark. "Looks like we're pretty well—"

"Language, Moth."

"In any case, looks to me like we've failed. Billions upon billions of days and nights with the Greater Sun rising and setting as peaceful as anything, and in one fell swoop the three of us ruin it beyond repair."

"Uncle Moth," Nod said reproachfully. "That's a bit much."

"It would be perfectly fine to say it if it were true, Nod. But it isn't. Not yet, anyway. The chaos down there can do us some good, since he won't come willingly."

"I told you we should have talked to the two of them," Moth said.

"You never said any such thing," Auntie said, giving the old man a smack on the back of the head.

"Well, I thought it anyway."

Auntie ignored him. "You two," she said, "head down and stay close to that boy. There's a raiding party getting close, and we can't afford to lose his head or ours. Wait for the fighting to start. When he's knocked unconscious—"

"But Auntie," Nod said, "how can we be sure that he'll only suffer a blow to the head?"

"Right," she said, standing up and straightening her heavily patched apron. "I forgot to mention. Bring a shovel. Make sure you don't miss."

CHAPTER FORTY-ONE

Violet never knew how long she remained inside the mirror. Indeed, she did not have any recollection of it at all, and while the image of that dear child pressing her palms to her cage and begging for rescue will haunt me until the day I die, for her there was no time elapsed at all from the moment she made the wish until the moment she tumbled, head over feet, out of a mirror in a forgotten room on the eastern edge of the castle and fell to the floor. She had been gone for thirteen days, and the castle had fallen into mourning.

And, what's worse, the war had begun.

But she didn't know that yet.

What she did know was this: the sensation of *something* transforming to *nothing* transforming again to *something*. Since neither you nor I have ever had the experience of *nothing*—how could we, as we are *something*—Violet explained it as similar to the sensation one has when dreaming. The action occurs, the world exists, but *you are not in it.* Conscious, yes; aware, yes; but as a nonbeing.

Her first sensations in her new body were in her hands—pricking fingertips, cracking knuckles. Then eyelids that blinked. The pull of hair on the scalp. Sweat on the back of the neck. As she felt the associations and amalgamations of a body forming itself in limitless space, she had the unmistakable feeling of the stomach pulling suddenly into the throat and the mouth spreading wide into a scream.

Violet was falling. Fast.

In a tangle of limbs and hair and heavy clothing, Violet crumpled against the stone floor.

"Ugh!" She sighed as she unscrambled her splayed arms and legs and wobbled herself toward standing. But something was different. Though she was able to move hands, feet, arms, and legs, each movement felt alien and strange—

and the *not-rightness* of it made her light-headed and nause-
ated. She looked down at herself, and though she could
move each toe, each finger, and bend each knee, there was
nothing that she saw that looked even vaguely familiar:
Violet was in a body that was not her own. She ran to the
mirror.

A new face. Amber skin that glowed. Wide-spaced
black eyes. Black hair, shiny as oil, falling in heavy coils
and snaking down her back all the way to her knees.

Lips like rosebuds.

Tiny feet clad in shoes made from the petals of lilies
dipped in gold.

A dress made from velvet spun from silk and shot
through with silver.

The calluses on her hands were gone, as were the scrapes
on her knees.

A real princess. Violet squealed and spun around, but her
hair was so heavy and her feet so small that she quickly lost
her balance and fell. She checked the long hallway to see if
anyone was watching. The hall was empty. (Did it strike
her as strange, my dears? It should have, of course, but it
didn't.) And the Princess righted herself unobserved.

She returned to the mirror, but her reflection lasted only

a moment. The image rippled before her eyes, and something very different appeared. A woman—golden eyes, golden skin, golden hair—smiling through the glass. Diamond teeth glinted through parted lips, their edges sharp as knives. Violet shuddered.

DO YOU LIKE IT, DARLING? the golden woman said— though her voice seemed to come not from the mirror but from the stones and the floor and the air. It was *inside* Violet. It crawled and wormed under her skin.

"I do," Violet said fervently, unconsciously rubbing at her arms. "I love it. I'm…" She paused. "I'm the way I'm *supposed* to be."

YES, MY DARLING! OH, YES! The golden woman's smile broadened. Her thin tongue flicked across her lips again and again. NOW, THERE IS THE SUBJECT OF PAYMENT.

"Of course," Violet said absently, admiring the soft flesh on her reedy arms—noting the lack of muscle and wondering how she would climb and ride with her new body. *Perhaps*, she thought, *I shan't need to.* And a knot began to form in her stomach.

DON'T SHOW YOURSELF TO YOUR FATHER—OR ANYONE ELSE. NOT RIGHT AWAY, the golden woman said. THEY WILL HAVE TROUBLE UNDERSTANDING WHAT HAS HAPPENED,

AND I DARESAY THEY WILL NEED MY ASSISTANCE. WHICH MEANS THAT I NEED YOU, DEAR, TO ASSIST ME IN FREEING MYSELF FROM THIS MIRROR. WICKED DEMONS TRAPPED ME HERE EVER SO LONG AGO.

Thick tears welled in those golden eyes. Golden lips trembled with manufactured sobs.

"That's terrible," Violet said. "Though you really shouldn't—"

GO TO THE STABLES AND GET YOUR HORSE. BRING A MIRROR. THE MOUNTAIN KING HAS AN OBJECT THAT BELONGS TO ME. HE HAS KEPT IT SAFE UNTIL THE DAY IN WHICH MY HEART'S BELOVED PRESENTS HERSELF AS MY CHAMPION. HE WAITS FOR YOU JUST WITHIN THE BORDERS OF YOUR COUNTRY—ONLY TWO DAYS' RIDE! PERHAPS NOT EVEN THAT. PRESENT YOURSELF TO THE KING, TAKE THE AMULET, AND RETURN IT HERE, AND EVERYTHING WILL BE WONDERFUL.

Lies, my dears. The Nybbas lied.

"That's it?" Violet asked, her neck straining against the weight of her hair.

THAT'S IT.

"Well, that's easy. And I'm happy to help. I'll get my mirror—I'll be but a moment."

And Violet ran down the empty hall.

And if the Nybbas had been just a little bit less success-ful with Violet's transformation, perhaps all would have gone according to plan. If Violet had been less delicate, perhaps, or if the details of her body were not as true to the stories, she may have made it to her room and to the stables without ever being seen.

But the load of thick black hair falling in waves down her back (a line, I must admit, I was rather proud of when I said it) was abominably heavy and pulled painfully at her scalp. And her tiny feet were much too small for her increased height, and she wobbled to and fro, unable to fully right herself. Her velvet gown weighed half as much as she did, and with her new delicacy, her lack of muscular agility, she hardly had the strength to walk, much less run, weighted by hair and dress. Though it wasn't far to her room, Violet was forced to stop no fewer than six times, catching her breath and regathering her strength.

And it was while she paused that she heard her father crying. Violet was a compassionate child, and loving. It was not that she disobeyed the Nybbas's instructions intention-ally. Indeed, at the sound of her father's grief-stricken voice, the Nybbas no longer existed for Violet. Neither did her new body, her new dress, her new hair. In that moment, Violet *did not remember* that she looked different.

She simply ran into the room.

"Father," she said, rushing to the astonished King, "don't cry. Please don't cry, Papa!"

The King stood in one of the castle's many parlors. His face was gray, his eyes darkened by worry and lack of sleep. Three generals, two ambassadors, and a hunting party all presented their news to the King—none of it good.

I was in the far corner of the room, ready to assist. Violet had been missing—in our time—for days upon days, and all searching had ended. We were now a nation at war. We were a nation in mourning. And my duty was to the King.

Still.

There was something strange in the simultaneity of our twin disasters—and whatever it was wormed under my skin like a parasite. *I should know this*, I told myself. *I should know what's going on.* A good teller, you see, prides himself or herself on the ability to draw on our history and myths, to provide perspective and context for those with more power than ourselves. It is our duty to our countries and our kings and queens, and I fulfilled it gladly. But of course now, now I understand that I, too, was under the spell of the Nybbas. I, too, was intentionally obfuscated and misdirected.

Or perhaps I was simply too cowardly to voice my true concerns.

Or perhaps it was both.

In any case, when I heard the child's voice coming to her father, my heart leaped within me. I rose to my feet, feeling as though I might be able to fly. I have no doubt that the King felt the same way, and so I understood how he responded upon seeing a girl (beautiful, shockingly beautiful!) come running into the room. A girl with Violet's voice. A girl who was not Violet.

"Please, please don't cry, Papa. I'm sorry I went away."

The King, seeing this foreign face that spoke with the voice of his child, recoiled in horror.

"*Don't touch me!*" he hissed. "Who do you think you are?"

I saw the girl jerk back as though slapped. Then she looked down at herself and appeared to relax slightly. "Papa," she said, "I know it's strange, but it's me. I swear. I...I made a wish."

"Guards!" the King called.

"No! Father, surely you can tell it's me. I was supposed

to be a real princess. A proper princess. So I fixed it, and now it's all right. No... excuse me! I am the Princess! Don't touch me!" Two guards took Violet's arms. She struggled and quickly lost her balance as two other guards grabbed her feet and carried her into the hall and toward the dungeons. She cried and pleaded and screamed for her father—her mother, too, though her mother was dead and gone, and no amount of beauty was ever going to bring her back.

The eldest general shook his head.

"How many fake princesses has that been, General?"

"That's the fifth one today, sir."

"Then, twenty-four in total since Violet disappeared." The general rocked back on his heels, pressing his fingers to his chin. "What has gotten into these people?"

And it was true—even from the first hour that the Princess disappeared, girls presented themselves to the King, claiming to be the Princess Violet. Then it was girls and women. Then girls, women, boys, and men of all ages. They ordered the guards about and tried to break into her bedroom and generally made a bit of a ruckus and nuisance. But there was something different about this one. While her indignation and surprise were not unusual—indeed, all twenty-four seemed to me to truly *believe* that they were, indeed, the Princess Violet—it was her voice. That *voice*! It was *her* voice. And how that voice came to be in the throat of a girl who certainly *looked* like a princess but was not *our* Princess, I had no idea. A spell, perhaps. Could the girl be a magician? Could she have stolen the voice but not the face of the Princess? Was such a thing possible? Surely, she was too young to be a magician—an art that required decades of study before the most basic spells could even be attempted.

Surely the girl couldn't be…but no, thought I. She couldn't be *Violet*.

I nearly gave voice to that possibility. And would have, had it not been for the King, white-faced and shaking, who uttered this: "The attempts at manipulation and impersonation are not, I believe, unconnected. I do not know the author of this plot, but I fear that it might be the brainchild of our enemy to the north. Therefore, any person claiming to be the Princess is to be immediately jailed and will remain there until this conflict is over. We can only assume that they are spies or worse. Anyone caught mentioning the imprisoned impostors shall also be imprisoned and questioned. If this is an attempt to rattle us and shake our resolve, it will fail. We will prevail. I will not see my people enslaved to the Mountain King."

Any concern I had, any inclination toward expressing my theory, died right there. I could not, I decided, risk imprisonment. I was terribly afraid of rats. And so I was silent.

CHAPTER FORTY-TWO

Despite the fact that Violet's new form was impossibly lithe and narrow, the guards found her difficult to carry due to the mounds of hair cascading from her poor scalp. Indeed, as they spirited her away down the hall and toward that terrible stairway that led to the lower reaches of the castle, her hair grew—it both lengthened and thickened into a great, snaking heap of fragrant black waves. It curled around the feet of the hurrying guards, winding prettily up their legs.

"A little help here," panted one guard, and three more

guards hurried over, each one taking up an armload of hair. By the time they reached the prison wing, the weight of hair required six strong men just to keep it off the ground.

"I don't know why you're bothering locking me up," Violet said. "It's not like I can move anyway."

"Hush, cursed child," said the guard holding her left arm. "You'll wait with the rats until you tell us what you've done with our Violet."

Our Violet, the girl thought. *When was the last time someone has called me that?* She also noted with some fascination the way the guard's voice seemed to break at the edges of her name.

The contempt, the *sneering* that she had heard so much before she disappeared into the mirror, was gone. Only worry remained. *Why?* she wondered. *What changed?*

"But sir," she began, "I *am*—"

"Quiet!" the guard barked. "That's *enough*."

They opened the door with a loud creak, the sound of which stirred the other prisoners from their stupor or sleep.

"Let me out of here!" shouted one girl.

"I demand to be set free!" shouted another.

"I am the Princess Violet," an old woman shouted. "Take me to my father at *once!*"

"You're not the Princess," a man said. "*I* am!"

"No, *I* am," a boy shouted.

"Liars!" shouted yet another girl. "It's me! I'm the Princess!"

"You see," said the guard holding Violet's middle. "You have lots of friends." His voice was bitter, grief ground to anger in his heart.

"You don't understand," Violet said, her words choking in her swollen throat, her wide eyes flowing with tears. "I *am* the Princess. I made a wish. I wanted to be a *real* princess. *Real* princesses are beautiful."

"*Violet* was beautiful," the guard holding her left arm said as he carelessly dropped her onto the hard stone floor. He made a sound somewhere between a grunt and a hiccup and a sob. "*Is*, I mean. Is beautiful. You are—well, I don't even know *what* you are." The guards filed out, slamming the door behind them, leaving Violet splayed upon the heap of her hair. They stood in the hallway, the backs of their heads framed by the barred opening at the top of the door.

"I am the Princess," Violet said, struggling to her knees. "A *real* princess."

"NO!" shouted a girl down the hall. "*I* am the Princess."

"NO! I am!"

"See." One of the guards pressed his face between the bars, his expression distorted into a mocking leer. "You'll have to come up with a more creative ruse. Seems everyone's the Princess Violet these days."

Violet teetered on her too-small feet, her balance thrown more and more askew by the weight of her hair. "But... I don't understand."

"Of course you do, *Princess*. You are in league with the enemy. You prey upon our fear and our grief. You are the worst kind of coward."

"No," Violet faltered, sinking to the floor. "My name is Violet. My mother's name is Rose. My father's name is Randall. I was born here in this castle in the winter. My mother said that a violet bloomed in the snow."

"Enough," the guard said, slamming the keys against the bars with a cold, hard clank.

"I am Princess Violet!" she shouted.

"NO!" came a voice from down the hall. "I am the Princess!"

"NO, I am," shouted the girl across the hall.

"NO, I am," shouted one of the younger guards.

"*Liars!*" Violet shouted. But the guards set their backs on her and marched away into the gloom.

Violet covered her beautiful, cursed face with her hands, sank back on the growing pile of her hair, and wept.

CHAPTER FORTY-THREE

It was no easy feat to drag a boy of Demetrius's size from the smoky haze of the battlefield into the tunnels. Despite the small stature typical of their kind, Auntie, Nod, and Moth possessed gifts of strength reminiscent of the insect world and were able to carry loads that exceeded their weight. Still, once inside the tunnel, the awkward sway of his bulk, his splayed limbs, and his lolling head all proved to be devilishly difficult.

"Does it really have to be *him*, Auntie?" Moth panted

and heaved. "Couldn't we have chosen someone smaller? A baby, perhaps?"

"Fancy bringing a baby into a place like this," Auntie said with a flutter of one hand, as though she wanted nothing better than to give Moth a smack but was prevented from doing so because he was on the other side of the unconscious boy. "There wouldn't be much of a point to it, in any case. So far we've found but two children who can hear us. A fat lot of good it would do to bring an unaware child into the bottom of the castle. It would only wet itself and call for its mother."

"The boy's been no use so far. The girl, neither."

"And yet we try, dear." Auntie sniffed, saying the word *dear* as though it actually meant *idiot*.

It took nearly an hour for the three of them to push, pull, and heave the boy into a small anteroom with a domed ceiling high enough for him to sit up. Auntie, Nod, and Moth dropped his limbs onto the ground and fell against the sloped stone walls, breathing heavily.

"Now what?" Moth said, rubbing his knees. "I won't lie, Auntie. These old bones aren't what they used to be. I'm not sure if I'll be able to haul the big'un any farther, if you know what I mean."

"Fortunately for your *bones*, Moth, we will pull no farther," Auntie said, raising herself to her feet and fixing a hard look at him. Far be it from her to actually *mention* the fact that though he was, truly, both old and feeble, back when he was nothing more than a little bobbin, crawling about on the shoulders of his remaining relatives, Auntie had already lived through five hundred and twenty summers. At *least*. The females of her clan were known for their longevity, but none held on to life more tenaciously than Auntie herself. Her joints cracked loudly, as though to make that point as she approached the unconscious boy. Moth simply grunted.

Auntie crawled up onto the boy, first examining the knot on his forehead—like a hard blue egg—and then peeking under his eyelids and into his mouth and listening at the nostrils.

"Nod, dear," she said absently, "could you please hand me my bag?"

"Will he be all right, Auntie?" Nod asked, handing the satchel up to the old woman crouching on the mountainous boy. "I hit him terribly hard."

"Not to worry, my child. The boy inherited his hard head from his grandfather. I once watched that man suffer a kick from the most enormous horse I'd ever seen. Right between the eyes. He simply shook it off and continued working. This boy will be just fine. Now where is that pigs-radish?" She fumbled through the endless pockets inside the satchel, grumbling all the while. Finally she pulled out a twisted little root, about the size of an earthworm. Clutching the boy's shirt for balance, she held the root under his nose, curled it under her long fingers, and crushed it, allowing it to drip its juices onto the skin between his nostrils and his lip.

The boy snorted, shuddered, coughed, and screamed. Auntie tried to smile, but Demetrius screamed louder, sitting up so quickly that he sent Auntie flying sideways. He hit his head on the stony ceiling with a crack.

"*Ow!*" he moaned.

"*This* is what we've put our hopes in, Auntie," Moth said, shaking his head. "Pardon me if I'm not whooping and hollering and dancing a jig."

"*Enough*, Moth," Auntie said, getting to her feet. "I've had *quite* enough."

"It's you," Demetrius said, shifting away from the small people on the ground and gingerly bringing his hands to his injured head. There was a lump on the back of his skull the size of a walnut. "Why can't you leave me alone?"

"Oh, come now," Moth said. "You and your little friend have been gallivanting through our corridors, mucking things up, leaving behind your terrible big'un stink—not to mention the crumbs from your stolen sweets—and who do you think cleaned up after your mannerless selves? Old Moth here, that's who." The old man glared.

Auntie shook her head. "He's not angry, dear," she said, giving Moth a hard look. "Just ornery. He's been very worried about that lump on your head."

"No, I haven't," Moth said.

"What happened? And what happened to my head?" The lump on the back of his head hurt to touch, but he let his fingers rest on it anyway. He could feel a few crusts of dried blood on one side.

"Oh, that was Nod. He's stronger than he looks, and the shovel was heavy."

"Shovel?" Demetrius said. "He hit me on the head with a *shovel*? What's the matter with you—"

"Oh, now, now," Auntie soothed. "We only did what we needed to do. You'll see."

And in truth, Demetrius believed her. While their initial appearance was shocking, he was no longer shocked. And the feelings written on their faces were plain enough. Worry. Panic. Fear. And the boy was moved.

"What is this place?" Demetrius said, rubbing his head. "And how did you get me here?"

"We are inside the castle. Deep inside. And we must go deeper still," Auntie said, walking closer to the boy—not so close as to touch him or frighten him, but close enough that he might know that she meant him no harm. "We need your help, child, and quickly, for the situation has gone quite out of control."

"All thanks to Nod," Moth said, dolefully seeking in his pockets for his pipe and, finding none, biting at his thumb instead.

"We *all* bear responsibility, Moth. All of us. Even the Princess."

"The Princess?" Demetrius gave the three small creatures a hard look. "What about Violet? Do you know where she is? Did you kidnap her, too? What does she have to do with it?"

Auntie sighed. "Everything, unfortunately. And nothing."

She paused, as though weighing her words. "And of course we didn't kidnap her. We didn't kidnap you, either." Auntie swallowed. "Well, not intentionally, anyway."

Moth began biting his thumb in earnest now, and Nod whistled.

"I see," Demetrius said.

"In any case," Auntie said, regaining her composure, "it's all terribly complicated, and we would save some time if we were walking. Well." She gave a sidelong glance to Demetrius. "*We* will walk. You, child, will have to crawl."

Demetrius pressed his hands against the low ceiling. There was hardly any light, aside from the paltry glow coming from the tiny metal lantern held by one of the small creatures, but he could see three tiny openings around the room, leading into dark, tight passageways. Demetrius felt a hot wave of panic roll from his stomach to his throat, burning as it moved. "I don't think..." Demetrius began, swallowing his fear. "I mean, I don't think I'll be able to. I'm too big." He pressed harder, as though he could break through the stone from sheer force.

"Oh, tosh," Auntie said, snatching the lantern. "You've already gone through the hard part, though, truthfully, we had to drag you. But these passages are nothing new to you and your little friend. We've been cleaning up after you for years." She walked into a passage, taking the light with her, her two companions following close behind. Demetrius sighed, flattened down onto his belly, and crawled after the light.

CHAPTER FORTY-FOUR

The war grew and swelled around us. It pummeled the walls; it rattled the windows; it whispered at the doors. Its voice was ragged and rusty and sharp. We choked on the smell. It crowded our eyes; it scratched at our ears; it knocked our bodies around and around. We thought war, spoke war, ate and drank and dreamed war. Soon we couldn't imagine a world without it.

The Great Hall was transformed into a hospital wing, and the library became a strategy center. Generals and diplomats from the west and the south arrived with armies and weapons and supplies in tow and proceeded to hurry through the hallways, their voices quick and sharp and urgent. They never stopped moving. The King, however, became more and more detached every minute. He deferred to the advisers. He relinquished control to this general or that general and began to agree to everything.

When the King simultaneously agreed to a total surrender *and* a fight to the death, the council of generals, sages, advisers, and magicians conferred with one another without the King. I was on the far side of the room with my beloved King, my ear tuned to their conversation. He didn't seem to notice what was going on and instead peered insistently into mirrors, and the surface of water glasses, and the slicked surface of the window. He would point, gasp, and then deflate.

"*My darling*," whispered the King. "*My child*," he breathed.

But there was nothing there. Just the mirror. Just the glass. Just the water. The King covered his face and gave himself over to weeping.

On the other side of the room, the generals, advisers, and magicians argued.

"It is obvious," one said, "that the King is incapacitated. We need a single voice of authority."

"Which should be me," the eldest magician said coolly.

"For your vast knowledge of military tactics," sneered the youngest general. "I was top of my class at the Academy. I nominate myself."

"*Idiocy*," cried an adviser. "The military is supposed to do as it is told. What is needed is a scholar and a statesman. I nominate—"

"Myself," said the magician who was called Albert.

"No, me!"

"No, me!"

The King ignored them. He was a man transported. The King stared at a mirror. Pressing his fingers to his mouth, his eyes shone and shone.

"Do you see her?" whispered the King.

"I see her," he whispered his own answer back.

He sighed, shook his head, and marched into the adjacent room. I listened to his words, though they seemed nonsensical and vague, like words heard in a dream. Slowly, I made my way toward the mirror that had so captured the attention of the King.

"My dear friends." King Randall stood tall in front of his advisers, his voice echoing strangely against the wall. His eyes shone. He smiled at the men and women staring back at him.

I turned away and stared at the mirror. My reflection wobbled, misted, and faded away.

No, thought I. *No, no, no.*

"While I understand and accept the gravity of the situation in which we now all find ourselves," the King said to his advisers, "and clearly, it is imperative for the safety and permanence of the Andulan Realms that we fight and win this war, that we do not accept slavery from the likes of our cousin to the north, I regret to inform you that because of the disappearance of our one and only child, the dear Princess Violet, I will be leaving the castle. Immediately."

A gasp.

A shout.

I hardly noticed. I stared at the empty mirror. A pair of eyes blinked back at me. They glittered like two hard jewels.

"I go in search of my daughter. Or..." He paused. "Not in search. Indeed, I know exactly where she is. I go to collect her. In my absence, I declare a temporary abdication of the crown and leave in my stead the crowned regent, the storyteller Cassian."

What? I thought.

"What?" they shouted.

Me? I thought.

"Him?" they shouted.

"It has been decreed," cried the King, slapping me hard on the back. "It is done. Cassian is lord regent. You will treat him as your king."

In the mirror, the jeweled eyes winked at me. They sparkled with delight. Sharp-tipped golden teeth glinted in a slowly widening smile.

"I know what you are," I whispered at the mirror.

OF COURSE YOU DO, the mirror hissed back.

CHAPTER FORTY-FIVE

Deep underneath the castle, the Princess Violet awoke on a bed of hair.

"Bother," she grumbled as she forced herself to her feet. Her hair had, for the time being, ceased to grow. Still. There were *mounds* of it, snaking down her back and pooling onto the floor. (And in her mind she cursed me by name, as it was my story that had birthed such a ridiculous notion in her young head. Who had ever heard of hair trailing on the floor? It was a terrible inconvenience, and I am sick, *sick, my dears*, that I ever put such a thing into a story.) *Well*, she told herself, *it resists tangles. So that's something*. At once, she began twisting it into a long rope that she looped around her waist and tied tightly into a knot. Though it still pulled painfully at her scalp and was terribly heavy to carry, she wasn't in danger of falling.

"Hello," she called. "Hello?"

From the end of the corridor, she heard the jangle of keys and the crackling of arthritic joints as a figure came closer through the gloom.

"Well," said the jailer—as pale and gap-toothed and grizzled and surly as any jailer you've heard about in stories. "If it isn't the *Princess*." With an ugly, mocking expression on his uglier face, he sank into an exaggerated bow. Violet smiled serenely.

"She's not the Princess," yawned a sleepy voice from nearby. "I am."

"No! Me!" said another.

"SHUT UP!" cried Violet and the jailer together.

"Honestly," Violet said, standing at her full height and holding her chin just so, as she had been painstakingly taught by her governesses and tutors. "I can't imagine how one can get anything done under such conditions. I commend you, sir, for your cool head."

The jailer blanched. He removed his knitted hat. "Why, yes." He cleared his throat. "Indeed. Thank you for noticing, miss."

"I state only the obvious, my good, good man." She inclined her head and gave a quick, genteel bow. The jailer opened his mouth to say something, then closed it, pressing his finger against his lips. "And I thank you for your service," Violet added.

There is something, my dears, that you must understand. Violet—*my* Violet—was a *real* princess. And no matter what lies the stories tell you, a *real* princess has nothing to do with opulent garments or a heart-shaped face or teeth like pearls. A real princess engages with the world in a state of grace. It is with grace that she listens and with grace that she speaks. A princess loves her people, no matter what their birth or station. Even ugly jailers.

"Is—" He cleared his throat. "Is there anything I can get for you, miss?" the jailer found himself asking. He was astonished, really. He couldn't remember ever asking if a prisoner needed anything. In fact, he couldn't remember a time in his life when he would have even considered *wondering* such a thing, let alone ask it. But the jailer asked. And, what's more, he was desperate to know the answer.

He clasped his hands at his chest and waited. His breath caught in his throat.

"You know, sir," Violet said very slowly, "I would give anything in the world for a basin of water to wash my face, and perhaps a mirror." She spoke lightly, casually. As though it wouldn't matter either way. But *oh*, how her heart trembled!

"Right away, miss," the jailer said, and scurried into the darkness to get them.

Violet turned, leaned her back against the bars, and rubbed her temples and hairline with her fingers. *There is nothing*, she thought, *more uncomfortable than too much hair.* She felt as though the weight of it might pull her scalp off altogether. She would have asked for scissors, or a very sharp knife, and she would hack at it all day if she had to. But it wouldn't do to push her luck. Best to take the mirror.

It didn't take the jailer long. The mirror was just a fragment—its sharp edges filed to soft waves. She took the mirror first, pressing its reflective side to her chest. The water in the basin was warm to the point of steaming. He brought a lump of soap, and a worn but soft cloth to dry her face and hands. He also brought a couple of apples, a hunk of hard cheese, and a bit of dry bread. It was, Violet could tell, all that he had.

"I can't take this, sir," she said, holding her hands up when he offered the food. But the man insisted, saying there was plenty more where that came from, and prisoners were fed but once a day, and while it was enough to last, she had missed the meal and would have to wait until tomorrow for nourishment.

She thanked the jailer, who found himself removing his hat and bowing at her. He turned, mystified, and walked away. Violet set the mirror facedown on the pile of straw in the back that she assumed would serve as her bed. The mirror heated and whispered. She knew exactly *who* was whispering her name, but *why*? That was another matter indeed.

She took a breath and cleared her head. Her head felt clearer now than it had for...ever so long. Was it the time in the mirror? Or the new body? Or was it simply that while she was suspended, she was not thinking? And when she was not thinking, she was not dwelling in thoughts of the Nybbas. And it had no control over her.

As she washed her face, Violet went over the facts as she

understood them. And as she sat, the things that she had *read*, and then ignored while she was wading through books in the library, came roaring into her mind, as clear and bright as bells. First, she *knew* that the voice in the mirror—that wish-granting trickster—was not to be trusted. That much was obvious. She knew that she had spent quite a bit of time inside the mirror. Two weeks, perhaps. Or more. Also obvious was that, in her absence, terrible things had been happening to her home. The council of grim-faced generals, the worn expression on the face of her father, the pandemonium outside—she had no idea what it meant, but she knew it couldn't be good.

War, she thought. *Riots.* It was all in the stories. Why didn't she see it before? Certainly, there were hints that the Nybbas delighted in both, and caused both when they suited its purpose. But what purpose, she wondered.

What does it want?

Violet crouched down, slowly chewing her apples and cheese. The Nybbas was able to twist the truth, to insinuate itself into the souls of men and women. This she knew from the stories. She knew, as well, that it had to do as it was told. And had done so thus far—it was just very good at convincing her to choose the things it wanted her to choose.

She chose the things that would strengthen it, nourish it, and give it power. *Very clever*, she thought. She had done this willingly. She had *given it power*. And now…well, she didn't know. But she was going to find out.

The Nybbas is clever, but the Nybbas is vain. And the vanity was her only chance. Violet took a deep breath and picked up the mirror.

The jeweled eyes flashed.

Violet smiled and simpered. "Oh, I thought he would *never* go away. Everything has gone wrong, my beloved, and it is all my fault." The tears rolling down Violet's cheeks were real. The repressed sobs were real as well. But she hung on to the lie of her words like a shield. She would lie to protect herself from a liar. "The King wouldn't recognize a real princess if she knocked him down. All of your hard work has been wasted, and it's all his fault." The mouth in the mirror twitched a hint of a smile. "What shall I do, my beloved? They've trapped me in the dungeon. They're *jealous*. I *know* it. They're jealous that I have your love and they do not!" Violet leaned close to the mirror. She felt her belly churning and her throat closing up. She prayed that the

creature didn't notice. "I want you to make them pay, my beloved. I want the kingdom I *deserve*. You are the only one I can trust. Please tell me what to do."

The face in the mirror blinked, then twitched. Then slowly, a slippery grin unfurled across its beautiful face.

OH, MY CHILD, it whispered. I WILL MOVE HEAVEN AND EARTH TO HELP YOU. BUT IF ONLY YOU COULD DO SOMETHING TO HELP ME... It tried to affect a miserable expression. Violet, who had spent the last few hours being very miserable indeed, wasn't fooled.

"Tell me what it is, my beloved. Tell me, and I'll do what I can to help you." Her heart fluttered desperately within her chest.

IT'S ONLY A TRIFLE, BUT I'M AFRAID IT SHALL BE TRICKY TO EXTRACT. THIS WRETCHED CASTLE IS HIDING IT, YOU SEE. BUT WHEN I AM RESTORED, I SHALL BUILD YOU A NEW CASTLE. WHEN I AM RESTORED, YOU SHALL BE THE GREATEST RULER THE MULTIVERSE HAS EVER SEEN. I WILL BRING ALL CREATURES AND GODS TO THEIR KNEES. EVERY POWER IN THE MULTIVERSE WILL BE MINE—I MEAN, YOURS—TO USE AS YOU WILL. I SHALL GIVE YOU MY HEART, MY SOUL, MY LIFE, AND MY POWER, VIOLET.

"Tell me, my beloved. Tell me what you want." Violet

shivered and shook. A thin trickle of sweat escaped from her mounds of hair and ran icily down her neck.

GET ME MY HEART, PRINCESS, AND I AM YOURS FOREVER.

Violet nodded, leaned her face to the warm glass of the mirror, and pressed her lips to the slippery grin of the Nybbas. "If you can magic me out of this prison," Violet said, "I will do whatever you want." In her heart she knew what she'd do. Break the mirror. Break every mirror. Cut the thing at its throat. Keep it from speaking. She hardened her mind to the influence of the Nybbas and painted a simpering smile on her lips like a mask. "Tell me how," she said.

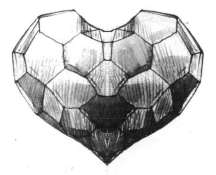

CHAPTER FORTY-SIX

The King left at midnight. I did everything, *everything*, my dears, that I could think of to dissuade him. I reasoned; I begged; I bargained. I even threatened to call in the guards to strap him in irons and throw him into the dungeons.

"There is no force anywhere in the mirrored world, Cassian," King Randall said, "that will ever keep a father from his child."

"Your Majesty," I began, but he shook his head.

"Even if you locked me up, I would find my way out again. You forget, I have done more to uncover the secrets of this castle than any monarch before me. It would only be a matter of time before my escape. Let me go with love, beloved Cassian, and not with anger. I *know* where Violet is. I *saw* her."

My heart sank. It was a trick. I *knew* it was a trick. But the crown on my head made me dizzy. The guards stood slightly apart, holding the open irons limply in their dangling hands, their eyes averted from the scene. I stood up, tried to appear if not *kingly* then *formidable*, perhaps, and cleared my throat.

"My King," I said, bowing to King Randall, "it is my opinion that you have been tricked. There is a reason, Your Majesty, for this...concurrence. The capture of your hunting party. The war. The vanishing of Violet. The glut of impostors. It can't be coincidental. It is my belief that we—"

The King held up his hand. "Enough, Cassian." He did not look at me. He looked at the mirror. The *mirror*! How I wish I had turned right then and there and smashed it to pieces with my fists! "You may arrest me if you like. You may bind me or bless me. My horse is fitted, and our provisions packed. I—" He paused. "I...*will not*—" The King closed his eyes and swallowed hard, pressing his hand to his heart before he could continue. "I will not return to this castle without my Violet. Nay, I *cannot*."

And with that, my King drew a tattered cloak and hood over his head and shoulders and mounted his horse. He raised his hands to the guards at the gate, who looked at me quizzically.

"Yes," I said to the guards, my voice like thistles in my throat. "Let him go." As the King rode out into the night, my heart shattered into pieces. I stood at the doorway, watching him disappear into the smoky chaos that our city—now camp of war—had become. Tents leaned upon other tents. Forges belched smoke while makeshift hospitals shook with the moans of the injured and the cries of those mourning their dead.

"Come back!" I called out, though I knew he did not hear me, and if he did, he would not have heeded. The King was gone, and I was alone.

After meeting with the council of war one last time, I approved a foolish, bullheaded plan to ambush the camp of the Mountain King. A plan so reliant on unknowns and false hopes, even a child could have seen the folly in it. But I had no strength to oppose, my standing among them being tenuous at best, before retiring to my quarters. The crown weighed heavily on my head, and my shoulders bent under the burdens of the world. Each time I passed a mirror,

I saw that face (those glittering eyes and that reptilian grin!) and heard its voice insinuating itself into my unwilling ears.

IT'S WHAT YOU'VE ALWAYS WANTED.

IT'S WHAT YOU DESERVE.

HOW NOBLE IN YOUR CROWN! HOW REGAL! HOW RARE!

LOOK AT YOURSELF!

But I would not look. I didn't trust myself to look. It was the Nybbas, I was sure. And the Nybbas was right. I did not want power. Gods, forgive me!

Thankfully, as I approached my quarters (my own quarters, thank you very much—I was not about to presume to stay in the King's room, though I now had the key) every mirror I passed was turned toward the wall. So relieved was I, it did not occur to me to wonder at it.

I opened my door. The room was dark and cold. No candles burned. No fire flickered in the hearth.

"Close the door, Cassian," Violet's voice came through the darkness. "We have much to discuss."

CHAPTER FORTY-SEVEN

Once again, Demetrius whacked his head against the curved ceiling of the tunnel, this time so hard he saw stars.

"That's a practice I can't recommend, dear," Auntie said without turning back. "I'd rather your brains remain unaddled for the time being. Once we make contact with the Old Gods, you can do what you want, of course."

"It's not my *fault*," Demetrius complained. "The tunnels keep getting smaller."

"That never used to be a problem. We've watched you

and your little Violet shimmy every which way through these tunnels. It's never bothered you before."

"It's not like I *tried* to grow. And besides"—he could feel his cheeks burning with shame as he said it—"she's not *my* Violet. Violet has always been her *own*." Demetrius pressed his lips together, listened to the hiss of his breath through his nostrils; his companions, he noticed, walked without a sound. "In any case," he continued, "I don't even think she's my *friend* anymore." His eyes heated and burned, and his throat swelled. He tried to swallow but couldn't.

Auntie clicked her tongue thoughtfully. "Hard luck, that. If it were true."

Up ahead, a slight skittering announced the return of Nod. If Demetrius had not been listening for it, he would never have heard it at all. Auntie shook her head in disgust. "The boy walks like a *human being*," she said derisively. "You'd think he tied stones to his shoes. Or cymbals."

Nod tore around the corner and sped—quite out of control—right toward Auntie and Demetrius (Moth silently thanked his lucky stars that he had the forethought to keep up the rear) and smashed headlong into Demetrius's shoulder, bouncing back and landing on the floor with a thud.

"Ouch," Demetrius said, surprised that such a small creature could hit that hard.

"Boy's never been much for subtlety," Moth muttered. "All speed, no control. His grandpap was the same way, may the Old Ones keep him."

Nod pulled himself off the floor, shook his head, and sat on his knees. "The King has left the castle, Auntie, just as you said."

"He *what?*" Demetrius almost shouted.

"*Hush*, child," Auntie said, smacking him hard against his nose. "You're sure, Nod? Completely? And the crown? Was the King wearing his crown when he left?"

"No, he ab…abi—" Nod stared at the ceiling as though he might find the word written on the stone.

"Abdicated?" Demetrius prompted.

"I think so. That old windbag storyteller has the crown now. It itches him terrible. The King wore a hood. Tattered thing, but warm by the look of it, so he won't freeze to death. And I added some food to his saddlebags so he won't starve, neither."

"Good boy. If we can get the crown away from that old fool, all's the better, but there are several things that we'll need from the King's study. Nod, dear, you didn't see the box anywhere in the King's saddlebags did you?"

"No, Auntie. And I checked everything."

"He wasn't carrying anything on his body? A satchel or a sack, maybe? Anything that might hold his papers?"

Nod rocked back on his heels. "Nawp, Auntie. Just himself."

"Good," she said, turning away from Demetrius and hurrying into the dark. "If the Nybbas knew about the research or the notes, it would have convinced the King to bring them. This, my dears, is borrowed time. Keep up, Demetrius; we're nearly there."

Demetrius struggled to keep moving, feeling the walls of the tunnel become more and more narrow with each passing moment. "Nearly where?" he asked, noticing that his voice, so muffled in the close space, had become suddenly echoed and expansive. He wiggled through the tightening corridor toward the thin light of Auntie's lantern.

"Here," Auntie's voice echoed back to him. She stood at the side of a precipice, her toes curling over the edge. Beyond, Demetrius could see only darkness. A cold wind swept upward from the pit, smelling of moss and damp stone. He shivered.

"What is this?" Demetrius asked. Somewhere in the tunnel behind him, Moth patted him on the leg.

"You'll probably want to close your eyes, boy."

Auntie pressed her fingers to her mouth. "This is the entrance to the core of the castle. This is where we leap. It's the only way to get down there. We're pretty sure that there'll be something at the bottom there to break our fall."

"WHAT?" Demetrius roared. "*Pretty sure?* You mean you've never even been—"

"Nod," Moth called. "Grab the boy's belt. Now, on three."

"If you've never even been there, how do we know we're not just falling to our deaths?"

"ONE!" Moth shouted. His voice echoed, cold and lonely, in the dark pit. It certainly *sounded* as though they were headed for their deaths.

"It's not how it works," Auntie said desperately, grabbing the shoulder of Demetrius's shirt and bracing her body to heave. "The Old Gods wanted our kind and your kind to work together in the face of—"

"TWO!" Moth shouted.

"Catastrophe," Auntie finished.

"But how do you know that's even true? That sounds

like a story. A myth!" Demetrius braced his foot and hand against the sides of the wall, but the three small creatures were much stronger than they appeared, and his grip was slowly slipping.

"My dear boy. We have faith."

"But I *don't*!" Demetrius said.

"Except that you *do*," Auntie said kindly. "Because you're here, and we're here, and that should be impossible. And if we don't do something, then there is no hope. And how can we go on without hope?"

"THREE!" Moth shouted, and with the three small creatures clinging to his clothing, Demetrius launched into the darkness and fell into the pit.

CHAPTER FORTY-EIGHT

I stood in the darkness of my quarters, breathing heavily. It was cold in there—the fire had been out for some time, it seemed—and though I shivered and shook, I knew it was not from the cold. "The candles are out," I said at last. "Let me call someone to get them lit."

"We have no need for light." Violet's voice cut the dark. "I am not interested, beloved Cassian, in the *looks* of things. I am far more interested in the way things *are*." She paused. I could hear her breathing.

"My heart leaps, Princess," I said, my voice catching in

my chest, "at the sound of your voice. Please. Let me see your dear face."

"You are wearing my father's crown," Violet said, ignoring my request. "How dreadfully sneaky of you."

"Sneaky?" I cried. *"Sneaky?"* My voice rose to a sickening whine that shamed me. Still, I carried on. "Princess—"

"Don't call me *Princess*," she said. "It's a term of little use to me anymore. My name is *Violet*. Call me that."

And oh! My dears! The ice in her voice. The glint of forged iron and sharp blades in each word. I pressed my hands to my heart and continued. "Of course. Violet. Your father has left the castle in a time of war to find *you*. He has turned his back on his people all because you decided to play a game of hide-and-seek. Where have you *been*, child?"

A cowardly question. For I knew where she'd been. I saw her in the mirror. I heard her voice. But I couldn't bear the weight of knowing. And so I ignored. I...obfuscated. I told myself I had imagined her face, that it was a trick of the light and the result of an overactive imagination. I lowered my head, letting the weight of my shame pull me down.

Violet sighed. "I have been of late in the dungeon, as neither my father nor *you*, Cassian, were able to recognize me. You sent me away."

"Violet, I—"

"You recognized my voice, Cassian. I could *tell*." She took a deep breath, and I could hear the repressed sobs rattling in the cold, cold room. "Soldiers—*my soldiers*—ripped me away. And you! You *knew*! You knew it was me."

"No!" I cried in shock. *"No."* But my voice was weak. Violet pressed.

"Did you know about the Nybbas?"

I fell silent.

"Did you know, Cassian?" Violet shouted.

"The Nybbas isn't real." I forced a whisper. "It's just a tale that old men tell old men in the hours before their deaths."

"You're lying," she said.

I slumped, removed the crown from my head, and set it on the table. "You're right." I walked toward Violet's voice and sat down on a stool, pressing my forehead to my knees. "The Nybbas is as real as you or I. But it's been trapped for two thousand years, since the Old Gods last saw fit to come to this world and set things right. Would that they would come today!"

"Not entirely right. They kept the Nybbas alive, didn't they?"

"I didn't want to believe it, Violet, I truly didn't. There are many who believed that the return of the Nybbas would signal the end of the world. Or the end of every world. Or the enslavement of every universe to the whims of a creature bloated by desire and selfishness and indolence. I just wanted to—"

"I do not care what you wanted," Violet snapped. "I just want to know how to kill it. This... *thing*. It invaded my mind. It changed my *body* and my *face*. It's invading my country. It's spreading madness in my people like a cancer. And I *want it dead*, Cassian. Can you help me or not?"

I shook my head. "The Nybbas is one of the Old Gods. A lesser god, to be sure. Weak. Unschooled. Never bothered much with learning how to better itself. Still, killing a god is tricky business. If the gods themselves couldn't do it..."

"You don't know how."

"No," I said sadly. In truth, dears, I had a few ideas. But I was *afraid* to fight. I was afraid to *die*. And part of me— the sniveling, cowardly part of me—felt certain that should a thing like the Nybbas take control, it would have use for a teller such as myself. It always did. I would survive—and possibly thrive in—such a transition. My dears, it pains me to admit these thoughts—indeed, I am sick unto my very soul to even consider that I once *had* them. But I did.

"Then you are useless. I intend to find out, and I intend to kill it, no matter what it takes. But first, as long as there are mirrors, every person is at risk, and every person becomes a threat. Every time it connects with someone, it grows stronger. Look at this castle. Look at the cracks! It's getting stronger this minute. You're the regent. Order the guards to smash the mirrors. We need to buy some time."

"But I can't!" I cried. "They'll think me mad! My control over things since your father left is tenuous at best, Violet. If they reject me, the nation will be leaderless."

"That will happen regardless, beloved Cassian," Violet said.

Though she was still shadowed, I could see the glint of a knife being unsheathed on the other side of the room. Violet held it shakily, away from her body. Still, her voice was resolute. And in my experience, it is the people pushed to the edge of reason who are more likely to—well, as I said before, I was afraid to die.

"Cassian," she said, "you know I love you, and I do not want to hurt you. But if you don't help me—if you refuse to assist me as I defend my people—I shall be forced to take action." She swallowed. "It will break my heart and shatter my soul to kill you, my beloved. But my love for my people is greater than my broken heart. And I will do what is necessary."

She spoke like a queen. She *was* a queen.

"Yes, lady," I whispered.

I stood, tore open the doors, and hailed the guards.

"The mirrors have been cursed," I cried out. "Don't look at them! Remove every mirror from the walls, lay them facedown on the floor, and smash them to bits. As regent appointed this day by King Randall the Bold, this is my first decree. So ordered." I ducked right back into my quarters to spare myself the incredulous stares that followed.

CHAPTER FORTY-NINE

Time slowed, then stopped. Demetrius felt his body in the darkness—he *knew* he still existed. He flexed his fingers, wiggled his toes, shut his eyes tight before opening them wide.

What is this place? he tried to say, but the winds from the pit swirled from below to above and back below, ripping away all sound before it could leave his mouth. *I am dying,* Demetrius thought. *Or I am dead.* He tried to focus his mind on the life he had—on his father, the memory of his mother, his friendship with Violet—and they all felt strangely far away. Like the memory of a dream.

He felt a pair of small, strong hands and nimble legs crawl up his back and hang tightly on to his collar and ear.

"Don't worry," he heard Auntie say—or not so much *heard* but *felt* her say. "We should reach the bottom soon." Demetrius noticed that she didn't sound all that hopeful.

Will we die when we land? He had no idea how long they had been falling, but it *felt* long.

"You won't. You're the one the Old Gods are supposed to talk to. *We* might. We're supposed to bring you to the heart of the castle, but the stories don't say anything about us surviving."

Well, why didn't you say that before? Demetrius thought, aghast. *You could have stayed up top!*

"Would you have jumped without us, son?" Auntie said—or thought, or transmitted, or however else she managed to press her words into Demetrius's brain. From the way her tiny body clung to his neck, Demetrius could feel her fear and sadness and panic that this moment might well be her last.

Well, gods or not, I won't let anything bad happen to you. Frankly, his sudden need to protect these small creatures (who had, after all, frightened him, then hit him with a shovel and kidnapped him into a network of underground tunnels, then heaved him into a pit) surprised Demetrius. Still, he knew it was true. He wouldn't let anything happen to them.

They didn't land with a thud, or even a splat. Instead, the pit just suddenly *wasn't*—like those odd transitions in a dream when one is sailing on a ship and then is suddenly sitting in a library, with no movement between space or time to shift from one place to another.

Auntie, Moth, and Nod rolled away from Demetrius and leaped to their feet, staring around the dim space with wonder. It was a hallway with a high, curved stone ceiling and smooth stone floors. Lining the walls were what looked like an infinite succession of doors, each made from polished wood and with a curved top and an iron handle.

"What is this place?" Demetrius asked, rising to his feet.

Moth shrugged. "It's supposed to be the heart of the castle, but it doesn't look much like the rest of the castle. The stone's all wrong." It was true, too. Most of the castle was built from dark stones with rounded edges, each slightly pockmarked with age. These stones were several shades lighter, with a smooth, shiny surface and sharp, tight edges fitted neatly together.

"Perhaps the 'heart of the castle' isn't in the castle at all," Nod said thoughtfully. "Like the heart of the matter or the heart of the problem. Maybe the heart of the castle is where everything starts." Nod's voice was off-kilter and dreamy. "Or where it stops," he added.

"Don't be an idiot, Nod," Auntie said, though, Demetrius noted, with a little less force than usual.

"But what are we supposed to do?" Demetrius asked. "And how do we get back?" There was, after all, no sign of the pit, no sign of an upward shaft, no way of knowing that they had come from anywhere except for the place where they *were*.

"I suppose we walk," Auntie said, moving forward. "Our people have been charged with bringing one of *you* to this place to see the Old Gods should the Nybbas ever attempt to escape its prison. We never knew what might happen *next*, you see. The stories never touched the issue of *next*."

Great, Demetrius thought. *We've traded our lives for a lousy story.*

He had no sooner thought this than the stones under his feet began to shiver and shake, and the high, curved ceilings began to rumble and moan.

"YOU'LL TRADE MORE THAN JUST YOUR LIFE, BOY," a voice boomed from the far end of the shadowed corridor.

Auntie swung around, her face blazing. "*What did you do?*" she hissed. "*Don't embarrass me, Demetrius, or so help me, I'll—*"

"THAT'S ENOUGH, AUNTIE," the voice boomed again, and the old woman went pale and silent. "BRING THE BOY TO ME. I'D LIKE TO TAKE A LOOK AT THE CHILD UPON WHOM THE FATE OF THE MULTIVERSE NOW RESTS. ONE OF TWO, I UNDERSTAND."

"No, sir," Auntie said, looking up at—well, *nothing*, as far as Demetrius could see. "We attempted to reach the Princess Violet, but—" She faltered. "We failed." Her voice choked, and her eyes filled with tears.

Nod rushed to Auntie and wrapped his arm around her. He whipped his head around as though trying to decide— not so much *who* he was talking to, but *where*. "It was me, your...your Old Godishness," Nod said bravely. "Auntie did her best. I'm the one who failed."

"*Hush, Nod!*"

"I won't, neither," Nod said stoutly, but Demetrius had stopped paying attention to the familial spat on the ground. Something distracted him.

That voice—that big, booming, ever-so-important-sounding voice—was laughing. And the laughter intrigued Demetrius. It was the type of laughter that he had heard a thousand times growing up—laughter that erupted without restraint from his mouth or Violet's mouth when they were very young, laughter he had heard since from the very young children in the walled city outside the castle. It was a joyful, almost giddy laugh, and completely unself-conscious.

"DON'T WORRY ABOUT VIOLET," the voice said with a sigh. "SHE'S TAKING STEPS THAT EVEN A GOD CANNOT TAKE. VIOLET WILL END ALL, AND BY ENDING ALL WILL SAVE ALL."

There was a long silence, and the confusion raging in Demetrius's heart was matched on the faces of his three small companions.

"IF SHE SUCCEEDS, THAT IS," the voice added in a broad, worried rumble.

CHAPTER FIFTY

At that very moment, the Mountain King was having a perfectly miserable evening. It was cold and windy, with a merciless drizzle pelting the camp. The war was not going well. Despite their preparations, it had been many generations since anyone had experienced the discomforts and horror of battle, and the soldiers of the Mountain King groaned in their tents and shivered in their damp bedrolls.

Not that the Mountain King noticed. Not that he

noticed much of anything. Not since he discovered his one true love.

He had a mirror—finely wrought and beautifully detailed, and his true love lived *inside*. Trapped, poor thing. But not for long. In the meantime, his tailor had sewn a special pocket at the front of all of his waistcoats so that he could *feel* the mirror next to him at all times. And though the news of the war was not particularly good (*"Dwindling supplies," his advisers warned, "and disgruntled soldiers"*), the news from the *mirror* was particularly fine. And *oh*, that voice! And *oh*, that mouth! Those eyes! Peeking out of the mirror was the most beautiful face he had ever seen. A face that rippled and flowed, that changed with emotion and diction and light. The Mountain King was entranced.

THE EMPIRE YOU *DESERVE*, the mirror told him.

THE BESPECTACLED DIMWIT FROM THE ANDULAN REALMS WILL NOT EVEN BE FIT TO POLISH YOUR BOOTS, the mirror promised.

WITH ME AT YOUR SIDE, WE SHALL BE UNSTOPPABLE.

The Mountain King needed no food nor drink nor sleep. He needed only his mirror. He stared at it and spoke to it and whispered his love as though it were a lullaby.

No one knew what to do.

The King is mad, the whispers began. And once they began, they began to grow; and once they grew, they began to spread. *The King is mad, mad, mad, and we are lost.*

The Nybbas heard, and the Nybbas smiled.

On the same night during which Violet reappeared in my study, when she was, at that very moment, tersely confronting me, the Nybbas whispered to the Mountain King.

IS EVERYONE ASLEEP?

"Everyone, my love," the King crooned. "There are only you and I, and I and you, and the world is now and ever ours." His words lilted and sang. He stroked the lovely face in the mirror. The Nybbas wrinkled its nose in disgust.

IF EVERYONE IS ASLEEP, MY DARLING, THEN YOU MUST PUT ON A SERVANT'S TRAVELING CLOAK AND SLIP OUT OF SIGHT. THERE IS SOMETHING YOU MUST DO, PRECIOUS LOVE, AND IT WILL NOT BE PLEASANT. BUT IT IS NECESSARY.

"Anything for my heart's treasure!" the Mountain King said, and he busied himself in finding a cloak.

Once disguised, the Mountain King slipped past the patrols and perimeter-keepers and hooked into a copse next to the curve in a small creek. The creek itself was so small that it didn't have a name—none, at least, that I ever knew, and none that ever appeared on a map. But children often called it the Creek of Flashing Rocks because of the particular abundance of a queer little stone that was scattered heavily over the creek bed.

The King sat down on a rock, sighed deeply, and pulled out the mirror. He held his breath in anticipation of seeing the ever-changing face of the Nybbas. He felt his love lodge in his throat like a hook. He could not swallow. He could not rip it away.

FOOL! the Nybbas cried. IDIOT! SABOTEUR! A mouth full of knives. Golden skin stretched tight across an elongated snout.

"My love!" the Mountain King cried, aghast. "How can you say these things?"

LOST! ALL LOST! MILLENNIA OF CAREFULLY WROUGHT PLANS HAVE ALL COME TO NOTHING! A reptilian tongue flicking out to catch tears from those hard, cold eyes. Thin lips widening into a crocodile grin.

"My darling! My precious! Tell me what to do! I cannot bear to see you suffer so!" He held the mirror to his chest, panic expanding through his body, crowding out his breath.

The image in the mirror rippled and flowed like water.

It transformed to light, then stone, then billions upon billions of stars glinting in the dark. One of those stars twinkled more prettily than the others, and the twinkling became larger, rounder, more defined, until it grew to lips, ears, eyebrows, a delicate chin, pearly teeth, and two hard, jeweled eyes. The Nybbas blinked and smiled.

THERE ARE ONLY TWO THINGS, MY ANGEL, THAT STAND BETWEEN US AND OUR VICTORY. ONE IS THAT NASTY DRAGON THAT THE ANDULANS NEGLECTED TO KILL. WHAT SORT OF COWARD HAS A DRAGON IN ITS GRASP AND REFUSES TO KILL IT?

"I shall do it for you, my darling! I shall slay the dragon as a sign of my love for you!" the Mountain King cried, though he had no idea how.

The Nybbas waved him off. NONSENSE, it said. YOUR BEST GENERAL HAS EVEN NOW WOKEN FROM A TERRIBLE DREAM AND WILL SEND HIS GUARDS TO DO THE DEED PRESENTLY.

The King found that his mouth had gone quite dry. "I—" he began. "I thought—" Someone else was to provide favors for his love? The very idea! The Mountain King felt his cheeks redden and his heart thump angrily against his ribs.

The Nybbas ignored him. THE OTHER PROBLEM IS THE
CASTLE ITSELF. THAT WRETCHED EXCUSE FOR A PRINCESS—
CURSE HER NAME!—PROMISED TO GIVE ME MY HEART. SHE
PROMISED! BUT SHE HAS TURNED TRAITOR. DESTROY ALL
THE MIRRORS, INDEED! NASTY, SNEAKY THING. SHE WILL
PAY, MY LOVE, MARK ME.

"An abominable child," the Mountain King agreed.
"Spoiled. And selfish. Everyone says so."

YES, YES, the Nybbas said impatiently. As it spoke, its
beauty began to thin and fade, as though in its excitement
it could hardly hold the form that so entranced the poor
King. The red lips stretched and paled, the brows pinched,
the soft cheeks pulled back as tiny scales crept forward.

AND HER TASK WAS SO SIMPLE. JUST A PHRASE. AN
INCANTATION. A FEW WORDS COULD BURN AND RATTLE
THE FOUNDATIONS OF THAT ACCURSED CASTLE, SETTING
MY HEART FREE. AND I WOULD HAVE BEEN FREE, OH MY
KING, OH MY LOVE. AND I WOULD HAVE BEEN YOURS. AH,
WELL, PERHAPS IT SIMPLY WASN'T MEANT TO BE.

And with that the image of the Nybbas began to fade.

"Wait!" the Mountain King cried. "What words! Let
me say them!"

MY LOVE, the Nybbas said, coming quickly back into

view. YOU ARE A DEAR TO OFFER, BUT I CANNOT ALLOW IT. YOU'VE DONE SO MUCH ALREADY. AND IT WILL HURT. VIOLET (MAY HISTORY SPIT UPON HER NAME) IS YOUNGER, AND THIS KIND OF MAGIC IS KINDER ON CHILDREN. I CANNOT BEAR TO SEE YOU IN PAIN, MY BELOVED. I WILL NOT ALLOW IT.

The image of the Nybbas leaned forward, its hard eyes wide with anticipation, an unbreathed breath pressing at its lips.

The Mountain King pressed the mirror to his chest. "I would endure all possible pain in all possible worlds, my darling," he said ardently, and watched in wonder as writing curled, as though by magic, across the face of the Nybbas. "Tell me. Tell me the words. I command it."

AS YOU WISH, MY LOVE, MY LOVE, MY LOVE.

It was as though an invisible quill etched each letter in scripted delicacy across the forehead, along the bridge of the nose, following the curve of each cheek. The same four words cut over and over again in the reflected skin of the Nybbas.

I will not—will *not*, my dears—tell you those words. I will never write them down. Suffice it to say, they are words that invite transformation, words that pledge loyalty, words that offer the soul—nay, the very self—to the use and misuse of a terrible god. They are words, I understand, that are the same in each universe, each distinct world, though they have only ever been used twice in history.

He said the words.

That poor, poor man.

The Mountain King's final moments were witnessed by a boy—no older than ten—who had been rounded up along with his older brothers and sisters to fight for the glory of their northern home. They had no choice in the matter. They weren't even asked. In any case, this boy, knowing that on the morrow he would be required to handle a bow or a sword and to kill or be killed in a senseless war, was unable to sleep. Well, really, who could blame him? He had seen that the campfire, around which his loved ones were currently huddled, had gone out, so he slipped into the forest to gather sticks and bits of peat. It was there, next to a stream glinting with shining rocks, that he saw a man talking to a mirror. He didn't know the man was his King—how could he? It was dark, and the man wore a simple cloak and no crown. The man crouched, cradling the mirror in his hands, declaring his love. He wept and sobbed and asked the mirror what he should do. The entire scene was so utterly mad that the boy decided to creep closer for a better look, thinking it would make a funny story to lift the spirits of his older brothers and sisters, as he couldn't bear to see them so downhearted.

He saw the man kissing the mirror, clearing his throat, and then, quite suddenly, he began speaking in a strange tongue—four foreign words, spoken in a strong, punctuated rhythm and repeated again and again and again. The boy held his breath. He had only ever seen magic—true magic, that is—once before in his life, but it was an experience that he never forgot. There was an energy around it, you see. You know, of course, how static electricity can make your hair stand on end, give you tiny shocks on your skin—now, imagine that, but on the *inside*. You wouldn't forget such a sensation in a hurry, and neither, my dears, did he.

The boy watched, transfixed. He listened as the weak-chinned man with the tearstained face recited those four strange words again and again. He watched as the words seemed to transform—they were no longer only *just* sound, but they were light as well. And substance. They looked to the boy like bright ribbons uncurling from the man's mouth and winding around his body like a snake, pulling tighter and tighter and tighter. And then, quite without warning, the ribbons sliced the man's skin and plunged inside. He didn't stop speaking those words, nor did he seem to notice. The ribbons entered at his chest, at his belly, and at his throat. They wiggled and shuddered, widening the entrance wounds into bloodless gaps in the man's body. The boy clapped his hand over his mouth in horror, terrified to let out a sound.

Finally, the man stopped speaking. His mouth lolled open, and his eyes rolled back, insensible. Still, the words continued—not from his voice but from voices inside him. Thousands of voices. Out of the man's wounds marched legion upon legion of tiny lizards—each with golden scales brighter than any fire, and jeweled eyes flashing mercilessly. When they fell to the ground, the earth around them smoked and singed. They poured from each wound, from the man's mouth and ears and the sockets where his eyes had been. His skin trembled and bubbled and rumpled as though it was nothing more than a sack. The boy covered his face and dropped to his knees.

The lizards swarmed and jumbled. They dammed up the creek; they crowded the trees; the land burned around them. The sack of skin that once was the Mountain King fell to the ground in a heap. The lizards stopped reciting the four words. They lifted their faces toward the sky and spoke with one voice.

"WE ARE THE SERVANTS OF THE IMPRISONED GOD," they said. "DESTROY THE CASTLE. RELEASE THE HEART OF THE NYBBAS."

Slowly, they moved as one along the path of the creek, reducing it to steam as they passed. And from the mirror left lying on the ground—the sound of laughing.

The boy ran to the camp, screaming that the world was ending. No one believed him.

CHAPTER FIFTY-ONE

"Tell me what you know, Cassian," Violet said from her place in the darkness.

"Let me see you, my child."

"You already have." Her voice was sharp. Accusatory. "You refused to know me *then*. Why would you choose to know me *now*?"

"We live," I said heavily, "in a world of our own choosing, child. We will insist the world is as we say it should be, until the world convinces us otherwise. Before today, I believed that the good King would remain on his throne.

I believed that what was right and what was good would be victorious and that the world we love would remain whole and prosperous and pure."

"And now?" the child's voice bristled with annoyance. I winced.

"Now there is nothing that is good." My voice was a cold, dead thing, and my heart was a stone. "The world we lived in is ending, or over. And there is nothing I can do. All that's left, Violet, is a story. One great story, which I shall gift to the world. Please sit where I can see you. I thought of this story the day you disappeared, and it has been tickling my mind ever since. And since I shall not, it seems, have the chance to tell it to the whole of the kingdom, then I shall tell it to you, Violet. My beloved. My best audience."

"Audience?" Violet said incredulously. "The country's at war. The—" She kicked a small end table, sending the vase atop it smashing to the floor. "The *entire world*'s gone mad, and all you can think of is telling a *story?*"

"It's all that I know *how* to do, Princess. Those who know how to fight are fighting. I will do the things that I *know*, as I know how to do them."

"Your stories, old man," the child nearly spat, "were

nearly my undoing. Tell me what you know about the Nybbas."

"I know nothing," I whispered. How, I wondered, could I tell the child that there was no hope? The only thing that had stopped the Nybbas before was the intervention of the gods. But the gods had long ago melted into their respective universes and all but disappeared. What were we but a basement in the multiverse? A forgotten broom closet in a many-roomed mansion. No one cared what happened to us. Or so I thought.

"Liar," Violet said.

"I know that it cannot be stopped. The Nybbas was kept powerless by lack of knowledge. If no one thought about it, dreamed about it, said its name, it dwindled. Even now. Even as we sit here, *thinking* about that cursed thing, it grows stronger, and it doesn't matter how many mirrors we smash."

"So you know everything."

I shook my head. "Only the broad concept. But the details I never knew. Only the eldest tellers ever know— and they don't learn until they go at last to the farthest of the Island Nations to the west to greet their last days. The only kings and queens who ever learn of it are the ones who sit on the Andulan thrones. But the King has gone off, and I fear that he shall never return."

"My father knows?" Violet gasped. She stepped forward. "My *father.*" I could not see her face, but even the shape of her shadow was a drastic alteration. *What did it do to you, my darling?* I wondered desperately. She took another step. "My father knows, and my mother likely knew, too. Well, of course they—oh dear!" The figure that apparently was Violet wobbled and tumbled backward. I leaped from my seat.

"Violet!" I cried, but when I knelt before her, I gasped. She was...*beautiful.* But not *herself.* And the wrongness of her face, the wrongness that *her* voice could come from *that* body, unnerved me to the core. "Oh, my child," I whispered, taking her hands. "What have I done?"

"What?" Violet-with-the-non-Violet-face asked, struggling to right herself. "Oh. Of course. I am changed. By the way, Cassian, I could kill you for this hair. Fancy imagining hair this heavy on the head of any poor girl! It's like balancing a crate of potatoes on my head."

"I—" My voice failed me, dears, as I helped her to her wretchedly small feet. "I thought—I mean, I thought I *knew*—that it was only a story."

Violet snorted. "Shows what you know. All stories are lies until someone believes in them. But I, for one, am sick to death of stories. Now, I want information. You're sure my father knew? About the Nybbas?"

"Of course he knew," I said. "It was his job to know."

"That means, Cassian dear"—and the girl drew herself to her full height and gave me a hard, steady stare—"that I am the new recipient of that knowledge. If my father knew, then he thought about it. If he thought about it, then he wrote it down. If he was even a portion as curious about this as he was about the dragons, he will have more notes than I can fit into a sack. Which means the place that I need to be is with his notes, and I insist that you escort me there at once. You see, Cassian, the King was in error to make you regent. I am the daughter of King Randall the Bold and Queen Rose the Benevolent. My country is *my* responsibility, and I, for one, will not rest for a moment until that—*thing*—has been stopped. My father's study, Cassian. Do you have the key?"

CHAPTER FIFTY-TWO

"So, let me get this straight," Demetrius said, rocking back on his heels and resting his head on his fingertips as he stared up at the ceiling. "One of your—*people*—gods or whatever, tried to take over every universe ever thought of. Then it enslaved an entire world and made plans to enslave *all* creatures of *all* worlds—including *you*, I might add, and you just *left it here*?"

"IT WAS THE ONLY OPTION," the voice boomed.

"Hogwash," Demetrius snorted. He wanted to hit something.

"Demetrius!" Auntie hissed. *"Show some respect!"*

"Why?" Demetrius asked. "You saw what's happening out there. People are *dying*. They're being *slaughtered*. Old women and men and little children and mothers and fathers, and for *what?*" He raised his hands. If he had a rock, he would have thrown it. *"Tell me why!"* he shouted.

"CALM YOURSELF, BOY," the voice rumbled quietly. "AND YOU, AUNTIE," it said, its voice becoming suddenly tender and deferential. "DO NOT WORRY ABOUT THE CHILD OFFENDING ME. INDEED, IT IS HE WHO HAS EVERY RIGHT TO BE OFFENDED."

"Why?" Demetrius asked.

"WE USED YOUR WORLD AS A PRISON—ONE THAT WAS INTENDED TO FAIL. IN TRUTH, I AM SURPRISED IT LASTED—"

"Intended to fail?" Moth asked, stepping forward.

"YES, MOTH. YOU SEE—"

"Intended to *fail?*" Moth interrupted. "What kind of gods *are* you? Thousands of years we've kept watch for you. We've kept the stories alive, passed down from parents to children to grandchildren. We've whispered to those idiot tellers and watched them think themselves *so clever*. And take all the credit, I might add! We've seen our numbers dwindle to *nothing*. Look at us! We are the only *we* left! All for a system *intended* to fail? I thought you lot were supposed to be intelligent designers!"

The voice laughed quietly. "EVEN THE MOST INTELLIGENT DESIGNER RELIES UPON TRIAL AND ERROR TO DISCOVER THE BEST SOLUTION. INTELLIGENCE DOES NOT MEAN INFALLIBILITY, NOR DOES IT MEAN IMMOBILITY. INTELLIGENCE MEANS THE ABILITY TO LEARN."

"Excuses!" Moth shouted.

"PERHAPS, OLD FRIEND," the voice said kindly. "BUT WE DID OUR BEST. AND THERE WERE CONSEQUENCES. STILL, VIOLET, EVEN NOW, IS LEARNING THE SECRET OF HER FATHER'S RESCUED DRAGON. EVEN NOW, SHE IS LEARNING WHAT SHE MUST DO."

"And what must she do?"

"KILL THE NYBBAS. SHE MUST DO WHAT WE COULD NOT. A GOD CANNOT KILL ANOTHER GOD. BUT WE CAN MAKE IT VULNERABLE. AND IT IS VULNERABLE AS LONG AS IT DOES NOT HAVE ITS HEART. WHAT SHE NEEDS IS BORROWED TIME."

"Will she die?" Demetrius whispered, suddenly realizing the depths of this fear—that losing Violet forever seemed almost worse to him than losing his father.

"I CANNOT SAY, CHILD."

"Cannot or *will* not?"

"A GOD CANNOT PREDICT THE FUTURE ANY MORE THAN YOU CAN. WE CREATE; WE SUSTAIN; WE LOVE. WE LEAVE THE SOOTHSAYING TO THE CIRCUS PERFORMERS."

"What am I supposed to do?"

"PROTECT THE HEART."

"No," Auntie said, though she was suddenly so aghast at herself that she clapped her hand over her mouth.

"NO?"

She closed her eyes and cleared her throat. "Sir," she said, "wouldn't it be better to destroy the heart? Like with a dragon's heart. With fire?"

The stone floor rumbled beneath their feet.

"IT'S TOO RISKY. THERE'S NO TELLING WHICH WOULD SUCCUMB FIRST. AND IF IT WAS THE CASTLE, ALL WOULD BE LOST."

"No telling?" Demetrius asked. "You mean you don't *know?*"

"WE USE OUR BEST GUESS. JUST LIKE YOU."

"But you're a god!"

"AND I KNOW MORE THAN YOU. BUT NOT EVERYTHING. THERE ARE STILL...SURPRISES."

"Still," Auntie persisted, "as a measure of last resort? If the heart could be destroyed, then—"

"NO," the voice said. "IT IS TOO RISKY. THE FIRE OF A DRAGON WHOSE HEART IS RESTORED CAN BREAK THE PRISON OF THE NYBBAS. RIGHT NOW THE PRISON IS THE ONLY THING KEEPING THE NYBBAS ALIVE. IF IT BREAKS FREE WITHOUT ITS HEART, IT WILL DIE—JUST AS ANY GOD SEPARATED FROM ITS HEART MUST EVENTUALLY DIE. THE NYBBAS DOES NOT UNDERSTAND THIS, TO ITS PERIL."

Demetrius shook his head. "I'm sorry, but I don't understand."

"LONG AGO, BOY, WE REMOVED THE HEART OF THE NYBBAS AS A MEANS OF ITS ENTRAPMENT—JUST AS IT HAD DONE TO THE RACE OF DRAGONS THAT ONCE WERE PLENTIFUL IN THIS WORLD. WE ENCASED THE HEART IN STONE AND USED IT TO BUILD THIS CASTLE. IF THE CASTLE IS DESTROYED, IF STONE IS RIPPED FROM STONE, THE HEART WILL BE RELEASED, AND THE NYBBAS WILL BE FREE. EVEN NOW, THE SERVANTS OF THE NYBBAS PREPARE FOR THE FINAL ATTACK, AT FIRST LIGHT."

Demetrius thought for a moment. "So the war is—"

"A TRICK."

"I see. So is all lost, then?"

"WOULD I BE TALKING TO YOU, BOY, IF ALL WAS LOST? THIS CASTLE WAS NOT MADE BY HUMAN HANDS. IT IS MY OWN DESIGN—THOUGH MOTH MIGHT SNEER AT IT. SURROUNDING US IN THIS ROOM ARE NEARLY TWO THOUSAND DOORS—EACH ONE LEADING TO A PARTICULAR ROOM IN THE CASTLE."

Demetrius spun around. "Really? They all lead here?"

"NO. NOTHING LEADS HERE. *HERE* LEADS EVERYWHERE ELSE. ONCE YOU GO THROUGH THE DOOR, YOU CANNOT COME BACK TO THIS PLACE."

"I can't bring Violet to you?"

"NO."

"But what if she doesn't believe me?"

"THERE IS NO HOPE WITHOUT RISK. FIND THE DOOR TO THE KING'S STUDY. THAT'S WHERE YOU'LL FIND VIOLET. TELL HER TO BRING THE DRAGON TO ITS HEART. TELL HER THAT THE DRAGON CAN HELP HER DESTROY THE NYBBAS."

"But how?"

"SHE WILL KNOW. OR SHE WILL FIGURE IT OUT. THEN BRING THAT IDIOT STORYTELLER TO THE FRONT LINES. HE MUST EXPLAIN TO THE COUNCIL THAT THE WAR THEY FIGHT IS A WAR IN ERROR. HE MUST WARN THEM THAT A NEW ENEMY WILL ATTACK. EVERY MAN, WOMAN, AND

CHILD NEEDS TO FIGHT. THE SERVANTS OF THE NYBBAS HAVE BEEN RELEASED, ALAS. AND THEY ARE COMING."

Demetrius hardly listened after the bit about the doors. Instantly, he ran from door to door, opening wildly. He opened a door that led into the Great Hall, and another that led into a storeroom, and another that led to the library, and yet another that led into a lady's dressing room. (That was the only one to which a rather red-cheeked Demetrius gently closed the door. The lady in question did not notice. Indeed, no one did.) Auntie, Nod, and Moth remained frozen where they stood.

"Don't just stand there! Help me look!" Demetrius shouted as he opened doors to workrooms and dungeons and kitchens and corridors.

But Auntie looked upward. "Sir?" she said. "I must know. I've lived ever so much longer than I should, and have done what I can to do what is right. But I must know. Do we..."—she gulped—"*return* to you? At the end. The stories say—"

"AUNTIE," the voice said gently. "YOUR PEOPLE ARE SOME OF THE OLDEST CREATURES IN THE MULTIVERSE. INDEED, IT WAS YOUR ANCESTOR WHO WAS MY FIRST FRIEND. YOUR

PEOPLE HAVE ALWAYS ENDEAVORED TO DO RIGHT, AND I HAVE ALWAYS APPRECIATED IT."

Except for the pounding of Demetrius's feet as he searched the names above the doors, the cavernous room was silent. "So," Auntie said. "The answer is no? Is it yes?" Her voice wavered in her throat.

"MY BELOVED, THE TIME HAS COME TO FIGHT A TERRIBLE POWER FOR THE GOOD OF ALL. WOULD IT MATTER WHETHER YOU RETURNED TO ME OR NOT? WOULD IT CHANGE WHAT YOU DO NOW?"

"No, sir."

"THEN CONTINUE, DEAR—"

"I can hear her! This is the one," Demetrius shouted, throwing his weight against the ancient door. It didn't move.

"It's stuck!" he shouted.

"WAIT! DEMETRIUS! BEFORE YOU GO IN—"

"Why won't the door open?" He smashed his weight against the door again and again.

"YOU NEED TO UNDERSTAND SOMETHING ABOUT VIO—"

"*Open, curse you!*" Demetrius shouted as the door inched open a crack. "*Violet! Can you hear me?*"

"SHE DOESN'T LOO—"

But the door opened, and Demetrius ran through.

The voice rumbled a sigh.

"See what I mean?" Moth said. "Intelligence. You're the one who set this nonsense up."

"GO. PLEASE. THE THREE OF YOU. IT CAN'T HAPPEN WITHOUT YOU."

"Well," Auntie said, regaining her brusque demeanor. "At least you admit it." And with that, she bustled after Demetrius, Moth and Nod trailing behind her.

CHAPTER FIFTY-THREE

The King's study had books lying open all over the desk. Ancient texts, journals, diagrams of dragon anatomy and dragon physiology. Violet shook her head.

"All this time. I didn't even notice what he was doing. All I cared about was what the Nybbas told me to care about."

"It's a silly, vain thing and encourages silly, vain thoughts. It wasn't your fault, Violet." I swallowed painfully, noticing the growing shame in my own chest. "You weren't yourself."

"It's no excuse," she said, running her hand over her father's notebook. She turned the page.

"When that thing that we do not name," it said in her father's slanted handwriting, "stole the hearts of every dragon in the multiverse and brought them here as slaves, much of their history became lost to them. Just as our history, from before we were brought to the mirrored world, is lost to us. Only scraps remain. Still, if these scraps are correct, then perhaps it is true that the dragon's heart can be replaced. That the danger posed by the heat of adolescence weakens over time. And, indeed, their hearts—those weak, delicate, breakable things—may be their biggest strength after all."

Violet didn't look up. Instead, she rested her forehead on the heels of her hands to brace the weight of that ridiculous hair.

"He talked to you about this?" she said.

"He did," I said. "Your father spoke to many people. Experts, thinkers, and storytellers."

"And is it true? About the hearts?"

I paused, running my fingers through my beard. "In my profession, we do not necessarily trouble ourselves with *facts*. And *truth* is a thing typically unfettered by...that which is *provable*. Sometimes there is a division between *accurate* and *true*."

Violet let out a terrific grunt and slammed her fist onto her father's desk. I jumped. "Beloved Cassian, have you always been this tiresome? Get to the point."

My skin crawled. The beating of the stones was getting louder. And perhaps this was to happen all along, or perhaps my *noticing* caused it to happen, but in any case, a hunk of plaster detached itself from the ceiling and smashed at my feet. I yelped and scrambled away. Violet barely moved. She gazed at me with those long, lovely eyes. The eyes that were not *hers*. I shivered.

"If the stories are true, Princess," I continued, "then without a heart in its body, the dragon is a shadow of itself—lacking in courage, lacking in soul. It is only *partially* itself. But when the heart is replaced, the dragon becomes *whole*, you see."

"So the Nybbas—it took the hearts of dragons so it could control them, and...I don't know. Rule things. Rule everything. So the Old Gods made the Nybbas know what it felt like—took its heart away, and with it its freedom— just like the dragons. So the heart would set it free?"

"Free from the mirror," I mused, searching through the King's books looking for . . . *something*. Anything. Any book this important wouldn't be marked, that's for sure. But where would the King have kept it?

Violet turned the page. "On Mirrors," the page announced in her father's hand. Violet leaned in closer, the weight of her hair bearing down on her neck, making her wince. "There are old stories," her father had written, "about tribes of dragons. Dragon societies. But how could it be, when the single defining characteristic of the dragon is fear? They fear one another, almost to death, facing one another only for the production of young, and that was so rare as to precipitate their near extinction. The question then is *why*. Why make dragons fear one another and fear the edge of the mirrored world? Was it, perhaps, because the—I will not write its name—feared that the dragons would find a way to escape? Did it fear the lack of fear?"

Violet asked, "Can the mirrored edge of the world be broken, Cassian?"

"Great gods, child! Why would you suggest such a thing?"

"When I broke the mirror," she said slowly, "the Nybbas screamed. And it was terrible, as though the creature was in pain. But it's trapped in the mirrored edge of the world, right? If the mirror were broken, would it kill the Nybbas? Or would it just weaken it? If it were screaming and in pain, could I finish it off?"

"It would kill all of us, Violet!" I cried, terribly alarmed. The child was mad!

"Maybe," she said. "And maybe not. Sometimes when one world ends, another one begins. But maybe it's worth it. We can't let what happened to our world happen to anyone else, Cassian. We are the only ones with the power to *try*." Violet stared at her father's writing and looked slowly around the room. Every book that her father had studied and loved had been placed carefully on the shelves, each one dusted and adored by the King's gentle hands. Violet's eyes welled up, and tears streamed down her beautiful-but-wrong face. "There are infinite worlds. You taught me that. And they are *innocent*. We can't let them come to harm, Cassian. We can't let that thing *win*."

"And I won't let you kill us all!"

"My mother would have wanted us to try. She would have stood up to it. You *know* she would have. Besides, we might not die. The mirrored edge of the world has been a prison. Aren't prisons meant to be broken?"

Madness! "Violet," I said. "I adore you and love you as if you were my own. But you are a child, and you cannot understand, and with your parents gone, I am the closest thing you have to a guardian. I am sorry to do this, child." I turned before she could stop me. "Guards!" I shouted, running to the door. "Guards!" The door flew open, but it was not the guards at all. In fact, it wasn't the hallway on the other side of the door. Instead, I saw a very different hallway, with a high, curved stone ceiling and polished wood doors as far as I could see. And a boy hurling himself into the room.

"Hello, Cassian," Demetrius said.

"YOU WON'T RECOGNIZE VIOLET!" a voice boomed from the other side. (And, so help me, I knew that voice!)

"Demetrius!" Violet cried, covering her face with her hands. "Don't look at me!"

But Demetrius, upon hearing her voice, couldn't see her through the blur of his tears, his heart hanging tightly to the friend he thought he had lost.

CHAPTER FIFTY-FOUR

Violet stood, ran to the far corner of the room, and pressed herself against the wall.

Demetrius walked slowly toward his friend. He was followed by three very small and very angry creatures. They looked human...mostly, but they were small enough to fit on my shoulder. I gasped.

"Look, Auntie!" the youngest of the three said, pointing up at me. "The idiot *can* see us."

"More proof that the world is ending," said one of the older ones. Male, from the look of him. "And more proof that the god we put all our hopes in is a charlatan and a fool."

"*Moth!*" said the old female. "*Blasphemy!* Show some respect!" She looked at me with a combination of criticism, judgment, and alarm. I wanted to start making excuses, though I wasn't quite sure for *what* yet.

Violet continued to cover her face with her hands.

"I'm serious, Demetrius. I don't want you to see me like this. I'm not *me*. And before. When I was so awful. That wasn't *me*, either, Demetrius. I swear it wasn't. And I am *so sorry*." And Violet gulped back a sob with a grunt. She squeezed her eyes tightly until they burned.

Demetrius slowly reached out his hand and touched Violet on her shoulder. "Violet," he said, "shall we play at stories?"

Violet laughed, and cried, and fell onto her knees, leaning her forehead against the wall.

"I'll start," Demetrius said. "Once upon a time, the world was wholesome and good. Or so we thought. But something was waiting—something foul. And it was biding its time."

Violet sighed deeply, running her narrow hands over

her forehead and along the curve of her skull. She grabbed her braided hair in her fists and hung on tight.

"Once upon a time," she said, "a boy and girl discovered a library deep in a castle. And the library hid a wicked secret. And they vowed to never return. But the girl lied."

Demetrius knelt next to her. "Once upon a time, a boy helped a misguided King capture the last remaining dragon in the world, and everyone's heart shattered to pieces."

"Once upon a time," Violet said, "a whole world tried to pretend an evil god didn't exist. They banned its stories. They banned its name. But it was slippery and tricky. And a princess let it out."

"Once upon a time," Demetrius said, "a wicked creature started a war. It did this for *fun*. For sport. And to provide the perfect smoke screen to hide its plans."

"Once," Violet said, "a girl lost her mother, and she blamed her friend. And she made a wish that she thought would heal the world. But she was wrong."

"It *is* you," he said, reaching his arms around Violet and holding on tight, pressing his cheek against her cheek. "Oh, Violet, I was so scared I'd never see you again." He stood, quickly wiped at his eyes with the backs of his hands, and stepped back. Violet sat up, her wide black eyes quite red now, and tear tracks running down her amber skin. Demetrius clucked his tongue. She was terribly beautiful.

"I'm sorry to tell you this, Violet," he said in a grave voice, "but you looked better before."

Violet erupted with more tears, more laughing, and Demetrius closed his eyes again, listening to her voice. "That's you, all right. Look, I need to tell you what we just learned."

And Demetrius told her about the escalating war, and about the well-aimed attack with a shovel by Moth, Nod, and Auntie, and about the terrible pit leading to the heart of the castle, and about what the god had said.

"The castle's the heart? Every stone? Then why did the Nybbas want *me* to get it? What could *I* have done?"

"I don't think you want to know, Princess," I said. Violet shuddered. She couldn't have known, of course, what had happened to the Mountain King—none of us could—and yet the closeness of her brush with the wickedness of the Nybbas shook her to the core all the same.

"In any case," I continued, "we shall have to think of a different solution. The King tried for months to break through to the dragon. Look at his notes! He wanted the dragon to find its heart as well—albeit, for different reasons. If the dragon wouldn't respond to *him*, with his background and training—"

"What do you mean, Cassian?" Demetrius said. "I could feel the dragon just as clearly as any horse. More so. It's—" Demetrius paused.

"Forthright," Violet concurred. "And *nosy*."

Auntie looked from the boy to the girl and back to the boy. "I thought it was impossible. No one's ever been able to reach a dragon before. Not since their enslavement. They're..." She searched for the word. "Prickly."

"Well, that is still true. But it's communicated with me. Didn't have anything nice to say, but still. The question is, will it help me? Will it *believe* me?"

Demetrius shrugged. "It won't have a choice. It has to. And we don't have much time. The god had instructions for you, Cassian, and for me. We are to fight, but first we have to warn the council. There's something coming— something awful. The war with the Mountain King is just a ruse, and we have to be ready for the *real* war." He turned to his friend and took her hand. "Violet, go to the dragon. Help it get its heart. The dragon's the key to killing that... thing. The thing that's causing all this. But the dragon needs your help. Or it needs to help you. We're not really sure. We'll try to buy you a little time, all the same. We'll keep the Nybbas away—or whatever the Nybbas is using to break the castle into bits. Go now."

He hesitated, took a sharp breath, and stepped toward Violet, wrapping his arms around her shoulders and hugging her tight. Violet held on for a moment, and then, without making eye contact, she wrenched her body away, spun on her heel, and ran out the door. The strange hallway was gone, and it was our own hallway, in our own castle with its familiar stones and familiar windows—all of which now thrummed and pulsed with that cursed, relentless heartbeat.

CHAPTER FIFTY-FIVE

Violet cursed her princess body with each step. She missed her old feet, her old hair, her old hands. She missed her face. Mostly, she missed the way that people lit up with love or recognition or even annoyance when she walked by. Now the few people left in the castle stopped in their tracks and stared. *They just care about the beauty*, Violet thought scornfully. *They don't care two figs about* me. She ignored the stares and went as fast as her tiny feet and delicate legs could carry her, which, I'm sorry to say, was not very fast.

When she reached the dragon's keep, she didn't even

bother announcing herself, nor did she climb to the top of the wall. "I'm setting you free," she mumbled as she undid the heavy latch and began cranking the windlass, slowly lowering the massive door.

FREE? THERE IS NO SUCH WORD, she felt the dragon think.

"Of course there is—" She paused. "I don't know your name."

IF I EVER HAD ONE, I'VE FORGOTTEN IT. "DRAGON" WILL DO. I'M THE ONLY ONE, AFTER ALL, SO NO ONE ELSE WILL COME WHEN YOU CALL. It paused. NOT THAT I WILL.

The windlass grew heavier and heavier, the closer it came to the ground. Violet's reedy arms shook. Finally, it slipped from her grip and jerked forward. The door hit the ground with a terrific crash. The dragon didn't move. It took another mouthful of leaves, chewed it, and swallowed.

"We need to go. There's something we have to do."

I DON'T NEED TO GO ANYWHERE. I CAN AWAIT MY SLAVERY HERE JUST AS EASILY AS ANYWHERE ELSE. It belched up a mass of chewed-up leaves and scales that looked, Violet thought, a bit like a compost heap. Except that it was on fire.

I'M SURPRISED IT'S TAKEN YOU SO LONG TO ASK ME, CHILD. I'VE BEEN WAITING.

"I've been a bit busy, but I'm here all the same."

THE VICTORY OF THE TYRANT IS NEARLY AT HAND. DO YOU REALLY THINK THAT I'LL BE ABLE TO HELP YOU?

"I know you can!" Violet watched as the dragon shyly peeked its head into the doorway. It blinked its one, glittering eye.

IT IS A RARE THING, GIRL, THAT ONE OF YOU CAN COME THIS CLOSE TO ONE OF ME AND LIVE TO TELL THE TALE.

"I assume that is true," Violet said, stepping closer. "But neither of us wants to see that *thing* in charge of this world or any world. Most of us would rather die. I think I know a way for *you* not to die, though I'm not so sure about everyone else...."

INTERESTING. AND WHY WOULD A HUMAN CHILD CARE SO MUCH ABOUT THE WELFARE OF A—WHAT WAS THE DELIGHTFUL TERM YOU USED? OH YES. AN "OVERGROWN LIZARD"?

Violet reddened. "You think you're special because I insulted you? You're not. I've been insulting a lot of people lately." She took a deep breath. "But for what it's worth, I'm sorry. My father—" She choked on the word. "My father cares very much about your welfare and captured *you* because he wanted to find a way to keep dragons from disappearing forever. He wanted to learn from you so that he could figure out how to help you."

AND WHAT DID HE LEARN? The dragon's eye shone in the darkness.

"My father thinks that long ago, dragons removed their hearts during adolescence but put them back in during adulthood. He thinks that at some point, the dragons lost this knowledge, though he's not sure how. He said in his notes that he thought if he put your heart back into your body, your heart would make you a whole dragon again. You would have your courage and your youth. Your body would be whole and sound again. That it would heal you."

NONSENSE!

"He said that it was because the Nybbas—"

DO NOT SAY THE NAME OF THE TYRANT! TO SAY THE NAME EMPOWERS IT. EMBOLDENS IT!

"Then let's kill it," Violet whispered. "You and I together. We'll find your heart, we'll heal you, and we'll break the mirrored edge of the world. That thing isn't as strong as you. It can't live without its heart. Or not for long, anyway."

BUT THE EDGE OF THE WORLD IS DANGEROUS! IT'S

FILLED WITH ENEMIES! The dragon cowered on the ground, covering its eye with its forearms.

"You only say that because you don't have your heart. It will make you brave again. I *know* it."

The dragon shook its head. I CAN'T LET YOU SEE WHERE MY HEART IS BURIED. I CAN'T! YOU'LL STEAL IT! YOU'LL STEAL ME! DO YOU KNOW WHAT IT'S LIKE—WHEN YOUR WILL IS NO LONGER YOUR OWN?

Violet approached the dragon, holding up her hands, palms out, to show that she was not a threat. "Actually, beloved, I know exactly what that feels like." The dragon didn't move but warily watched as the girl approached. It blinked its one, shining eye. "It's true that I could steal your heart. But I won't." She stood just in front of the wide jaws, felt the heat of its breath on her skin. "It's also true that you could gobble me up in an instant. You could burn me to cinders or rip me to shreds or deliver any number of terrible and ghastly deaths. I can't tell you what to do. I can only hope. I can only trust you. Just as you must trust me." She reached forward and laid her hand on the dragon's nose. It closed its enormous eye and began to make a sound—a deep, rumbly sound that came from the core of its body. It sounded like a cat's purr, but deeper, broader, and louder. It rattled Violet's bones. But it was a *good* sound, a *safe* sound. A sound like family. "I didn't know dragons made that sound," she said, smiling slightly at the creature.

WE RARELY DO, the dragon replied. ONLY WHEN—

But Violet didn't learn *when* a dragon makes its purr. At that very moment an arrow sliced by, landing next to Violet's left foot.

"Over here, Marshall!" a man's voice called through the darkness.

"It's escaping! Fire, men! Fire! Don't let it get away!"

Violet held up her hands. She stood between the archers and the dragon. "Stop!" she shouted. "It's not going to hurt you!"

"Shoot the Andulan filth while you're at it," another man's voice called out. "The Mountain King only asked for the death of the dragon, but he'd be pleased to hear there's one less Andulan—"

If he said something more, Violet didn't know. Instead, all she knew was the tip of an arrow on her skin—bright and hot, like an iron coming out of a raging forge. Though she knew later that it all happened in less than a second, it seemed to her to last a lifetime or more. The tip of the arrow. The bright apex of pain. Her skin swelled, then erupted around the arrow's tip, as though swallowing it whole. And then the arrow was part of her. Or she was part of the arrow. She fell back, harpooned, as the pain spread from her shoulder through her chest, down her spine. She felt another jolt of pain on her left leg.

Then: a dragon's roar.

And a bright cloud of light above her head.

And in those last seconds before losing consciousness, Violet thought for sure she saw the earth leap away, and the path, the wall, the wood, even that great, shining dragon, all spun farther and farther into the air until, at last, the darkness swirled around them and she was gone.

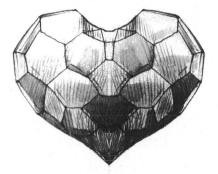

CHAPTER FIFTY-SIX

I must confess, my dears, how the bravery of those two children diminished me so. Was I like that, I wondered, when I was young? So willing to act, so willing to launch a resistance to unspeakable power? Alas, I think that I was not. I, who should have risked heaven and earth to protect that dear girl and that dear boy, found myself simply pulled in their wake—my heels dragging along the ground.

It shames me to think of it.

After Violet left the room, I sat down on a chair by the fire, gripping the handles and hooking my ankles around the legs, bracing my body against moving. "There are limits, Demetrius, to my bravery," I began, but Auntie snorted.

"There are no limits at all. You can't put a fence around nothing. If your bravery does not exist, then we can't well limit it, can we?"

"That's not entirely fair, Auntie," Demetrius said.

"You don't know the half of it, boy." Moth climbed onto my knee and pointed his finger toward my face as though it were a weapon. "We've been watching this fool for a while now. Uses stories to puff himself up and stories to smash people down and stories to keep from doing the right thing when the time comes. To say he has the bravery of a flea would be an insult to fleas."

"Be that as it may, I cannot be asked to fight. I can say that my *story* of this battle will be, most likely, more glorious than the battle itself—"

Auntie kicked my shin in rage as Moth and Nod erupted in a fit of shouting.

Demetrius sighed. "The King made you regent, which means that you are the one to direct the council of war, which means that the fate of the kingdom is in your hands. *Yours*, Cassian. Have you ever told a story that *doesn't* have the King riding into battle for the sake of his country? No. You haven't. For the first time in your life, Cassian, you'll be doing something that *matters*. And the story you'll tell about this battle will be *real*."

"That was a lovely speech, son," I said loftily. "But you will have to convince the generals by yourself. I shall *not* tell them to make nice with the armies of the Mountain King. And I certainly shall not be the one to inform them that a creature they don't believe in has warned us of the antics of a creature they've never heard of."

"But the god said—"

"To you. Not to me. I shall remain by the fire. It's my professional right and responsibility."

Demetrius shook his head. "Fine," he said. "Nod? If you wouldn't mind..."

At that moment I felt something leap onto the back of my shoulder. I felt great locks of my hair being wound around a small arm and a small leg, and I felt something very sharp and very cold against the pulsing vein in my neck. I made a move to swat poor Nod away but was rewarded with a sudden increase in pressure from the blade on my neck and the fists pulling my hair.

"It's not in my nature to kill people," Nod whispered in my ear. "Don't make me do what we'd both regret. Lower your hands, please."

"Beloved Cassian," Demetrius said in the formal voice with a low bow, "I'm terribly sorry that it has come to this, I really am. But we must do what must be done. Stand up, Cassian, and call a meeting. You must address the council. The god said that the attack will come at first light, which means that we all must be ready."

And before I could contradict him—before I could say a blessed thing, Demetrius opened the door, hailing the guards in the corridor. "The regent Cassian, stand-in for the King, wishes to hold a council of war. Immediately. Alert the necessary personnel and see to their arrival." There was a moment's hesitation, but only a moment's. He was so force-ful, so *commanding*, that the guards instantly saluted him. (I thought at the time, dears, that it was the influence of the god that did it, that perhaps the *god stuff* still lingered on him after his time below in the heart of the castle. But no. Deme-trius had always been like that. I just had been too blind to see it.) Four went hurrying away to gather the necessary peo-ple while two more waited at attention to escort me to the parlor-turned-war-room in the eastern wing of the castle.

Demetrius turned to me and grinned. "Come on, then," he said. I stood, hesitated for a moment, and received a smart kick on my left ankle from Moth.

"Now!" he snapped. "Enough dallying." To emphasize the point, Nod gave my hair another nasty yank and pressed the blade more firmly against my skin. (To be fair to the dear boy, it was the flat of the blade and not the edge. He also apologized, though quietly, so his uncle would not hear.)

We walked into the hall. Tiny cracks wormed along the walls and spread through the ceilings and the floors. The stones vibrated and pulsed, and the rhythmic beating became louder, faster, more triumphant.

"Oh dear," Auntie said, looking at the quivering stones. "We'd better hurry, Demetrius. We don't have much time."

CHAPTER FIFTY-SEVEN

Captain Marda watched the fire through her spyglass, but it didn't do much good. It was too bright, too...*strange*. It didn't spread or flash or roar the way a wildfire is supposed to do. There were no columns, no plumes of ash, no tornadic twists of flame. Indeed, her eyes should have been watering from the smoke. She should have had to tie her kerchief over her face to ease her breathing. But no. The air was clear. The flames bulged and wobbled like a living thing—a many-tentacled monster with a multitude of hard, bright eyes flashing in the dark.

And whatever it was, Marda could see it was growing. New sections were emerging from the woods, emerging from the riverbeds, pouring over the horizon. They were coming from everywhere.

"What *is* that?" she asked, shaking her head. *Nothing good*, she decided.

She closed up the spyglass and slid it into her satchel, pressing her fingers to her mouth.

"Rob!" she called. "Neda! Lilan!" Three messengers came running across the stone battlements, their legs wobbling over the cracks in the rock.

"Send out the high alert. Ring the bells. Notify the other captains, and one of you—Lilan—take this message to the castle: 'The thing across the field waits and grows. We will send a squadron to meet it before it can reach the city.'"

The three messengers bowed shakily, turned on their heels, and ran into the night.

Captain Marda turned toward the shining horizon. "We will not be cowed by the likes of you," she said out loud. "We will not permit you to touch one stone of the city."

The golden mass increased its rhythmic writhing across

the field. She held her breath and listened. Was it her imagination, or did the breeze begin to sound like a voice—a collection of voices—whispering *soon, soon, soon?*

Without warning, the wall under the Captain's feet started to rumble and shake, and the world around her was filled with the sound of the cracking of stones, each one beating like a broken heart.

CHAPTER FIFTY-EIGHT

When Violet woke, she could hardly move. The ground beneath her feet was uncannily warm, as was the breeze blowing into her face. Her right arm hurt to bend, and her eyes were swollen shut.

"What's happened?" she said to no one in particular, noticing with some distaste that the breeze blowing at her smelled uncannily like sulfur.

I'VE BROUGHT YOU TO MY HEART, CHILD, the dragon whispered inside her head. IF YOU TRY ANYTHING STUPID, I WILL RIP YOU TO SHREDS.

"Well, that's gratitude, isn't it?" Violet squeezed her eyelids together as tight as she could before forcing them open. Her left eye opened a crack, but her right eye was still glued shut. "That's the last time I take an arrow for the likes of you." She tried to laugh but coughed instead, wincing all the while. "Are the arrows still there?" She was afraid to look.

The dragon sighed. It brought its snout close to her body, the heat from its breath running over her skin like water. While it didn't take the pain away, it did certainly ease it quite a bit. *Did my father know that?* Violet wondered.

YES, the dragon answered. YOUR FATHER DID KNOW, THOUGH HE DIDN'T ASK ME ABOUT IT. AND EVEN IF HE HAD, I DOUBT I'D HAVE ANSWERED HIM. I WASN'T UP FOR TALKING MUCH.

"Why?"

WOULD YOU TALK TO YOUR CAPTORS?

Violet tried to sit up, but the pain knocked her flat. "I *would* and I *did*. If I hadn't, I would still be locked up, and you would be killed, and we would not be having this nice little conversation." She shook her head. "You know, for a dragon, you are a bit of an idiot."

YOUR PEOPLE HAVEN'T HAD THE EXPERIENCE OF CAP-
TIVITY. IF YOU HAD, YOU'D UNDERSTAND.

"Well, my people are about to have all kinds of captivity experience if we don't kill that... whatever that thing is. A god, I guess. But I thought gods were supposed to be good?"

AND YOU THOUGHT DRAGONS WERE SUPPOSED TO BE BAD, the dragon whispered icily. SHOWS WHAT YOU KNOW.

Violet reached down to her leg. Her clothes were torn and wet with blood, but the arrow was gone, which was a relief. The arrow in her chest, however—that was still there. She touched it once with the tip of her finger and shuddered.

I WAS ABLE TO GET THE SECOND ARROW OUT. The dragon's whisper in her head became suddenly gentle. Tender. BUT THE ONE IN YOUR CHEST IS DEEP. YOU'LL BLEED. A LOT. I COULD HELP THE HEALING PROCESS A BIT, BUT I COULDN'T BE SURE IT WOULDN'T KILL YOU. IF I'M GOING TO KILL YOU, I THINK I'D LIKE YOUR PERMISSION.

"Well, that's terribly polite," Violet said. With great effort, she lifted herself onto her elbows and forced both eyes open. The arrow was tucked into the far side of her chest, in that little hollow just under her shoulder. She

looked away. "In any case, the arrow wound is going to be useful for us." Violet grunted, then growled with pain as she poured her weight onto her feet and staggered to a stand.

HOW CAN AN ARROW WOUND BE USEFUL?

Violet closed her eyes and let her face spread into a slow smile. "Show me your heart, and I'll show you."

CHAPTER FIFTY-NINE

To say that the council was unhappy to see me, my dears, would be a bit of an understatement. The members had not forgiven the King for placing me in charge, nor had they forgiven me for accepting. (Not that I had much of a choice—or any, mind you—but that did not remedy their vitriol toward me.)

Moreover, I was calling a meeting in the middle of the night, in the company of a small child. (And not just a small child, I could feel them thinking. The child of the liveryman. A no one. A nothing.) As well as three very small creatures who I insisted were present with us, but whom none of the council could see.

"Am I to understand," guffawed one particularly ancient council member (Wyfryn was his name, a skeptical old fellow and not one for listening to stories), "that we are now expected—in a time of war—to take orders from a confirmed lunatic?"

"Confirmed by whom?" I cried, indignant.

"By *reason*," Wyfryn said nastily. "Destroy all the mirrors, indeed! Inventing curses and magics when the barbarians in the north cry out for our blood and servitude. The very idea!"

"But it's true," Demetrius said. The council erupted.

"Who let this boy in here?" Wyfryn shouted.

"This is a council of war," shouted a general. "Not a nursery school!"

"Get the boy out of here at once," roared another general.

Demetrius, always such a calm boy, so implacable even in the face of panicking animals and outraged human beings, bowed his head for a moment. And because the old men and women of the council *expected* the boy to stamp and pout and throw a fuss, his calm, unflappable demeanor shocked them into silence. Or, more likely, it was simply the presence of Demetrius himself. Something about that boy made people want to listen. The gaggle of squawking old men became instantly calmed. Demetrius cleared his throat.

"I know this isn't what you want to hear, but the enemy at work here is *not* the enemy we are fighting against. The war that idiot Mountain King wages on us right now is a ruse. Something to put us off our guard. Something very powerful is—at this moment—inside the castle. *Inside.* Lay your hands on the stones if you don't believe me. Feel them beating. Look at the cracks. They've been getting worse for weeks."

"Fairy tales," Wyfryn spat, though I noticed his hands shaking as he looked upward at the spidery cracks growing across the ceiling and down the walls.

"I think we both know that isn't true. You are my elders, all of you, and you have from me the respect that is due. But I've heard the voices of the protectors of the castle— the protectors who made the tunnels that the Princess Violet and I roamed through from the time we were little. The protectors who were left here by the Old Gods in case the Nybbas—" A shocked gasp shot through the room.

"How does he know that name?"

"He dares speak it!"

"Its story is forbidden!"

Demetrius continued, undeterred. "In case that *thing* should find a way to awake, enlarge, and empower itself. My beloved elders, *this has happened.* It's happening right now. The Mountain King has been manipulated by flattery and false promises. He has been duped. All it wants is its heart. Surely you can *feel* it. It's beating right now. And getting stronger every second."

"I feel no such thing," Wyfryn said. "And I've just about heard enough. Guards! Remove both of these miscreants from our sight!"

What happened next was quite a bit of shouting, the loudest of which came from my*self,* who erupted in a long and misguided tirade about my rights as the new king, saying that I would see to it that each one of them spent the rest of his or her days rotting in the lowest reaches of the dungeons, and making other statements of an equally low and cowardly manner that I, quite frankly, am thankful have been lost to time, and world, and dimension.

"Stop," Demetrius commanded as the guards rushed in. "You must listen," he shouted as they bound my wrists and pushed me roughly from the room. Demetrius, in contrast, fought and struggled, and no fewer than six guards were needed to hold him, bind him, and carry him away. This was made more difficult thanks to the actions of Nod, Moth, and Auntie, who managed to stymie the guards—a slice to the leg here, a toppled chair there, and once, an entire painting removed from the wall and smashed over one soldier's head. "*Please!*" the boy cried, nearly in tears. "You have to believe me. I went to the center of the castle. I found the path to the temple of the Old Gods deep underground. And one of them spoke. We are in terrible danger. A rogue god, imprisoned in our mirrored sky for two thousand years, is straining at its bonds and seeks to destroy the castle and enslave our people. It did it before, and the results were terrible. We need to protect the castle. Every man, woman, and child."

"Your lies become more fanciful by the moment, boy," Wyfryn said. "The Old Gods are dead. Their final act was the building of the multiverse. Everyone knows that. Guards, stop the boy's mouth until you reach the dungeons. The last thing we need is for the child to start spouting heresy to the kitchen staff."

But neither Demetrius nor I made it farther than three

paces into the corridor. It was there that we met Captain Marda, her band of young—terribly young!—soldiers standing behind her with their knives unsheathed and their arrows nocked. Standing between two child soldiers was an elder lieutenant of the Mountain King's guard. He was unarmed, but he did not look like a prisoner of war. His face bore no contempt, no scorn, no rage. Only terrible, terrible fear. And his eyes were fixed on the leather sack in Captain Marda's hand. And inside the sack, something wriggled and fought. A foul-smelling steam poured through the cinched opening, and the Captain held the sack at arm's length, though, despite that, her hand was dark red and starting to blister. Her jaw was set, and she gave a grim smile.

"I order the lot of you to stop and unbind your prisoners." She turned to the war council gathering at the doorway, and bowed low. "Begging your pardon, my beloved, but your refusal to listen to the boy is both imbecilic and suicidal. He speaks the truth, and I can prove it."

"Indeed, sirs," the northern lieutenant said, bowing low. "The war, as we knew it, has altered. Or, more specifically, it is ended, and a new one has begun. Our King is missing. Or dead. Our armies have been scattered. And a terrible enemy has been cutting us down, one by one."

"Lies!" Wyfryn cried, his ruddy face transforming to purple. "Insubordination! Captain, you shall join these two in the—"

But he stopped. All mouths hung open, and all eyes focused on that trembling, writhing sack.

Because whatever was in that sack could speak.

"WE ARE THE SERVANTS OF THE IMPRISONED GOD," the sack said. "RELEASE THE NYBBAS."

CHAPTER SIXTY

Violet forced herself to her feet, holding on to the side of the dragon for balance.

YOU PROBABLY SHOULDN'T STAND. The dragon's thoughts wormed into her own, as though they had always been there.

"Don't worry about me," Violet said. She coughed violently, each cough pushing a shard of pain into her body, lodging it deep. She spat blood onto the ground. The dragon's breath was keeping her from dying, for the time being. But it was a temporary measure and only, Violet knew, delaying the inevitable.

I am dying, she thought.

I should be afraid to die, she marveled.

But she wasn't. There was a task to do.

MY HEART IS HERE, the dragon said. UNDER THIS GROUND. THIS IS, IN FACT, MY GROUND—FOR THE PLACE WHERE WE BURY OUR HEARTS IS SACRED TO DRAGONS. WE SHOW IT TO NO ONE. AND WHEN WE MAKE OUR YEARLY PILGRIMAGE TO VISIT OUR HEARTS, TO FEEL THEIR HOT BEATING AS NEAR AS OUR OWN BREATHS, WE ASK THE OLD ONES TO GIVE US THEIR BLESSING, AND WE PRAY THAT OUR YEARS IN SLAVERY ARE NEVER REPEATED IN THIS OR ANY LIFE.

"Yes, yes, very interesting," Violet said impatiently. "And now it is time to dig it up. But to replace your heart, we need a blood sacrifice. The ancients were terribly clear on that. Fortunately, we have an abundance of blood—and a willing sacrificial victim." Violet patted the arrow in her chest, sending a new, hot jolt of pain, nearly breaking her in half. "I'll have to cut you, but the heart will heal you up once it's back in. Or my blood will. That's what my father's ledgers said, anyway."

AND THEN WHAT?

"Then everything." Violet sank to the ground, the strain of speaking nearly sapping her entirely. "All your fear?

Well, it won't be gone exactly, but you'll be able to face it. In other worlds, long ago, dragons lived in tribes. They had families and societies and even nations. Because back then, everyone knew that a dragon put its heart away until the heat of adolescence faded. When dragons replaced their hearts as adults, the hearts didn't incinerate. They heated and glowed like liquid iron."

AND THAT WILL HAPPEN TO ME?

Violet shrugged, then winced, then coughed. She spat blood again. The sight of it made her dizzy—or perhaps the injury made her dizzy. Or the fact of dying was itself dizzying. Already her vision seemed to darken around the edges. She forced herself not to notice it. "Hopefully," she admitted. "The truth is, you're kind of—" Her voice trailed off.

OLD?

"Well, yes. My father was worried about it. I'd be a pretty awful person if I didn't tell you it was risky."

AND THEN?

"Break the mirror. You destroy the mirrored edge of the world before the Nybbas regains its heart. Once it's out of its prison, separated from its heart, it can be killed."

WITH FIRE?

"Yes." *Hopefully*, she added, in the silence of her heart.

YOU ASK ME TO DO THIS. DEATH INSTEAD OF SLAVERY?

"No." Violet squeezed her eyes shut. "I ask that *we* do it. I wouldn't ask you to do it alone. And besides, we might not die." *Or,* Violet thought to herself, *at least you might not.*

The dragon stretched its neck upward and tilted its face toward the sky. Violet felt the inky black scales rippling over its flank, felt the shudder of fear, followed by heat, then cold, then heat again. She closed her eyes, and opened herself to the dragon's fear. She felt it as the creature felt it—knowing full well that the dragon's reflection at the limit of the sky was too far away to even see, but that just *knowing* it was there was reason enough to set the bones rattling and turn the bowels to water. She pressed her palm against the dragon's side and held her breath, focusing all of her attention to her own heart, and her heart's insistence that she not *ignore* her fear but act *because* of her fear. That her fear alone was motivation enough. She felt her heart clanging in her chest, loud as a mallet struck hard upon an iron door.

I'd give you my own heart if I could, she thought. And she meant it.

I KNOW, the dragon thought in reply. STEP BACK. It took three deep breaths, and, turning its face to the ground, shot a white-hot breath hard at the rock. It bubbled and melted

362

and opened into a widening gulf. Violet watched in fascination as the rock transformed to mush, then to liquid, then to steam. Finally, when the dragon had a hole about one man deep and four men wide, it reached in and pulled out a box made of glowing metal, large enough to hold a young goat. This the dragon opened, and pulled out another box, also metal, though not so hot—it steamed and smoked, but only the edges were red. Inside that box was another, not metal, but something black and hard and shiny. The dragon pulled out the box and held the object close to its body. The creature shot Violet an apprehensive glance.

"What is the box made of?" Violet asked.

ME, the dragon thought, though its thinking was so reticent that Violet could hardly grasp it.

"You?"

WELL, NOT ME, EXACTLY, came the slightly exasperated reply. BUT I MADE IT. MY OWN SCALES, MY OWN BREATH, MY OWN TEARS. The dragon sighed. THIS IS ME PROTECTING ME.

Violet nodded. "Lie down on your back. The arrow in my chest—" She gritted her teeth and clasped the arrow's shaft in her fist. "It's more useful for us than those soldiers could have known. Once I remove the arrow—"

BUT YOU CAN'T! The dragon's thoughts rang through Violet's skull like a bell. YOU'LL DIE!

"My beloved," Violet said sadly, "I'm already dying. At least this way, I won't die in vain."

And before the dragon could protest, Violet leaped lightly onto its abdomen and, with an anguished cry, pulled the arrow out from her ribs. She let the blood flow onto the creature's chest. To her surprise, each drop sank instantly into the scales, disappearing entirely. Where the blood fell, the scales turned from glossy black to brilliant, blinding white. She squinted. The world around her wobbled and flowed as each ounce of strength leaked from the hole in her chest.

"Get ready, my beloved," she said as she positioned the sharp tip of the arrow over the scales. The cut was smooth, sure, and easy. The dragon's ribs opened like a hinge, exposing the intricate and delicate workings of its body to the naked eye.

Oh, Father! she found herself thinking. *If only you could see!*

But aloud she said, "Now! Now, my darling! Replace the heart!"

And the world around her thundered and flashed and went suddenly dark.

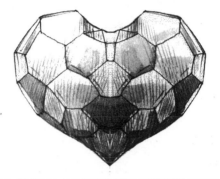

CHAPTER SIXTY-ONE

Captain Marda reached into the bag and pulled out a small, golden-scaled lizard. Its skin shone like molten gold, and I found myself wondering whether her hands would blister and burn as she held the creature. It struggled and thrashed against her grip. Its mouth, madly snapping at the air, was curiously filled with row upon row of bright black teeth, each one barbed and tilting inward. Even more curious, its mouth was *only* teeth. No tongue, no palate, no soft tissue around the throat. A mouth that looked as though it could never be used for eating. Or speaking, either, not that I expected a lizard to talk, and yet a voice came out of the creature—not from its *mouth*, mind you, but from the creature *itself*. "FREE THE HEART OF THE NYBBAS," it said—which is to say, its *body* said—over and over and over again. That lizard was a *weapon*. A moving, reactive, sentient weapon, but a weapon all the same. I shuddered to look at it.

"My lords and ladies," Captain Marda said. She did not tell her band of young soldiers to lay down their weapons, nor did the armed guards surrounding the council lay down theirs. They looked to the Captain, then to the unarmed northern soldier, then back to the Captain. Still no one seemed willing to make the first strike. Had there not, everyone reasoned, been enough of us killed? Could we bear it if a drop of Andulan blood were spilled by Andulan hands?

Captain Marda cleared her throat. "My beloved," she added, because it was proper. "I wish to show you something, that you might understand the nature of the threat that is, even now, drawing closer to the castle, our home." She turned to one of her soldiers—a girl younger than Violet. "Lilan," Marda said, "if you please."

The girl paled slightly but did not hesitate. With heavily

gloved hands, she grasped the lower half of the creature's body, and Captain Marda unsheathed her knife. The cut was quick and bloodless. Indeed, the knife sliced through the creature silently and easily, without the resistance of bone or sinew. But before we could wonder at it, the Captain began barking orders at the girl.

"Hold tight now, soldier. Don't let that thing touch the castle."

Lilan, now quite red in the face, gripped the halved creature with both hands, holding it as far from her body as she could. And in an instant, I understood why.

A head peeked from the bloodless wound. Two hard, glittering eyes blinked in their golden sockets. Two bright shoulders wriggled free, followed by the upper half of a body. And, in Marda's hand, the other half of the creature sprouted a new tail, new hips, and new flanks. Where there had been one, there were now two.

Captain Marda grabbed Lilan's doubled lizard and threw both of them into the sack. They wriggled and thrashed and screamed.

"This is what we're up against. A swarm of... *creatures*—though they are unlike any creatures that I've ever seen. A swarm of weapons. There are millions of them, and they have been gathering from all corners of the world—though from where, exactly, and *how*, I cannot say. But it seems that they are done amassing and are now on the move. And while they are slow, they are relentless. By my estimation, they will arrive by morning."

The northern lieutenant spoke up. "These...things cannot be beaten by the sword. And while one can do damage, a dozen can rip a man to pieces. This I have seen." He shut his eyes tightly, and his face clouded over. "We lost an entire camp. Good soldiers. Children too young to be soldiers, but soldiers all the same. We panicked and scattered. I do not know how many were lost."

The Captain cast a shrewd eye on the guards binding and gagging poor Demetrius, who still struggled in their hands, his eyes wide and horrified, unable to look away from that terrible sack. "Would you care to release that boy, soldier? He looks as though he has something to contribute to this conversation."

"No," Wyfryn began, his voice weak and faded. "There is nothing. He's just a—"

"*Release him*, soldier," the Captain interrupted, her voice so forceful that the young soldier obeyed at once. Wyfryn tried to say something else, but the words garbled in his mouth and leaked into a whine.

"Captain," Demetrius said once the gag was out of his mouth, "the Princess Violet is alive. That name the lizard spoke? The Nybbas? It is the name of a god—a wicked god. And it is trying to enslave our world, and every world. Violet was tricked and transformed by the Nybbas. It is imprisoned and hobbled in the mirrored edge of the world, and cannot act without being ordered. Not without its heart. We have to protect the castle. The heart *is* the castle. It's inside each stone. As long as the Nybbas does not have its heart, it's vulnerable. Or that's what the runty god said. Violet has gone—" Demetrius's voice cracked, his worry for his friend nearly breaking him in half. "She's gone to get the dragon, and the two of them will find a way to defeat the Nybbas—to destroy it. We *have* to buy her some time. Once the Nybbas has its heart back, there won't be a thing we can do about it. We have to keep those creatures away from the castle for as long as possible, or everything has been in vain."

"The creatures are devilish," the lieutenant said, "but they are not insurmountable. Nets deter them. So do ditches.

Anything to disrupt the swarm, turn it in on itself, will buy you some time. And if the sword is useless, perhaps we should try fire."

Captain Marda turned to the council who, every last one of them, looked at the floor. Some of them—Wyfryn included—were muttering words like *preposterous*, and *fanciful*, and *fairy tales*. While others just stood in a stunned silence, every once in a while stealing glances at the thrashing sack in the Captain's hand. "Since the King appointed Cassian as lord regent, it matters not what *you* have to say. You served at the pleasure of the King, and now it is Cassian whose pleasure matters. Your illegal arrest notwithstanding." She turned to me, and though she bowed, her eyes were as sharp as a sword to my heart. "Beloved Cassian," she said. "Last I checked, you were still regent. What are your orders?"

And perhaps it was the sudden realization of the terrible danger that my darling Violet was in, or perhaps it was the pleading look on the face of Demetrius, or even the tiny dagger in the hand of an invisible Nod pressed firmly against my throat. In any case, I felt the spell of the Nybbas fall away from my soul like a spent cocoon. I shook myself, feeling suddenly free.

I was ready, at last, to do the right thing.

"Gather every man, woman, and child. Every person with two hands and strength enough to heft a shovel or haul wood or push a cart. We will be ready to fight by morning."

CHAPTER SIXTY-TWO

When Violet woke, she was warm, comfortable, and cradled in a pair of arms, her cheek pressed to something smooth and alive, the sound of a heart's beating thrumming against her skin.

In her mind's eye, she saw herself as an infant, gently bound in a soft cloth and tied securely to her mother's body. She felt a memory of her mother's hands, and that memory was immediate and tactile and terribly alive. Her hair, her skin, her dark, husky voice—all were as close as breathing. Violet nearly shattered with grief. Very slowly, she opened her eyes. It wasn't her mother's arms around her—of course it wasn't. Her mother was dead and buried.

The arms holding her, the heart beating next to her own—they belonged to the dragon. It rocked her back and forth as though she were an infant.

PLEASE WAKE UP. OH, PLEASE, PLEASE WAKE UP, the dragon silently pleaded.

"Mama?" Violet whispered in her stupor. Then she coughed. Then groaned. "I mean, Dragon."

YOU'RE ALIVE!

"I am?" Violet looked around. The wound in her chest had been dressed and bandaged with a shiny, pearly substance that adhered directly to her skin. Dragon tears, Violet guessed. It ached terribly, but the bleeding had stopped.

DON'T MOVE. YOU'VE LOST A LOT OF BLOOD.

"Where are we?" But once the words were out of her mouth, she knew. The sky met the earth like the edge of an upturned bowl, and curved smoothly upward and outward, until the reflections in its surface blurred into a broad, slick shimmer.

THE EDGE OF THE MIRRORED WORLD. The dragon's thoughts were hushed and amazed. YOU WERE RIGHT. I'M NOT AFRAID. I CAN HARDLY *REMEMBER* EVER BEING AFRAID.

The dragon stared at its reflection, enlarged and enormous in the sky's concave surface, a look of wonder on its face. It turned its head this way and that. It blinked its one bright eye. I SUPPOSE IT WOULD BE RUDE TO SAY THAT I AM BEAU-TIFUL, BUT I DO *FEEL* THAT IT MUST BE SO.

"You didn't have to bring me here," Violet said, forcing herself to her feet. She saw the reflection of her body—her wrong body—in the curved mirror of the sky. She gri-maced and looked away. It made her sick to see it. "You could have let me die."

The dragon turned its head toward the girl, gazing at her sadly. NO, it said. I COULDN'T. I COULDN'T LEAVE YOU AT ALL. I TRIED TO LEAVE YOU—TRULY I DID. BUT LOVE HELD ME BACK. IT IS, IN THE END, ANOTHER KIND OF SERVITUDE. BUT I CHOOSE IT. AND THAT MAKES ALL THE DIFFERENCE.

Violet looked away. *Does love bind us?* she wondered. *Or does it set us free?* She did not know, but looked up at the mirrored sky instead. The Nybbas was in there. *Somewhere.*

A HEARTBREAKING SCENE, said a whispery, slithery voice from the other side of the mirrored edge of the known world. It sniggered unpleasantly. I THINK I MIGHT CRY.

Violet watched in horror as an image of her*self* (herself

as she *was*, as she was *supposed* to look before she foolishly asked the Nybbas to change her) uncurled from the rim of the land and grew to hideous proportions against the curve of the mirrored sky, an unnaturally broad smile snaking across its face. The Violet-shaped image threw back its head and laughed, its mismatched eyes leaking tears.

"You!" Violet cried, ignoring the wound in her chest, picking up a rock and throwing it at the image's belly. The pain knocked her sideways. She toppled over with a thud. The rock bounced off with a metallic clink and fell to the ground. It didn't leave even a scratch.

ME, the Nybbas said, tossing back the tangled curls that were *supposed* to belong to Violet, and running its tongue along that dear chipped tooth. THOUGH I MUST APOLOGIZE FOR MY APPEARANCE. It cast a smug glance down at itself. I CAN ONLY ASSUME IT'S DUE TO YOUR INCESSANT AND UNGRATEFUL LONGING FOR YOUR ORIGINAL FORM. It examined its bitten nails. CAN'T THINK WHY. AND AFTER MY KINDNESS AND *EVERYTHING*.

"You're a thief." She gritted her teeth and threw another rock. The dragon-tears bandage pulled away from her skin a bit, and the girl started to bleed. The rock bounced, and the Nybbas smiled wider with Violet's mouth. "And a cheat," Violet screamed. Another rock. More blood. "And I want my face back!"

It rolled its eyes. I'D PART WITH IT WILLINGLY, IF I COULD. THIS APPEARANCE IS...AN UNINTENDED SIDE EFFECT, AND AN UNPLEASANT ONE AT THAT. I WILL CAST IT AWAY ONCE MY USEFUL LITTLE TOOLS HAVE THEIR WAY WITH THE CASTLE. AND I, AT LAST, WILL BE FREE. ALL I'VE EVER WANTED, VIOLET, ASIDE FROM MY OWN FREEDOM, WAS YOUR FRIENDSHIP, AND YET YOU'VE SPAT ON MY SIMPLE REQUESTS AND TREATED ME LIKE *GARBAGE*.

"No," Violet said quietly. "I haven't. You are worse than garbage. You are a liar. And a charlatan. *And you are no one's friend.*"

The Nybbas-in-the-shape-of-Violet shrugged. NO MATTER, it said. YOU HAVE BEEN USEFUL, MY CHILD, AND I WILL REMAIN GRATEFUL FOR YOUR WILLINGNESS TO EMPOWER ME WHEN I NEEDED POWER AND FOR BREEDING CHAOS EXACTLY WHEN CHAOS WAS REQUIRED. I SHAN'T FORGET YOUR HELP. INDEED, EVEN NOW, AS MY HEART IS IN MY GRASP, I KNOW THAT I SHALL EASILY BE *ABLE* TO KILL YOU ONCE I HAVE THE STRENGTH TO STEP OUT OF MY PRISON, BUT I THINK I SHALL *NOT*. I THINK I SHALL GIVE YOU A

FIRSTHAND LOOK AT THE LOVELY DEVASTATION YOU HAVE
CAUSED FOR MY BENEFIT.

Now! Burn it! Violet thought wildly at the dragon. *Burn
the sky. Burn its prison. Burn it now!*

The dragon opened its throat, and fire poured out onto
the sky, directly at the image of the Nybbas-as-Violet. The
mirrored sky glowed orange, then blue, then white. The
Nybbas fractured into a hundred, then a thousand, tiny
replications of itself.

STOP! the Nybbas screamed. PLEASE STOP. I'M A PRIS-
ONER! I'M WEAK AND PATHETIC. PLEASE DON'T HURT ME. It
whined and sobbed. It sucked its snot and lisped through a
litany of pleading. Violet thought she'd be sick.

Don't stop, my beloved, she thought desperately at the
dragon.

CAN'T . . . BREATHE . . . she felt the dragon think. MY
FIRE! And feeling the dragon's growing panic like a brand-
new arrow—hot and bright and terribly sharp—in her
abdomen, Violet fell to her knees.

You can do it. I know you can.

The sky bubbled and wobbled. Violet braced herself.
But the dragon coughed, then gasped, then fell to its side,
panting for breath.

"Dragon!" Violet screamed.

The mirrored edge of the world smoothed over, and the multitudes of images of the accursed Nybbas swirled together into one. The ground rumbled and shook, knocking Violet to her knees.

"What was that?" she asked.

The Nybbas sighed. And smiled.

THE FIRST STONE HAS FALLEN! it cried. MY FREEDOM IS AT HAND!

CHAPTER SIXTY-THREE

Slowly, by blink and by sigh, Auntie, Moth, and Nod became visible to everyone present. At first, it was a flutter at the edge of the eye. Then the flutter became a blur, and the blur became a figure, and the figure became an individual, complete with expression, intention, and cunning action. People gasped, then pointed. One very old woman said, "I knew it!"

Two guards—a brother and a sister as alike unto each other as two daisies on a single stem—fainted dead away at the sight of Nod swaggering next to me, his spear slung across his back and his tiny blade tucked underneath his left shoulder. Wyfryn, an idiot to the end, gave a small, tight scream whenever he laid eyes on one of them, followed always by a shake of his head and a mumbled assertion to himself that he could not see what was not there. After a moment or two of *that* nonsense, Captain Marda ordered the council member gagged, his hands bound in front of his body like a prisoner.

"He'll not waste his time in the dungeon, mind you," the Captain called over her shoulder. "There are ditches that need digging. And they won't dig themselves. And come to think of it, someone should go down there and release anyone who is willing to stand in defense of the country. Which reminds me." She stopped, spun on her right foot, and marched over to Auntie, bowing low. "We have not been properly introduced, mother," the Captain said, stretching out one hand for Auntie to step up on. "I am Marda, formerly Mistress of the Falcons, and now Captain of the Front Guard. I am sorry that I am only just now able to see you, or I would have endeavored to make your acquaintance before this moment. In any case, I have a feeling that you might have a piece or two of useful information, and I, for one, would like to hear it." Auntie flushed for a moment—but only a moment—before nodding curtly and clearing her throat. She had, after all, quite a bit to say.

And, flanked by the young soldiers, both the Captain and Auntie made their way to the front lines, pausing to shout orders and send the underlings running, but conferring all the while.

Within an hour's quarter, the entire castle—nay, the entire city—was mobilized. Old women left their kitchens, and children left their nurseries, and old men taught the young every trick they'd ever learned in their soldier days. The prisons were emptied; the forges blazed; the tavern keepers loaded provisions into carts and brought them to their fellow citizens amassing outside the city walls. Deep ditches were dug, barricades built, and massive nets knotted to stymie the servants of the Nybbas. Slow them down. Keep them at bay.

We faced an enemy we would not defeat. Indeed, that we *could* not. We were laying down our lives to buy time.

As the night wore on, every man, woman, and child was outfitted, armed, and readied for battle.

The enemy was coming. We could hear their voices in the ground, in the stones, in the air, and in our very skin.

SOON.

SOON.

SOON.

NOW.

CHAPTER SIXTY-FOUR

Demetrius and I stood with the men and women of the Andulan Realms—in addition to the assembled remnants of the scattered armies of the north—and watched the servants of the Nybbas approach. His arms and his back and his voice were sore. His hands were bloody and swollen—much of their skin rubbed away from a night of shoveling and hauling and stacking and hoping. He had worn three pairs of leather gloves to nothing, and his trousers were ripped at the knees, his tunic torn at the elbows and across the back.

He was utterly, utterly spent.

But it was not over. They were coming. Even now, the ground rumbled as they approached.

"Brace yourselves," Marda shouted.

"Brace yourselves," cried the people.

"Courage," whispered Demetrius. And oh! That boy! In truth, he hardly looked like a boy to me any longer. He had the strength of a man now, and the courage of ten men. Demetrius turned to me. "Courage, Cassian," he said, and gave my shoulder a squeeze.

And my heart leaped.

And my fists gripped my cudgel.

And I was ready.

A great, golden, seething mass moved as one across the fields. It was slow, methodical, and relentless. In its wake, everything green was ground down to the root, everything woody pulverized to pulp, everything stone smoothed into sand.

The broad ditch, which seemed so insurmountable the night before, looked now no deeper than a scratch. The piles of dead wood and living wood and broken furniture and cast-off lumber, and the torn-off pieces of people's homes, the hand-knotted net from torn-up linens—these seemed no more intimidating than a candle's wick.

We are lost, I thought.

The great mass grew nearer. The torchbearers approached the wood piles.

"Wait!" Captain Marda shouted.

A sound grew from the assembled crowd. A guttural, gamy, growly sound. It was quiet at first, but it began to grow. Men, women, and children picked up their weapons—clubs and sticks and sacks. Nothing that could cut. Only implements to beat the things back. The torchbearers held their flames close to the piles of wood.

"Wait," Captain Marda said.

The sound bubbled into a rumble and widened into a roar. Despite his ragged voice and his tender throat, Demetrius found that his head was tipped back, his lungs powerfully ripping his voice out of his chest and hurling it into the air. His swollen hands clutched a club in one hand and his sack in the other. His injuries—though real, and though *painful*—disappeared. He was ready.

The mass grew closer.

"Burn it!" Captain Marda shouted. "Let it burn."

Demetrius noticed that the Captain looked behind her as she said this. He turned. On the castle's battlements, he saw three more torches. And three more piles of—what was that? Bedding? Rags? He couldn't see. But he *could* see who held the torches—Auntie, Nod, and Moth.

"NO!" shouted Demetrius, but no one heard him.

The torchbearers threw their torches onto the piles of wood. The fire lit and spread. Behind them, in the castle, the three Hidden Folk did the same. "We're not supposed to do that!" Demetrius shouted. He dropped his club and sprinted through the chaos toward the fire.

Marda grabbed his shoulder and, with a quick jerk, lifted the boy into the air and spun him around. "Let it be, soldier," she shouted.

"You don't understand," Demetrius shouted through the din. "The god said—"

"I'm more inclined to believe that old woman than any slumbering oaf. We are outside of what the Old Gods understood, and we are on our own. All that's left for us to do is fight." And with that, she patted Demetrius on the back and ran to the front lines.

The mass of lizards widened and arced around the city walls. The flames on the wood blazed hot and high as the servants of the Nybbas plunged headlong into the ditch. As Demetrius feared, it did not stop them for long. The ditch filled with lizards, and the lizards tumbled over one another and pressed against one another, until there was so much lizard and so little slope to contend with. The coming hordes simply walked across the mass of their brethren.

"GET AWAY FROM THERE!" Demetrius shouted toward the castle. Auntie, Nod, and Moth waved at him from the battlements. They waved and waved and waved.

CHAPTER SIXTY-FIVE

The ground shook again.

"Dragon," Violet called, pulling herself back up. "Burn again, beloved! It was working."

NO! The Nybbas-as-Violet dropped to its knees (*My knees!* Violet thought) and pressed its hands together. PLEASE DON'T HURT ME.

The dragon reared and opened its throat, but a distant voice stopped it cold.

"Violet!"

Both Violet and the dragon turned toward the sound of

the coming voice. *It can't be*, they thought together. The Nybbas, wearing Violet's face, looked up, wiping away its crocodile tears.

Violet—the *real* Violet—froze. "Father," she whispered.

And indeed, coming over a small rise, his horse thundering and snorting as it ran, was the King. His eyes were not on Violet on the ground. He pulled his horse to a stop, dismounted, and walked toward the sky. His eyes—round they were, and glassy, and *glittering*—were on the wicked god with his daughter's face. He did not notice his child—his true child—blood-soaked and injured and walking unsteadily toward him with her arms outstretched. He looked instead up at the *image* of Violet in the mirrored edge of the world, hideously enlarged, though shrinking now to normal size.

"Father," Violet said again. But her father ignored her. Instead, he pushed right past his own daughter and pressed his palms against the surface of the mirrored sky. The Nybbas—all smiles, all happy tears—pressed back.

"I knew I'd find you, my child," King Randall said, running his hands along the mirrored edge, as though trying to find an opening. "I knew my footsteps would lead me home to you."

OF COURSE THEY DID, the Nybbas whispered with a sly smile. BUT QUICK. YOU MUST PUNISH THAT DRAGON AND THAT GIRL. THEY TOOK ME AWAY, FATHER. Fake tears, fake sobs. Violet felt herself sick to see such lies come from her own face, her own mouth. The Nybbas leaned in closer. YOU MUST KILL THEM, MY FATHER, it said in a low voice. KILL THEM BEFORE THEY KILL ME.

"What?" The King stepped back, his face cloudy and unsure. "What are you talking about, my darling? I can't kill the dragon. I'm trying to save the dragon."

Violet shot a quick look at the dragon as though to say, *There! You see?*

The dragon roared. It flew upward and shot another round of fire at the sky. The Nybbas howled. Its stolen face and stolen body reddened, multiplied, and swirled. It became five Violets, then ten, then a thousand. The earth shook again, snapping violently this way and that. Violet grabbed her father and pulled him away from the mirror.

STOP! The images of Violet spun back into one, and it swelled and loomed as large as a giant overhead. MAKE IT STOP! the Nybbas said desperately. YOU SEE WHAT THEY'VE DONE, FATHER?

Violet took the King's face in her hands. "Father, that's

an impostor," she said. "*I* am Violet. That *thing* in the mirror, it's not me at all. It's stolen my face and my voice and has changed me into"—she gestured to her new body with unveiled disgust—"into this. We need to—"

DON'T LISTEN TO IT, the Nybbas shrieked. IT LIES! IT LIES! IT'S A NASTY, SCHEMING—OH!

The Nybbas, with Violet's face, Violet's body, fell to its knees. It clutched at its chest. WHAT'S HAPPENING? It panted as smoke erupted from its mouth, its nose, each eye socket, each ear.

"Violet?" King Randall asked tentatively, laying his hand back on the mirror.

The dragon shot its flame once again, and tiny cracks formed, tracing an outline of a body—long arms, long legs, hands and feet like points. The shape framed the image of the thirteenth god.

Violet stared at it in wonder. *I know that shape*, she thought.

The Nybbas clutched at its chest. MY HEART! it screamed. IT BURNS!

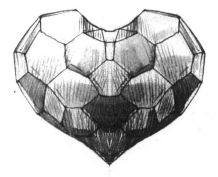

CHAPTER SIXTY-SIX

Demetrius fought valiantly. The servants of the Nybbas could not be sliced in half, lest they regenerate, nor could they be stabbed, as they had no hearts, and no blood to leak out. However, their heads could be smashed—a temporary measure, as they still regenerated, but in the meantime they tripped on their own feet, wandered blindly, mewed like kittens. Apparently, they could not destroy what they could not see.

New fires were lit, and as he fought, more and more fuel was being added to new fire lines. Chairs, wagons, beds, toys, and tables—everything burned.

Demetrius stood at the front of the pack, smashing the lizards with more gusto than he would have thought possible. He fought blindly, wildly. He aimed for the heads, making sure not to split their bodies with his blows. The lizards swarmed and tangled around his feet. Demetrius kicked and raged at the tiny beasts.

"Get away from us!" he shouted. "We do not want you here!" He knocked lizard after lizard into the growing fire, but soon they swarmed around his legs, sending him sprawling into the golden, writhing mass. He felt their terrible teeth pulling at his skin as easily as if it were custard. Demetrius closed his eyes. *I'm sorry, Violet,* he thought.

"Idiot," he heard Nod say as he grabbed lizard after lizard and hurled them into the air.

"You're alive!" Demetrius shouted—or tried to shout. In truth, it was more of a croak. Moth stood on Demetrius's chest, kicking the lizards with his boots and knocking their heads with a large wooden spoon.

Auntie had a basket of coals strapped to her back, and thick black gloves on her hands. One by one, she grabbed a lizard, shoved a coal into its mouth, and sent it on its way— where it would stumble, teeter, and explode.

"Must we expend all our energies, Demetrius dear,"

Auntie asked as she tossed another wriggling (and doomed) lizard away as if it were nothing more than a toy, "on rescuing your poor self from another sticky end?"

Demetrius pulled himself to his feet. "Why did you set fire to the castle? The god said—"

"Hmph," Auntie said, shoving another coal into a lizard, then grabbing it by the tail and swinging it out of sight. "If I put my stock in every pompous fool that came along, we'd all be in a mess of trouble."

"Demetrius." Captain Marda appeared through the smoke. "Help me with this barrel." She turned to the three Hidden Folk and inclined her head. "Auntie?" she asked. "Is it lit?"

"We weren't supposed to—" Demetrius began.

"The god is intelligent but not infallible," Auntie said grimly. "He also said that intelligence meant *ability to learn*. Which means he could stand to learn a few things. If the Nybbas simply needed to tell someone to set the castle on fire, don't you think he'd have done it by now?"

Demetrius had no answer.

"No," Auntie continued. "He needs those *things*. And they hate fire. So fire it is."

"Spill and light!" Captain Marda shouted, leaping

lightly onto one of the carts and heaving the barrel to the ground.

"What?" Demetrius yelled through the din. But the Captain didn't hear him. She pushed out another barrel, the top of which flew off the moment it hit the ground. Thick oil spilled over everything. And, in fact, on every cart, someone heaved off the barrels, popped their tops, and let the oil—all kinds of oil, at that, for cooking, for lamps, for the smooth workings of machinery—spill onto the ground.

"Get back behind the line!" the Captain shouted. And before Demetrius could ask, he saw just what kind of line she meant.

Soldiers with torches ran to the toppled barrels. If any barrel was still closed, the soldiers smashed it open. They lit the oil.

And the whole world burned.

CHAPTER SIXTY-SEVEN

The dragon flew at the mirrored sky, belching flame. The sky glowed red, then blue, then white. And the outline cracks deepened into fissures around the form of the Nybbas.

Violet stared.

The outline had sloped shoulders. And a narrow head. And its pointed hands and pointed feet were as sharp as spears.

It's almost like— She shrugged the thought away. She would not think about the painting. She would not think about the dragons with the empty eyes or the pile of hearts. She would only do what was necessary. There was only *now*.

We are going to win, she told herself firmly.

The dragon coughed, sputtered, and reared. It took a deep breath and blew fire once again.

"It's working, Dragon!" Violet called.

The King unsheathed his sword. "Your prison is breaking, my darling. It's only a matter of time before I get you out." And he charged the mirror at a run, aiming the tip of the sword toward a broadening break.

GET AWAY! GET AWAY! The Nybbas cast a panicked eye on the growing cracks. Its body—its *stolen* body—continued to smoke and heat.

Violet winced, as if it were her own arms, her own skin that was slowly burning alive. *Is it truly my body?* she wondered. *Or is it just an illusion? Is this body, this wrong body, an illusion? Will I open my eyes and be* me *once again?* Smoke poured from each hairline crack, and the Nybbas screamed.

"But...Violet." King Randall was confused. He looked up at the huge figure in the mirrored sky. "You are trapped," the King said, smashing at the mirror with his sword. "I'm here to get you out." But though the cracks spread and deepened across the breadth of the sky, the King's sword had little effect. The sky was made of stronger stuff than swords forged by men and women. The mirrored sky was built by a god.

STOP! The Nybbas tore at its hair (*my hair*, thought Violet) and clawed at its eyes (*my eyes*, thought Violet) and wept like a child. (*Faker*, thought Violet. *Schemer. Liar. You cannot weep without a heart!*)

WHAT'S HAPPENING? it yelled, desperately grabbing at its smoking chest. It turned back to the King, its wild eyes glittering with confusion and rage. DON'T TOUCH ANYTHING! DO YOU HEAR ME? THIS IS MY MOMENT OF FREEDOM. MY MOMENT OF TRIUMPH. AND *THIS* IS NOT SUPPOSED TO BE HAPPENING!

"Oh yes, it is," Violet said. She turned to the King. "Father, you need to leave. I don't know why the Nybbas guided you here—but I have no doubt that it did. You need to get on your horse and get away. Whatever that thing wants—"

But she said no more. The ground rumbled and cracked, knocking the King to his knees. It split and yawned, causing a rift that stretched from well behind them all the way to the lip of the land, and snaked up the sky. The Nybbas howled in pain.

The earth shook again, snapping under the King's feet and sending him tumbling into the rift. The King cried out and then was silent.

"FATHER!" Violet shouted, leaping and stumbling over the shifting rocks and into the break in the land. Cursing her weak arms and her oddly balanced body as she climbed, she scrabbled and scrambled into the rift. Her father was slumped at the bottom, bleeding heavily from his head, his left leg bent away from his body at a sickening angle. The ground shifted and grumbled. Violet lifted her father from the dirt, hoisting his weight onto her narrow shoulders and teetering to a stand.

"Dragon!" Violet called. "Please. Get him out of here."

The dragon circled above and landed next to the rift. It stretched its long neck into the gap. Violet grasped her father's chest with one arm and the dragon's neck with the other.

"That voice! I know that voice," the King said. "Violet, is that you?" Blood flowed from the wound on his forehead into his eyes.

"Yes," Violet said, kissing her father on the cheek. "Hang on to my shoulders if you can, Father," she whispered, "but don't strain yourself. I'll hold tight either way."

The dragon dragged them to the surface. Violet hoisted her father to his feet and placed him in the arms of the dragon. She gazed into the beast's one, shining eye and laid her hand on its chest, right over the heart.

"Dragon," she said. "Take him in your arms and fly him away from here. Some place safe. And you stay safe." She grabbed the hilt of her father's sword and slid it from its sheath. She gave the dragon a hard, wild stare. "The sky is already cracking, and I will break it myself. I will fight that thing, and I will kill it. And I want you to live. And I want him to live."

VIOLET—

"I am the Princess. And I love you. I love you both. And I am giving an order."

A queen's voice. A queen's face. A queen's tears. There would be no dissuading her.

"Violet—" her father said.

"In a minute, Papa," she said. And to the dragon, "GO. *Now.*" The dragon unfurled its wings. "*Go,*" she said again. It launched into the air, kicking the dirt into eddies around her feet. *I love you,* she thought, *I love you, I love you, I love you.* And she felt her love radiating from her body like flame. She felt it go toward the dragon and her father and beyond. She felt her love shoot outward, from one end of the mirrored sky to the other. Toward Demetrius. And her mother. And the whole kingdom. And the whole world. And her love was sharp and hot and *dangerous*.

Violet turned her back on her father and the dragon and faced the Nybbas.

CHAPTER SIXTY-EIGHT

The outline around the Nybbas's body deepened, with the stolen face of Violet trapped inside.

YOU DID THIS! the Nybbas said.

"Yes," Violet lied. She lifted her father's sword and smashed it against the surface of the mirror with a cry. She didn't even leave a scratch. The sword sprang back, the metal reverberating painfully up her arm. Violet staggered and reeled. Still the cracks in the sky from the dragon's fire continued to spider outward. She struck again.

AFTER ALL MY KINDNESS.

She struck again.

AFTER MY GENEROSITY.

She reared back, grunted, and struck again. Nothing happened. What if she couldn't kill it? *What then?*

AFTER EVERYTHING I—WHAT IS THAT INFERNAL LIZARD DOING? TURN AROUND, SLAVE! I AM YOUR MASTER! I SHALL DANGLE YOUR HEART BEFORE YOU ON A STRING!

Violet followed the Nybbas's gaze and saw the shiny black form of the dragon streaking against the sky, heading straight toward the Greater Sun.

What are you doing, my beloved? Violet thought at the dragon.

The dragon opened its throat and poured its fire into the sun and sky. And the sun broadened and widened and burned. And the sun was the sky. Or the sky was only sun. And the dragon was a tiny black mark in a blinding gleam.

Still, its heart spoke. And Violet heard it.

VIOLET, DO NOT GRIEVE. WHERE THE SKY IS HOTTEST, I WILL RELINQUISH MY FIRE AND DESTROY THE THING THAT DESTROYED MY PEOPLE. I DO THIS BECAUSE I AM MEANT TO DO IT. BECAUSE LOVE TRANSFORMS OUR FRAGILE, COWARDLY HEARTS INTO HEARTS OF STONE, HEARTS OF BLADE, HEARTS OF HARDEST IRON. BECAUSE LOVE MAKES HEROES OF US ALL.

"Come back!" Violet yelled.

STOP! the Nybbas screamed.

Violet felt the dragon's words thrumming against her heart.

I LOVE YOU, VIOLET. AND MY LOVE IS AS INFINITE AS WORLDS. AND IT CONTINUES BEYOND MY—

And the dragon disappeared.

Into the fire.

Into the cracking mirror.

Into heat, and destruction, and the death of all.

And the sky broke open like a melon, and everything went dark.

CHAPTER SIXTY-NINE

The war ended as the sky cracked.

We saw the servants of the Nybbas cease their writhing, cease their destruction. We saw them shudder and crumple to the ground. We saw the light in their terrible glittering eyes flicker one last time before going out forever.

We saw the mirrored sky above our heads light up and burn from end to end. We saw it crack like a plate and shatter.

I ran to Demetrius. I grabbed him in my arms.

I protected his body with my body.

And the sky rained down.

CHAPTER SEVENTY

"DRAGON!" Violet shouted. She heard nothing. She could not feel its voice. Instead, there was only the howling of the empty sky, the winds of infinite worlds, screaming across the land.

As the sky shattered and darkness fell, the outline of the Nybbas's body remained. The jagged edge of the narrow head, the sloped shoulders, the blade-sharp edges of the pointed hands and feet, all took on a cold, glowing light. The figure stepped forward. It wobbled in the wind. It was made of mirror—as thin and insubstantial as a paper doll. But huge. It towered over Violet, its two-dimensional shoulders twisting this way and that. In its reflective sheen, Violet saw images of the burning world, the crumbling mountains, a castle reduced to cinders.

The Nybbas wobbled, shifted, its form fluttering in the gusting winds of the burning sky.

It turned its head toward one hand and then the other, marveling at the sharp tips—no fingers, just two shining blades.

AHHHHH, the Nybbas whispered. UNEXPECTED, BUT SURELY TEMPORARY.

"I didn't expect you to be so...*thin*," Violet said, her voice a harsh rasp, a scathing curl in her upper lip. She picked up a rock from the ground and threw it at the mirrored creature. It didn't seem to notice. But Violet saw a small notch left in the shine of the mirror where the rock hit, and tiny cracks spidering outward.

The Nybbas drew itself up. THOUSANDS OF YEARS IN A MIRROR, CHILD. JUST GIVE ME TIME. Its edges glittered; its body radiated triumph. YOU HAVE FAILED, it screamed. I AM ALIVE! I AM ALIVE! The voice came from the figure, but it rumbled out of the earth as well. It vibrated the air and rained down from the empty space that once was the sky. It was everywhere.

Violet looked up. She saw her reflection in the leg of the Nybbas—her *wrong* self. She also saw her *true* face on its chest. And she saw the castle that was her home, encased in flame.

The heart—that *thing's* heart—was destroyed. Violet knew it. She could see the burning castle. *Strange that it cannot*, she mused. That was why its body smoked. Why it cried out. That is what hurt it so.

Destroy the heart, destroy the Nybbas. That's what the god had said. But the heart was destroyed. Violet pressed her lips together.

So the Nybbas was mortal. And she had her father's sword. Her fingers curled around the hilt. Violet set her teeth and growled.

"You are not free because you have your heart," she said. "You are free because we broke your prison. But your heart has burned. It is destroyed. And you are just as mortal as the men and women who gave their lives defending their homes." Her voice caught. *My people!* she thought. *My home!* "And you will be just as dead."

I HAVE GROWN WEARY OF YOU, VIOLET, the Nybbas said. It took two long strides toward her, the points of its feet piercing deeply into the ground. It raised its hand and sliced down in a long, clean arc, its sharp edges stinging the air with a high, bright sound. But a wind blew, and its body shifted, and the Nybbas missed.

Violet ducked under the flash of the Nybbas's sharp arm, extended her sword toward the creature's leg, and made contact where its knee should be. The sword clanged hard, and its body rang like a bell. And the creature began to crack—a slow, thin shattering along the Nybbas's leg. It didn't notice. Not at first.

I SAID, I *HAVE GROWN WEARY OF YOU.* INSUFFERABLE CHILD. It swung again, but the winds continued to blow. It missed—almost, the tip slicing across Violet's cheek. She cried out but didn't falter. She struck again, this time at the creature's torso. Cracks as thin and complicated as spider-webs traced outward, spreading across the midsection.

DEAR ME, ARE YOU STILL TRYING TO WIN? IT SEEMS TO ME— The Nybbas gasped. Its legs folded in three places and dropped like an accordion. WHAT'S HAPPENING? It plunged its spiked hands into the ground and looked up and bellowed forth a great, anguished cry. WHAT HAVE YOU DONE? I'VE WAITED SO LONG!

The Nybbas shattered slowly. A shard from its shoulder detached and fell to the ground. Then a shard from its hip. The Nybbas slashed at Violet, who dodged the blows and struck at its torso, its shoulders, its narrow head.

STOP! the Nybbas screamed. PLEASE, PLEASE, PLEASE. Its voice was a squeal, a whine, a pathetic sigh.

Violet struck again. She shattered its left arm. It fell to the ground in pieces.

PLEASE.

She struck its right leg. It exploded in dust.

I AM NOT WHAT YOU THINK.

She struck the center of its chest—the empty place where its heart should be.

The figure froze. It bent its head toward the sword still lodged in its chest. It shuddered once as the cracks zigzagged and spiraled, as they spread as fast and wild as exploding stars.

And in a spangle of glass, the Nybbas was gone.

Violet was in absolute darkness. The ground rumbled and shuddered and leaped beneath her feet, as though in great waves. Violet felt herself tossed lightly into the air before coming crashing down, landing hard on her back. She covered her face with her hands.

(Was that a chipped tooth?)

(Was that a pug nose?)

(Was it *her* face?)

"I am lost," she cried out.

"NO," said a voice. "NO, CHILD. YOU ARE QUITE FOUND."

CHAPTER SEVENTY-ONE

At the center of the empty, roofless sky, we saw them.

Twelve old gods, as tall as towers. And as small as pinpricks.

Strangely, *both*.

And behind them—though only for a moment—we saw the multiverse the way a god sees it—worlds upon worlds upon shining worlds. A great sea of universes. We saw how they surged and swelled. We saw them crash against the shore. And we nearly wept at the beauty of it.

The Old Gods rubbed their eyes and yawned. Their

bodies shifted and readjusted, as though only recently formed—or, in their case, re-formed. One of them—the shortest and stumpiest of the lot, turned to Auntie, Nod, and Moth.

"YOU DID WELL, MY BELOVED," the runty god said.

CHAPTER SEVENTY-TWO

The twelve gods stood on the surface of the land just as the world around us shrank. Mountains curled inward and disappeared; forests contracted; landmarks once impossibly far away became so near we could have called out to them. Oceans—that just hours earlier required a ride of many days to reach—lapped against the fields that once were heavy with crops but now appeared as sand dunes covered with tough, thick grass.

We tasted salt in our mouths. From tears? From the surf? Was there any difference?

We saw the people of the Northern Mountains, the Southern Plains, the Eastern Deserts, and the Island Nations to the west all walking on foot toward the burning castle—its once-beautiful ramparts now a smoking ruin in a shrinking landscape.

And we saw Violet—plain of face, mismatched eyes, pug nose, and the most beautiful thing in all the world—kneeling on the ground, holding her father, stopping his bleeding with her hands.

(She had blundered through the darkness.)

(And in the darkness her wrong body became her right body.)

(And in the darkness, her father, lying on the ground.)

(And in the darkness, the world she knew fell away.)

The ground around her was wet. She was met by the runty god. The child stopped, swallowed. "I know you," she said.

"YOU DO," the runty god said.

"I have failed you."

"YOU HAVEN'T."

"My father...he won't wake up. And my dragon..." Violet's voice choked in her throat. Demetrius ran to his friend. He laid his hands on her face, wiping the tears away.

He pulled a cloth from his pocket and pressed it on the King's open wound.

"YOUR FATHER IS WOUNDED. HE WILL HEAL. NOT PERFECTLY, MIND YOU, BUT HE WILL HEAL ALL THE SAME. THERE ARE WORSE THINGS," the god said kindly. "AND THE DRAGON GAVE THE LAST OF HIS FIRE AND THE LAST OF HIS LIFE FOR A CAUSE GREATER THAN HIMSELF. THERE IS NO BETTER THING."

"But—" Violet said, her desperation hot and sharp in her throat. "The dragon is dead because of me. It's my fault."

"YOU GAVE THE DRAGON HIS LOST COURAGE AND HIS LOST LOVE AND HIS LOST HEART. HE WAS A FULL DRAGON AT LAST, SOMETHING MANY OF HIS BRETHREN NEVER KNEW IN THEIR LIFETIMES. HE HAS REJOINED HIS TRIBE. HE HAS GONE ON."

"On?" Auntie said hopefully. "Do you mean—"

"NOT YET FOR YOU, MY DEAR," the god said. "BUT YES, THERE IS AN *ON*."

"Oh." She gasped. Auntie fell to her knees and covered her face in her hands. "I *did* know it. I *did* believe. It's just that—"

"THERE IS NO BELIEF WITHOUT DOUBT, CHILD. JUST AS THERE IS NO LIFE WITHOUT DEATH. AND NO DEATH WITHOUT LIFE."

Auntie nodded, picked herself up, and walked back, as stately as she could, into the shadow of Captain Marda, who bowed to the old woman.

The land shuddered and rumbled under our feet, pulling toward the castle like water down a drain. People pointed and cried out. But as the land of our world contracted and shrank, we noticed with increasing curiosity that new land, new landmarks, were coming into view. And the sky, no longer mirrored, was a brilliant blue. And it seemed to go on forever.

"What is this place?" I asked the Old Gods. "There is a story of a land of endless sky. An ancient story. I thought it was the stuff of dreams."

"IT IS YOUR TRUE HOME. THE WORLD YOU HAVE KNOWN WAS A PRISON BUILT FROM AN ANNEX—A BASEMENT WITHIN A LARGER WORLD. BUT THAT PRISON IS NOW BROKEN. YOU ARE FREE."

"How can we be free if the world we have known is gone?" Violet asked.

"YOUR ANCESTORS' ANCESTORS WERE TRAPPED INSIDE THE MIRRORED WORLD AND ENSLAVED TO A WICKED AND SELFISH GOD. THIS WIDE BLUE SKY, THIS ENDLESS GREEN LAND, THIS IS YOUR TRUE HOME. BUT IT WILL NOT BE EASY.

HERE IN THIS UNDISCOVERED COUNTRY, THE PERILOUS SHORE, YOU WILL FIND FRIENDS AND FOES AND HARDSHIPS AND JOY—ALL IN EQUAL MEASURE. ARE YOU READY?"

No one spoke. No one was ready. We looked at one another in fear.

Finally: "I am," Violet said. "I am ready."

The runty god smiled. "THEN, VIOLET, YOU SHALL LEAD YOUR PEOPLE INTO THE WILDERNESS AND BACK OUT AGAIN. YOU SHALL HELP THEM TO FIND A HOME. YOUR LIFE WILL BE HARD. AND DANGEROUS. AND YOUR PEOPLE WILL NEED YOU."

"But you won't be alone. No one can do that alone," Demetrius said, stepping forward and taking her hand. "I'll help."

"AS YOU ALWAYS HAVE."

And with that, the runty god vanished, along with his brothers and sisters. And we were left alone.

And it was time to go.

CHAPTER SEVENTY-THREE

The next days were a jumble of activity, with Violet and Demetrius at the center of it all. Supplies needed to be gathered, animals tended, the wounded treated, and the dead buried. Violet sent riders ahead to map the terrain and to scout potential camps, territories, and settlements. Demetrius and his father saw to the horses and the goats and the sheep and the pigs, and sent the cattle to munch on sea grass, though they knew the cattle would wrinkle their noses at it.

Auntie, Nod, and Moth assisted with the wounded, and

the physicians were astounded at the vast stores of knowledge carried in the head of that tiny, withered old woman. They paid her every respect and deference and did their best to keep from offending or disappointing her. This was not an easy task.

The King convalesced in a knot of pain. His danger had passed, and we knew he would not die. But he would not be the same. "Even in the darkest winter," he said to anyone who listened, "a Violet blooms in 'the snow," and then he would fall to weeping, and only the sound of his daughter's voice would soothe him.

The land under our feet—the once vast and productive fields of rich Andulan farmland—had shrunk to the size of a garden that might feed one man, but not the thousands of empty bellies that now followed the girl. Not a princess any longer—we had no use for such terms—but a girl who led her people all the same.

Toward a new home.

Into a new world.

On the morning when Violet and Demetrius set out, they shouldered their rucksacks and gathered the sick and wounded and infirm into carts. They herded their animals and led their people into that wide green country. They

craned their necks up to the sky and marveled at the blue dome, the shockingly white clouds, the single, yellow sun. They were beautiful and hopeful and brave.

And the people followed—the different peoples of my world together.

I watched them as they walked to the limit of the horizon. The sky grew purple, then orange, then gold over their heads, and the light spilled onto their shoulders and shimmered on the ground. As the single sun sank, it glowed large and red above the lip of the land, hovering like a beacon before melting away.

And they marched toward the darkening sky.

And they marched toward the glint of innumerable stars.

And they vanished from sight.

I stayed behind. The castle is nothing more than a heap of blackened stones, but it is still my home.

The only things that live here now are memories: the press of people gathered around the firelight as a story unspooled at their feet. The screech of children down a long, dark hall. The cluster of books around the bent figure of a King. The downy head of a precious child peeking out from the protective crook of her mother's arms. And on those tiny lips, a flicker of a smile.

The memories press themselves against the stones. They breathe their life into the cracks. And I tell the story. The *true* story.

I tell the story of a story gone terribly wrong, and a wicked god, and a heartbroken King, and an idiot story-teller, and a stalwart friend, and a girl undone, and a whole world lost.

I tell the story of a girl with an iron heart, who loved the world and made it new again.

ACKNOWLEDGMENTS

Many, many thanks to Steven Malk, Kristy King, Genevieve Valentine, Ted Barnhill, Julie Scheina, Pam Garfinkel, and Jennifer Regan for their willingness to wade through the different versions of this story, for their patience with my petulant whining, and for their gentle encouragement as I slogged through the drafting (and redrafting, and re-redrafting) of this book.

Many more thanks to Ella, Cordelia, and Leo, who heard this story when it was still leaking, unbidden, from my mouth as I told them stories in the dark. How could I write stories without you to listen to them, my darlings?

Physicists have long written about their theories of multiple universes, and most have done so using complicated equations and large words that I pretend to understand but do not. Not really. Thank you to Brian Greene, whom I have never met, but whose book *The Elegant Universe* haunts my dreams. And to Michio Kaku, who makes me glad that I live in a universe that has smart people who are willing to explain complicated things in language that rubes like me can understand. Or pretend to understand, anyway.

Scientists and poets are cut from the same bright fabric: They pull at the threads of truth from the edges of our understanding and weave them into the center; they wind bright knots, as tight as vises, binding idea to idea to idea; they cast their filaments ever outward and link our souls to the stars.